PULLING AT THE STARS

BETH MARIE READ

woodhall press

NORWALK, CT

Library of Congress Cataloging-in-Publication Data available
ISBN 978-1-949116-14-4 (paperback)
ISBN 978-1-949116-15-1 (e-book)

Layout Artist: Casey Shain
Copyeditor: Tracy Salcedo
Proofreader: Tess Pellicano

w o o d h a l l p r e s s
Woodhall Press, 81 Old Saugatuck Road, Norwalk, CT 06855
Woodhallpress.com
Distributed by Ingram Publishing Services (800) 937-8000

For Madison

Author's Note

It is important to recognize that every victim of domestic abuse has their own individual story to tell, and yet many stories, sadly, have common and overlapping details. This book was created as a tool to empower domestic abuse victims in a relevant way. Every character and situation in this novel is fictitious.

ONE

I knocked. Nothing. Buzzed. Again, nothing. My father and I were waiting outside a rundown apartment building in Harlem, New York.

"Nina, don't you have a key?" my father, Luca, asked.

"I didn't get one yet."

Nina was my nickname. My birth name is Pasqualina Panicucci, the most Italian name you could imagine, and it suits my family well. My mother's family came from Northern Italy, and my father is Sicilian. I always wished I inherited the Sicilian skin, but of course, I am the light northerner with green eyes and long brown hair. At least I still tan in the summer.

When I was born, my mother insisted I be named after my great-grandma Pasqualina. I have always hated my name, so around the age of six, I decided that everyone would call me "Nina."

Anyway, my roommate should have been home, but I guess she forgot what time we were arriving, which annoyed me, but I wasn't going to make a big deal about it. After all, it had been my dream to move to New York City to pursue acting ever since my first performance as "Lullaby League Girl 2" in *The Wizard of Oz* in Kindergarten. I became addicted to the limelight after that, so my mom signed me up for acting lessons. I was the first Freshman to ever land a lead role in my high school's fall play. I even did a few local commercials. It was the first day of living my big dream, so I wasn't going to let her tardiness fuck *that* up. Finally, I saw her walking down the street with a grocery bag in her hand.

"Is she a drag queen?" Papà asked under his breath.

I thought the same thing when I first met Grace; it was rather anticlimactic when I discovered that she was, in fact, just a girl.

"No, and don't say that so loud," I whispered back and nudged his arm.

She had cobalt blue hair that she swirled up on the top of her head like soft-serve ice cream, and always wore matte hot-pink lipstick. Her skin was so pale it was practically transparent—a stark contrast to the colorful skin in the heights of Harlem. She stood five feet tall and was anorexic thin.

"Hey, Nina! Nina! It's me, Grace!" she said. "I'm glad I met you outside because there has been sort of a little problem with the room."

"*What* problem?" My smile faded to wide eyes.

"Um—remember when I said that my other roommate had moved all of her stuff out?"

"*Yes—?*"

"Well, she didn't. Actually, the apartment really belongs to *her*. She has been having a lot of, um, mental issues? Anyway her mother took her back upstate to get better. She is renting her room to you, and she decided to keep her furniture here for when she returns."

"When she returns? What do you mean? I thought I had the room?"

"Well, actually, I don't really know if she is returning or not. She says she is, but her mom tells me that she isn't. It's confusing, but either way, you are here, and the room is there, and I have been shifting some things around to accommodate."

She'd *better* accommodate considering I already gave her one month's rent *and* a security deposit.

Meanwhile, my father single-handedly removed all of my furniture, including my queen-size bed, dresser, and massive desk, out of his trailer on to the street. I went upstairs with her to scope out the space. The apartment looked like an Andy Warhol painting gone wrong. The front door opened to a long hallway painted sky blue. Streaks of green plaster stretched across its walls in random and unfinished strokes. The bathroom sat halfway down the hall and was painted gold with a reddish-pink marble floor. Farther down was a lemon-lime kitchen featuring a clock made out of broken shot glasses. The living room, now stuffed with bedroom furniture from the crazy mental roommate, had purple trim, yellow walls, and a herd of cows painted on the ceiling. Grace's room was about the size of a closet and had posters of Audrey Hepburn sprawled across it from floor to ceiling, covering the electric blue walls.

My room was the craziest of all. It had a Pepto-Bismol pink concrete floor, peach walls, a lime green ceiling, and teal trim. It smelled like cherry car fresheners. The worst part about it was the fact that my door didn't reach the height of the vaulted ceiling, leaving about a foot of empty open space in between. I wouldn't think it was much of a problem until I awakened every morning to Grace eating cereal one grain at a time, being sure to clank her metal spoon against the bottom of the ceramic bowl with every bite.

My father and I managed to squeeze all of my furniture into the apartment and, finally, I was out on my own.

I wished my mom could have been there, but she died when I was fourteen. She had been sober nearly four years before her death. Shiraz was her demon of choice and it all crashed down one day when I was ten. She had dropped me off at a burger joint and sent me in by myself to get food while she binge drank in the car. I was walking back with a box of fries and sodas when I heard her car door open and the sound of a glass bottle dropping to the pavement. She swerved the car as we drove home and her speech became slurred. That's when I realized what was happening. My father gave her an ultimatum that day: Get help or get out.

She made the choice to become sober, join AA, and started going to temple once in a while. Oh yeah. She was Jewish. Papà is Catholic—Roman Catholic—and very serious about it too. So serious that he made me go to mass three times a week with him for years. Church wasn't terrible and I made a few friends there, which made it tolerable, but I liked temple better. They had snacks there. Before long, my mom turned into an activist and helped several members of the community sober up and heal from the traumatic effects of alcoholism through art. She was a phenomenal painter. She studied art in New York City before I was born and, if she were there that day, she would have been so damn proud of me. I had never seen two people so happy with each other as my parents were in her sober years. They renewed their vows in Italy and eventually made plans to expand the family, until she got sick.

My father clung to the church for comfort after she was diagnosed, so she smothered me with attention. We started having "Breakfast Wednesdays," when we'd go out for breakfast before school. I was almost always late to my first class. She helped me pick out a gorgeous off-the-shoulder dress for my first high school dance and hushed my father when he said it revealed too much skin. We continued the tradition while she was indefinitely in the hospital, and munched on saltines and Jell-O talking about all the plans I had for my future. Her name was Camilla and she succumbed to skin cancer on a Monday.

After my mom died, I realized that life was too short not to live my dream, so at twenty-one years old, I finally had the guts to up and do it. There weren't many kids from my high school graduating class that actually left our small town, let alone Connecticut, but I got the hell out as soon as I could.

Papà helped me finish unpacking and handed me a fifty-dollar bill.

"Use this for groceries, and maybe a lock for your room."

"Papà, stop. I'll be OK."

He kissed me on the top of my head. He was short, but I was still shorter.

"I know. Live your dreams, Flower. *Ti amo.*"

"I love you, too."

I saw him to the elevator and watched him drive away from my new bedroom window, caressing the golden hamsa hand that hung from my neck, thumbing the sharp sapphire in the middle of the hand. It was my mother's necklace.

The first thing on my to-do list was to find work. Most people would have found a job *before* moving, but you know, whatever. After a week of looking, I ended up getting a temporary job on Wall Street working for a dentist as her receptionist, since her regular girl was out on maternity leave. She paid me very well and I worked for about two months banking up some cash. I woke up at six in the morning Monday through Friday and rode the train all the way from 135th to Wall Street. I would come out of the subway into the hustle and bustle of the stockbrokers and bankers, and head over to my "coffee guy." After a week of faithfully visiting his coffee truck, he started having a cup of joe ready for me, just the way I liked it, perfectly timed.

In the afternoons, I strutted over to the smoothie truck for a kale and orange something-or-other blended with bee pollen. That was the "hip" thing—bee pollen. It was in everything from smoothies to brownies. I'm surprised the coffee guy didn't sell bee pollen-infused coffee. They claimed it was healthy, but to be honest, I couldn't tell a bit of difference drinking it or not.

It did, however, make me feel like a trendy New Yorker, and it also led me to my first city hookup.

He bumped into me, and I could tell it was on purpose, but I pretended not to notice until he did it again.

"Excuse me," I said, rolling my eyes.

It was my last day on the job and we were standing outside the smoothie truck. He was about six feet tall with dirty blonde hair, fierce green eyes, and smooth, tanned skin. He was lean and wore a slim-cut charcoal suit with a teal-colored tie and matching handkerchief sticking out of his pocket.

"No, excuse *me*," he said and proceeded to cut me in line.

"Oh, come on! I'm standing right here! Hello! Do you not see me?" He ignored me and continued on with his order.

"Are you kidding me? Seriously, come on! I'm *right here*!!"

I tapped my foot while he paid.

"Kale, mango, orange smoothie with one scoop of bee pollen, right?" He handed me my drink.

My jaw dropped.

"You come here every day, and I've stood behind you in line at least five times, yet you've never noticed. My name is Marco. What's yours?"

I couldn't move. I looked him up and down and soaked in his magazine-perfect body. "Uh ... Nina. Hey, hi. Um, yeah, my name is Nina. Pasqualina, but you know, just call me Nina. Nina is fine." My heart pounded fast, half in fear, half in excitement. Even though it was mid-October, I could feel the sweat drenching my armpits as I took the smoothie from his hand.

"Pasqualina. Italian? Me, too. Marco Roncalli. Northern Italian I take it? My family comes from Treviso. What about you?"

To be frank, I didn't know much of my Italian heritage. My great-grand-parents got off the boat and assimilated as quickly as they could into the American lifestyle. That was the extent of my knowledge. I didn't speak a lick of Italian nor did I know anything about the country. "Um, just north I guess." His pregnant pause expected a more in-depth answer, but I remained quiet. "Well, I should get back to work. Thanks for the drink." I turned to leave.

"Wait!" He blocked me with an arm that smelled like a Gucci advertisement. I looked up at him. "Giuseppe's. Eight in the evening. Tomorrow." He half-saluted, turned, and walked away.

"Giuseppe's?" I said. "Wait! Where is Giuseppe's? Hello! Can you stop for a second? Where is Giuseppe's?"

He kept walking away as he yelled back, "Eight o'clock!"

Bewildered, I walked back to work.

Giuseppe's happened to be the most popular Italian restaurant on Mulberry Street in Little Italy. I looked it up when I got home and was astonished. Apparently, they didn't take reservations and it was at least a two-hour wait outside on the street to get a table.

"Dang! Who are you going *there* with?" Grace asked as she looked over my shoulder.

"I don't know. Some guy from the smoothie truck."

"A truck guy is taking you to Giuseppe's?"

"Not *the* truck guy, some stockbroker I met *outside* of the truck. He bumped into me today and bought me my favorite drink. He said he's stood in line behind me before and memorized my order. Honestly, I don't know whether to be afraid of a stalker or flattered."

"Is he hot?"

"*Way* smoking hot."

"I bet he's harmless."

The next day was Saturday and I spent the entire day getting ready. I took my last paycheck and went shopping at an expensive boutique in the Lower East Side. I found a black skin-tight dress that hugged my slender curves. Under it, I wore a pair of black lace panties that did nothing but ride up my butt crack, but they showed off my ass and I had to be prepared *just in case*. I opted out of a bra. Being a size 32A, who needed one anyway?

It was eight o'clock. I stood outside of Giuseppe's by myself looking for my hot date in the crowded line of people outside of the door, but he was nowhere to be found. I figured I would at least get in line and hold us a spot. Ten minutes later, I was starting to get worried. Just then I heard some commotion at the front of the line. There was Marco stepping out of his white Mercedes and giving the keys to the doorman. He scanned the crowd and came over to me. He grabbed my hand and said, "Come with me. I don't wait in line."

We passed by the doorman and the hostess seated us right away in a small intimate corner of the restaurant.

"Do you like seafood?" he asked.

"Yes! Anything and everything."

When the waiter came over he ordered a bottle of wine, and before any menus came Marco said: "Two Roncalli specials please." The waiter nodded his head.

I stared at him speechless with an empty-headed smile on my face.

It was the most delicious Italian dinner I'd ever had in my life, even better than my grandmother's cooking. Marco went on to explain that his family owned a production company that served several popular television shows, which left him with millions of dollars, a penthouse five-bedroom condo in the W hotel, a Mercedes and career anywhere he wanted.

"I head up a hedge fund," he said and puckered his lips with pride.

He swooned me with his Mercedes up and down the FDR while we talked about this thing and that thing, and eventually retired to his luxurious condo. The view was incredible. His entire living room wall was floor-to-ceiling windows. The sparkling and colorful lights of Tribeca reminded me of the Lite Brite toy I had as a kid. I'd never seen such a beautiful apartment; it was a far stretch between his place and my Harlem room-for-rent. I was embarrassed and tried not to touch anything.

"Come here," he said.

I followed him through two solid mahogany French doors into a colossal bedroom with a king-size bed flowing with fabrics that made even the Pottery Barn look cheap. He grabbed me by the waist and kissed me softly, backing me up and pressing me against the wall in silence, shutting off the light as he pulled my zipper down. His touch was delicate and devoted.

"You're beautiful," he whispered.

The words blazed in my ear and prickled through my toes. I covered my small breasts with my arms as my dress fell to the floor. He lifted my chin and said it again.

"You're beautiful."

Removing my arms from their outpost, he began kissing down my neck. I scooped my hands under his shirt and pulled it over his head. I could feel his muscles through his skin, which begged to press against me. He laid me down on his feather-soft bed and found his way inside me. I wasn't expecting it; his anticipation was too abrupt, but I entertained it and eventually my body caught up. After five minutes with half his body's weight on my chest, and grabbing my ass until it was purple, I took over. I used his rhythm to push him off me and slam him down on the mattress.

"Let me do this." I started with my hips. I hated being on the bottom anyway, especially because when a guy barely knows you, he barely knows how to get you to climax.

He spread his arms out to his sides. He wouldn't even touch me or try to arouse me more. Did he really think his dick was *that* good that he didn't have to use his hands? I shifted myself around until I was hitting the right spot, and closed my eyes tight until the image of a sexy, built, shirtless model appeared in my mind. We were in a rooftop bar at sunset and he was serving me a cocktail. He came up next to me and put his fingers to my lips and stripped naked. He picked me up and I could feel giant hands caressing me as he placed me on the bar, and soon I wasn't making love to Marco, I was making love to the bartender.

I was just starting to get myself going when Marco started to come. I had to put my acting cap on and fake an orgasm. Why do we girls always feel like we have to fake an orgasm when a dude sucks in bed? We should just be honest and be like, "Dude, you suck in bed." But whatever, I faked it, and that was that.

Afterwards, he called room service and ordered a snack. We snuggled and watched some trashy late night TV until three in the morning. I was falling asleep when he reached over and handed me three twenty dollar bills.

"Hey." He nudged me. "Take this with you when you go."

"What's this for?" I wrinkled my eyebrows.

"Your cab. Don't you know it's impossible to get a train this time of night? I'll pay for it, no worries."

"Oh," I said. "Yeah, of course."

I was confused, but took that as my cue to get dressed. I think he sensed my disappointment and asked if I would see him again the following Saturday, which happened to be Halloween. I accepted and wrote down my address for him to come pick me up. I was slightly embarrassed by my neighborhood but too excited to really care.

He walked me down to the cab stand at the front entrance.

"Eight o'clock on Saturday. I'll see you then, Nina." He flashed his intoxicating smile, gave me a gentle kiss on the back of my hand, closed the door to the cab, and sent me on my way.

Saturday came. I didn't know whether to wear a costume or not, and I couldn't ask him because I realized I had forgotten to get his number. I played it safe and wore a white dress I had in the closet that resembled something Marilyn Monroe wore, and figured I could claim it as a costume if I needed.

I gushed to Grace about Marco and told her about the dinner, the joy ride, the W Hotel and, of course, the "hot" sex. I had spent all week dreaming and talking about my night with Marco, overdramatizing his abilities and convincing myself he was a sex god, even though he definitely wasn't. But he *was* rich, and suave, and I still had a good time with him.

"Where do you think he will take you tonight?" she asked.

"I don't know, but he'll be here soon. Do I look OK?"

"Super hot!"

I felt good. I was confident and ready for date number two with a man I knew was way out of my league, but with whom I couldn't help falling. It was time, so I put my high heels on and sat in the living room to wait. Grace had made other plans and left.

A half hour later I got up to check the shot glass clock. I figured he was running a little late, just like last time, so I didn't think anything of it and grabbed a couple of crackers out of the pantry to hold me over. He was taking me to dinner, or at least so I thought. He didn't really say what we would be doing now that I thought about it. I sat back down and turned on the TV.

When ten o'clock came and went, I decided that it was probably time to take off the dress and throw on my pajamas. Humiliated, I sat on the couch in my purple-striped fleece pajamas, which were sure to ward off any man if he saw me in them. I snuggled up to a pillow and tore into a pint of cherry ice cream. I fell asleep on the couch with the TV on until a loud commercial woke me. I reached for the remote and was about to turn it off when the commercial caught my attention. It was for a Jewish organization, and explained that if you are of Jewish descent, they would pay for an all-inclusive two-week trip to Israel, and give you the option to "make aliyah," whatever that meant.

I clicked the channel to the *Sex and the City* marathon. I popped open a bottle of Merlot, not even bothering to pour it into a glass and submerged my abandonment in drunkenness.

I never heard from Marco again.

TWO

"Nina, I need the rent money now. You are five days overdue, and I can't carry the whole rent by myself. This is the second time you've been late and I really can't have you doing this anymore. I'll see you at home."

I deleted the voicemail immediately after listening, trying to put it out of my head. I had been putting the rent off because I didn't have the eight hundred dollars I owed Grace. After my temporary Wall Street job ended, I looked for more work but couldn't seem to find it. I felt frustrated because I came to New York City to be an actress, not a waitress or someone's receptionist. City life was harder than I thought it would be, and my dad couldn't hold my hand or pay all of the bills anymore. I had to get a real job, but I couldn't get acting out of my mind. Instead of applying to regular paying jobs, I scanned the call sheet for an agent. I had spent two hundred dollars on headshots, another hundred on prints, and a hefty amount in postage mailing them out to various agents around the city. That left me with just under eight hundred to my name.

When I got home, Grace was still at work. It was late afternoon on a Thursday, and the brisk January air seeped into the apartment through the cracks in the window frames. I put on some water and made a cup of hot tea with honey, grabbed a blanket and opened up the living room window. I stepped out onto the fire escape and sat on the black-painted metal stairs, eight stories above the street. The cool air made clouds with my breath. The apartment building was on Riverside Drive and overlooked the Hudson

River. Off in the distance, I could see the George Washington Bridge lit up, and getting brighter as the winter sun set behind it. I pulled out a cigarette, lit the tip, and sucked in menthol-flavored chemicals. A gust of wind blew at me, protesting my contamination of the city's only virgin air, so I pulled my hat down over my ears and snuggled tighter into my blanket wondering what the hell I was going to do.

There had to be a quick way to make cash in a city like this. I took a sip of tea and took out my phone, pulling up a job search app. I surfed and sifted through job after job that I wasn't qualified for even in my dreams. I only had a high school education and a few years of acting classes under my belt. Most of the jobs required at least a bachelor's degree, even to be a receptionist. My finger clicked on the "spa services" section. Six months before I moved to New York, I became certified in a practice called Reiki. "Reiki the leaves," my friends teased. It is an old Japanese technique that reduces stress and pain. I had never thought of selling Reiki before, but in a city where eating bee pollen every day was "normal," I figured it should fit right in. I e-mailed seven different spas inquiring work.

I had been outside for about an hour when Grace startled me by opening the window.

I rolled my eyes. "Grace, can you just give me a second please?"

"No! Did you get my voicemail? Nina, I need the rent. I paid your half for you and now I'm totally wiped out. I need to go grocery shopping, and I need your half *right now*. If you can't pay the rent, then you need to leave so I can have a roommate who is actually responsible. And is that my teacup? Why are you using my stuff! You better wash it!"

"Why don't *you* move out, and I can get a roommate who doesn't look like a drag queen!" I yelled.

Her jaw dropped. She slammed the window shut and locked it.

"Great. Just great. Let me back in, not like it's thirty degrees out here!" I slammed my palm against the glass. "Grace! Let me in or I'm calling the police and they will bust open the window for me!"

She came over, unlatched the lock and marched back to her room. I opened the window, grabbed the teacup, now practically frozen, and took my first step back inside.

"Shit!"

My foot slipped on a small patch of ice and I braced for my fall. The teacup tumbled to the ground and shattered.

"This is the worst day ever," I grumbled. I slid into the apartment and shut the window behind me.

Later that night, Grace came out of her room to talk, but before she could say anything I aggressively began the conversation.

"Listen, I know you are mad about the rent, and I promise I'm going to buy you a new teacup. I'm sorry about the drag queen thing." I barely paused so that she couldn't get a word in. "The truth is, I've only got seven hundred and sixty dollars and I can give all of that to you right now." I grabbed a check out of my purse, signed it and gave it to her. "I don't know how I will come up with the other forty, but I will, and I'll have it for you by the end of the week, OK?"

She let out a long dramatic sigh, rolled her eyes, and said "OK" as she grabbed the check and spun around with her nose in the air, marching back to her room.

I pulled up my e-mail and noticed that I had a response from one of the salons.

"Dear Nina, Thank you for your inquiry. Please send us a photo of your-self and your measurements. Sincerely, Asma and Alexa."

"Measurements? That's weird. Maybe for uniforms?" I thought.

I picked out a picture from my headshot session and indicated that I was an "extra small for tops, size two for bottoms."

Their response was almost immediate. "Please meet us tomor-row for dinner at the Burrito Grab n' Go place on 33rd and 2nd." I jumped in the air, and ran to Grace's room, pounding on her door. "Grace! I have a job interview tomorrow! Grace! Check it out!" I held my phone in my hands with the e-mail open to show her, but I heard no response. I knocked again and a second later heard a shoe hit the door at full force. "Well, I'll have your money soon."

I shut off the lights, and when my eyes adjusted to the darkness, I walked to my room and closed the door.

Twenty-four hours later, I was on my way to the interview. I walked into Burrito Grab n' Go and looked around for two women. They knew what I looked like from my picture, but I didn't know what to expect. I decided to order some food with the five-dollar bill I found in my coat pocket earlier that day, but all that got me was a side of tortilla chips and tap water. I took my snack to a small table next to the window that overlooked the crowded city street. I picked at the chips as slowly as I could. I had heard once that if you eat slowly, you get fuller quicker. Since I had given Grace all of my money, I couldn't buy anything else to eat. I had six apples and a big bag of egg noodles at my apartment, which I figured would last me three or four more days. Just then two ladies approached me with their plates overflowing with greasy burritos and sat down.

"Pardon us, but are you Nina?" one of them said.

"Yes, that's me." I stood up to shake their hands and tried to be as polite and professional as possible.

The two women were somewhere in their mid-thirties and total knockouts. Asma appeared to be Middle Eastern and had long black hair that reached the small of her back and was curled into gentle soft waves. I had never seen such a beautiful and flawless complexion in my life. She had eyes brown like rich coffee beans and pouty lips covered in a blanket of glossy red lipstick. Alexa was something out of *Cosmopolitan*. She had short, bleached-blond hair curled tight up onto her head and the bluest crystal eyes. She had high cheekbones accented with rose-colored blush and her double-D breasts were barely covered in a deep V-neck sweater. I looked down at my plaid shirt and jeans and realized I should have dressed up a little. They sat down next to me and the aroma of their burritos made my mouth water.

"I hope we didn't keep you waiting long. It looks like you've eaten already?" Asma said.

"It's no problem. I ordered chips, and— I'm not hungry," I responded.

They looked at each other and exchanged a glance.

"Well, Alexa, why don't you grab a couple side orders of queso for those chips and, oh hell, just grab a burrito, too," Asma said as she winked at me and smiled.

"You eat chicken?" Alexa asked.

"I do."

Alexa got up and placed an order while Asma and I sat at the table getting to know each other.

"I grew up in Minnesota," Asma said, "but always felt that New York was the place for me. The day I moved in and was walking down the street to the subway I felt right at home, you know? Like all was right in the world, and things were the way they were supposed to be."

"I know that exact feeling! It happened to me, too! In one sense I was terrified to move here, but as soon as I did, everything just clicked," I said.

While we waited for Alexa to come back, Asma shared a few stories about her home state, her family, and her new Boston terrier, Manny, making me feel more comfortable around her.

"What did I miss?" Alexa said plopping the hearty chicken burrito down in front of me and winking.

My cheeks flushed with embarrassment, but I managed to make out the words, "thank you," before diving in.

"Nina here was just telling me about when she first moved to New York," Asma said.

"Really? What made you move here, if you don't mind me asking?" said Alexa.

"Well," I started with my mouth full, "I really want to be an actress, but I'm realizing now how hard it is to actually break into the business. I thought it would be a lot easier. I look around and I feel like everyone is five foot six and a size two with green eyes and brown hair. We all look the same and we are all trying to be a model or an actress. How can I compete with a million clones of myself? I'm still trying, but I need to have a job that can support me financially, too, which I guess is where you come in?"

Alexa chuckled, "Of course! We got your e-mail and your picture. You are just the cutest thing! I feel like you would fit right in with the girls in our massage parlor. Did Asma tell you anything about our business?"

"No, not yet. I didn't realize it was only a massage parlor. You know, I'm not a certified massage therapist— I can only do Reiki."

"Oh don't worry," Asma said, "We properly train all of our girls in our special massage techniques, and we also feel that your Reiki will be a nice asset to our clients."

"What kind of techniques do you use?" I asked.

The two women smiled simultaneously.

"Alexa, why don't you give her a little insight into our company."

"Sure. I would like to start by saying that our business is one of many in this city, and our girls don't have to work many hours and get paid very well. A lot of our girls came to us just like you— their wallets stuck between a rock and a hard place, but now are financially free."

She leaned in and I could smell her sweet floral perfume. She was on my level, speaking to me like a long-lost friend. I half smiled and looked back and forth between them.

Asma continued, "Our massage parlor is special and different from others you may have experienced. We service only *men*," she whispered.

"Oh, *that* kind of parlor?" It occured to me at what they were hinting.

They stared blankly, waiting for me to indicate that I truly understood what they meant.

"Like, a 'happy ending' place?" I whispered.

"See Asma, I knew she was smart," Alexa said. "Yes! That's what we do."

On any other day, I would have stood up and walked out, but I really needed cash, so I inquired more about their "salon."

"So, do your girls sleep with their clients?" I asked.

"Oh no, dear, no. Anything that would ever threaten our girls with diseases and such, we don't do," said Asma. Alexa made a discrete motion with her hand, which no one in the busy restaurant noticed.

"Oh, so, just—hand stuff?" I asked, relieved.

"Yes, exactly," Alexa said. "Now, I want you to consider it. You are a beautiful girl, and our employees can make up to a grand per night."

"God, I *need* that money," I thought.

Asma handed me her business card. It was entirely blank but her name and phone number. "Do you have any questions?"

I sat still and silent for several seconds. "Can I think about it and call you?"

"Of course," Asma said. "Take all the time you need. Just know that we are always here, and the business we have built is safe. You will always be safe with us. Understand?"

"Yeah."

We sat around the small table for another fifteen minutes, eating our dinners and listening to more of Asma's dog stories. She was light-hearted and kind, and funny. The two women seemed genuinely caring. After we finished eating, we said our goodbyes.

"Let us know what you think, Nina. I have a good feeling about you," said Alexa.

"Me, too," chimed in Asma.

We parted ways on the street. It was nearly freezing, and the wind tunnels whipped frigid air at my face, but there was too much on my mind to feel it. I decided to walk the hundred city blocks home. It took me an hour and a half to get there, but I needed to clear my head. Was I really considering this? Were times *really* that bad? I supposed I could just move back to Connecticut, but where would I go? My father had already sold our house and moved into a one-bedroom apartment on the shore. No. I had to stay. But could I do this? Could I really be a *prostitute*? Maybe prostitute was the wrong word. It's not like they had *sex* with their clients, and how much different was it than that night with Marco? I slept with him, and he gave me cash. Same thing, I guess, only I would be making a *lot* more money at the parlor.

"Only hand jobs," I thought aloud. "It's only hand jobs."

A lady in the street turned and gave me a confused look, then proceeded to walk faster ahead of me.

"I can't," I thought. "What if Papà finds out? I'll never tell him. I can do this. I can! Right? It's not so bad. The money is *great*. Maybe I can buy a new door for my bedroom, or even get my own place. Hell, if I worked enough I could buy a damn apartment instead of renting one."

Soon I was in a full-blown daydream, watching myself walk down Fifth Avenue with a Louis Vuitton bag, a fur coat and Louboutin heels. I saw myself walking into a high-rise condo overlooking Central Park. I could tell my dad I scored an acting job. He might believe that. A gust of cold rain slapped my face back to reality. By the time I rounded my street corner, I had made up my mind. I pulled out my phone and the business card Asma gave me.

"Hello Asma? It's Nina," I texted. "Yes—I'm interested."

THREE

The next day I was given the address to the parlor and asked to show up for training. This time I had better-prepared myself by wearing a push-up bra and teasing my hair a little. Now mind you, even with a push-up bra I had zero cleavage, but it did make my boobs look slightly bigger. *Slightly*.

When I arrived, the parlor was not what I expected. I rang the bell to the second floor and Asma buzzed me in. I went up the stairs and to my surprise, it looked like an ordinary three-bedroom apartment. One bedroom was the "office" where a desk, a filing cabinet, and a few chairs were set up. The living room was typical and set up with a couch, TV, and area rug. The kitchen was fully stocked, and beautiful paintings hung gallantly on the walls. It was in the other two bedrooms that all the "magic" happened. Each room was stocked with a massage table and a cabinet full of lotions, oils, and small vibrators "for their balls," I was told. Some of the men liked that. Asma and Alexa led me into one of the rooms and had me hop onto the table.

"We're going to show you how we massage the men to kind of get them—*going*—if you know what I mean," Alexa said.

"It's easier than you think. Men are animals, that's all!" Asma threw her graceful hair back and laughed.

"Lay down on your stomach. We always start them off on their stomach." Alexa patted the top of the table, and I hopped on. "Now, when you are massaging them, you want to use long and fluid movements, up and down their back like this," she continued. "And, when you feel it is appropriate, take out your titties, and just kind of jiggle them sensually on their shoulder, as if by accident, but you know, it isn't," she laughed again.

Titties. What a gross word. I hated hearing it, especially when referring to my own body, but I went with it anyway.

"But they are too small, they don't jiggle," I laughed.

"Then shake that booty like you mean it!" Asma giggled. "Don't worry, you have all the right tools."

We all burst out laughing. Despite the less than ideal language, I was actually having fun. This couldn't be *so* bad, right?

"Ok, so when you get them all worked up, you want to flip them over onto their backs. Make sure you take off all of your clothes. Men are visual. Some of our clients like the lingerie, but most want to see you naked. We have records of everyone, and we will let you know who likes what but, as a general rule, you'll want to at least take off your bra at this point," Asma explained.

Alexa opened up a drawer in the cabinet and took out two towels and some oil. "I always use oil on my clients. It makes them go quicker," she said. "You want to have one towel on hand to clean them up after they squirt, and another towel to hand them so they can finish cleaning themselves. After they are set, you can wash yourself off in the staff bathroom next to the office."

"Good to know," I said.

"Some of our clients," Asma added, "like to take a shower afterwards, so we leave them alone to do that if they want. Do you have any questions?"

"No, honestly, this seems really easy."

"Great," they said in unison.

"So now, we just need to pick a new name for you," Asma said. "For your protection, we don't ever use a real name, and we will never post your face on any of our advertisements."

"Well, that's good to know," I said.

"Like we always say, you are *safe* here with us," Alexa said. "So, about that name, what are you thinking?"

"Is this technically my 'porn star name'?" I asked. "Growing up, my friends and I would joke around about what our porn star name would be, but I never knew that I would actually *have* one," I laughed. "What is it—your middle name and the street you grew up on right? How does Marie Birmingham sound?"

"Pretty awful actually," Alexa said, as we all laughed.

"How about Dominique?" Asma said. "It sounds sweet, yet exotic."

"Oooo, it sounds French," I said. "Dominique. I like it."

"When do you want to start?" Alexa tilted her head and smiled.

I remembered that I owed my roommate money and thought it was probably best to start as soon as I could. "Can I start now?" I asked.

"I knew I liked you," Alexa smooched my forehead and hugged my head close to her breasts. "Come back here at seven o'clock. Some of the other girls will be here and you can shadow them for a little while."

"Great! See you then!" I said.

I was excited to make some money, but as I headed back to the parlor that night, it struck me that this wasn't some game or a fantasy. I was actually going to massage a man I didn't know, and jerk him off for money. I pictured it in my head as I rode the train. I saw myself stroking a man who I envisioned looking like Marco, trying to get my confidence up that this was something I could do. Was I even *good* at hand jobs? I would sure find out.

When I walked through the parlor doors, three other girls were there— Candy, Mandy, and Veronica. "Typical," I thought. Everyone was really nice and positive and smiling. It definitely was not the idea I was given by Lifetime movies about the lives of prostitutes. I always thought they were grungy-looking women with their guts hanging out of their too-tight tube-tops, sucking dick in an alley for ten bucks. This was quite the opposite. The girls immediately took me in the office for a makeup overhaul. They dressed me up in a slutty costume with more hooks and straps and fishnet than I'd ever seen before. My makeup looked impeccable and I sat trying to figure out how I could accomplish it on my own.

"We have a client, ladies!" Alexa said as she hung up the phone. "He's two blocks away. Candy, you are up first. Take Dominique with you for observation, OK?" Then she pulled me aside.

"Listen," she said, "I want you to be in the room and try some of the things I taught you. Candy is really good about sharing the spotlight. Also, she said she would split her tip with you, so you'll make some money."

"Sounds good to me," I said. My heart was beating so hard I was sure everyone could see my fluttering chest.

The client showed up. We all remained in the office with the door closed, except Candy, who opened the door for the man and led him into a massage room to get undressed. She returned to the office five minutes later, completely naked, to look at his records.

"He prefers full nudity and is a two-minute man. This one should be easy." Alexa said. "Dominique, are you ready?"

"Sure." I followed Candy back into the room.

I gasped quietly to myself as the bedroom door shut behind me. This man was *nothing* like I pictured, and was the furthest from the image Marco left in my mind. He was severely overweight and smelled of cologne and garlic. Black hair grew thickly down his neck, back, and thighs. His protruding dimpled butt looked like two Jell-O molds swaying back and forth. His feet sticking out from the end of the table were calloused and housed yellow toenails.

Candy tossed a bottle of oil at my stomach, relaxing my scrunched face.

"So how have you been, Mr. Strong? How's your girlfriend doing?" Candy asked.

"She's good," he muttered. "We've been traveling a lot."

His accent was thick, Turkish perhaps.

"Girlfriend?" I thought. "The dude has a girlfriend and he's coming over here for a hand job?"

I didn't have time to meditate on it because Candy signaled me to start massaging. I slopped some oil between my hands and closed my eyes. I thought that maybe if I kept them closed, I could pretend he was a cute dog.

"German shepherd," I thought. "Golden retriever."

I did just as Asma and Alexa taught me. I stroked his back and his neck with my oily hands and continued all the way down to his legs. After about ten minutes, Candy asked him to turn over onto his back.

There it was: Mr. Strong's pathetic, miniscule, erect penis. I don't think I had ever seen, or will ever see, a penis that small. "That explains it," I thought. Luckily, Candy took over the hand job part and all I had to do was shake my ass a little and stroke his legs. Just then I felt something creep up the back of my outfit and grab my butt cheek. Mr. Strong was grabbing my butt! He rubbed it and squeezed it, and then stuck his finger straight into my vagina.

"I'll give you six hundred if you fuck me," he said to me.

"Holy shit," I blurted out. I looked to Candy, but she said nothing. In fact, she stopped jerking him off until I answered.

He swirled his finger in my vagina again, smiled, and said, "Come on."

Candy grabbed a condom out of a small bag taped up underneath the table and handed it to me. "It's up to you," she said.

"I didn't think we did that here." I stood confused.

"It's our little secret, and Mr. Strong pays cash."

Mr. Strong looked at me and smiled, and flicked his finger, gracing my g-spot. He was not attractive, and the sight of his pecker wasn't exactly erotic. The rent money went through my mind. I absolutely did not want to have sex with him, but I was so broke, and I really needed the cash.

I took the condom, rolled it onto his dick, and mounted him. I was grinding my hips into him for all of thirty seconds before he came. I looked down at his face, frozen in a pleasure coma, and immediately regretted every second I had spent in the room.

Candy was still watching. I got down from the table, and she slapped me five. "Thanks for scoring us some extra cash," she snickered.

"Us?" I thought.

Mr. Strong pulled off the condom, cleaned himself up and handed Candy a wad of cash before heading to the bathroom. Eight hundred to be exact. One fifty for the "service charge," fifty for our tip, and six hundred for my vagina. She counted out the money and handed me three hundred and twenty five dollars. She tucked her "share" into her bra she had already clipped on.

"Um," I said, treading carefully. "He gave that six hundred to me. I should have a lot more than this."

"Without me," Candy said, "You wouldn't have any of it. And if Asma and Alexa knew you fucked him, you'd be fired anyway."

She walked down the hall back to the office. Mr. Strong was in the shower, and I stayed in the bedroom for a minute to think about how I wanted to handle the situation. I took a long hard look around the room. It was dark, though some candles were lit. It smelled like sex. Gross, dirty, disgusting sex.

"Did I *really* just have sex for money?" I reflected.

I was in denial. I was ashamed, and I was also very scared. A million thoughts ran through my head. Will I get pregnant? Will I get an STD? No, I used a condom— but, *what if?* How do I explain this to someone? Oh my God, I can never tell *anyone!* I need to get tested for STDs. Maybe tomorrow

I'll see a doctor. All for six hundred dollars and I didn't even get all of it!

I was enraged.

Stripping naked, I unstrapped all of the clips, ripped off the fishnets, and wrapped myself in a towel. I stomped down the hall towards the office and slammed the door open.

"Give me my money, Candy!" I yelled.

"Come again?" Asma said.

"I fucked Mr. Strong for extra cash and Candy took half of it," I said, staring at Candy. "You fucking dirty whore!" My finger was inches from her face.

I called *her* a "dirty whore." How ironic. I grabbed my clothes as Asma stood up. "I said I want my money *now*."

Candy took the money out of her bra and threw it at me. "Here." She grabbed her chest as she laughed.

I picked up the bills off of the floor.

Alexa was dumbfounded. Just as she was about to say something to me, I put up my hand and yelled, "Don't talk to me."

I grabbed my purse, quickly dressed myself, and left.

When I got home, I left the money I owed Grace in an envelope on the kitchen counter and took a two-hour shower.

I cried hard until I puked, and then cried some more. This is not what I envisioned the city to be. New York was supposed to be glamorous. I was supposed to find love. It's the city where dreams come true, but only for the rich and privileged, I suppose. The city for the rest of us was a hellhole. A constant struggle of trying to pay rent and keeping any dignity in the process. I put on three layers of clothing and stepped out onto the fire escape. I looked down at the street below and lit the last cigarette in my pack. I was embarrassed and ashamed of myself. I had sex with a man I didn't know, but at least I paid my rent. If my dad saw me now he would probably perform an exorcism.

I climbed back inside through the window and lay awake in my bed until the sun came up. Eventually, my body forced itself to pass out, and I woke in the afternoon to my phone ringing.

"Hello?" I said.

"Hi, may I speak to a Pask, uh—"

"Pasqualina. Call me Nina."

"Hi, my name is Tyler and I am Karen Picard's assistant," he said.

Karen Picard sounded familiar, but I couldn't pinpoint where I had heard the name.

"OK?" I said, confused.

"Karen owns Studio 8 Talent Agency," he said.

"Oh my God!" I jumped out of bed. "Hi!" I yelled.

"She wants to know if you could come in for an audition at six o'clock tonight."

I snapped out of my pity party and accepted, scribbled down the Midtown address while scanning my closet for an outfit. Finally, a real chance, and it couldn't have come at a better time. I spent the afternoon putting the parlor out of my mind as best as possible and rehearsing a monologue I had memorized. I did breathing exercises and tongue twisters to make sure I was warmed up and ready for my audition. I flipped through some of my notebooks from an acting class I had taken at a local theater before moving. I still kept pondering the fact that I would need to stop in at a walk-in clinic at some point to get swabbed for STDs, but this audition was more important, at least for now. I'd have to put it off until tomorrow.

When I stepped off the subway, I turned the corner and found myself on Fifth Avenue. I clenched the cash from the night before still in my coat pocket, and thought, "To hell with that stupid parlor and to hell with their scum money too."

FOUR

When I got close to the address and saw a line out the door, my heart sank. I thought this was going to be a private audition, but clearly it was more of an open call. It was a good thing I got there early. I took my place in line and observed the other people around me. The agency seemed to have picked people of all shapes, sizes, and colors, which made me feel less of a clone and more like I had an actual chance at this. Most of the prospects had their heads buried in their phones.

I took out my own phone and scrolled through page after page, catching up on the lives of my old friends back in Connecticut. A few of them were recently engaged and plastered pictures of their rings all over their profiles. I didn't realize how alone I was until this moment. New York City is a place bustling with millions of people, but it was then that I realized I had failed to make one single friend in the months I had lived there. I wouldn't exactly count on Grace being my friend. Not as of late anyway.

I waited in line for an hour before I made it into the hallway where auditions took place. I was next in line when the boy in front of me walked out of the studio. He was crying. A girl waiting outside for him asked him what had happened.

"She had a lot of feedback. She's just, well, she kind of rips you apart."

He wiped away some tears and looked at me.

"Break a leg, just don't let her words punch you too hard," he said to me as he walked away.

"Great."

I walked into the room and, to my surprise, it was a decent-sized black box theater. In the front row sat Tyler, the man who had called me, and Karen Picard herself. My guess is that she was somewhere in her sixties, but because of several face-lifts, she portrayed forty-five-'ish.' She wore heavy makeup with blue eye shadow, fake eyelashes, thick eyeliner, and bright orange lipstick that popped off her smooth, dark-as-twilight skin. Her hair was bleached blonde and pin-needle straight. Her bangs were thick, and cut straight across in a perfect line. Her acrylic stiletto nails were shaped fiercely to a point, like a lioness's. She wore an elaborate, tight-fitting, short skirt, and extremely high heels. Her boobs were obviously fake and looked even faker in her corset shirt.

"What's your name?" she asked.

"Pasqualina Panicucci," I responded. "But you can just call me Nina."

She skimmed down her list and put a check next to my name.

"Whenever you are ready, *Nina*."

My breaths became short and my hands started to shake. I took a moment and stepped to the back of the theater. I turned around and closed my eyes, imagining myself on the shores of a beach, clearing my mind until I could hear the waves crashing and the seagulls cawing. I tensed and released my body one limb at a time, relieving the pressure, rolled my head back and forth and relaxed my jaw. These were all exercises my years of acting classes had taught me and proved to be useful in high-stakes auditions. Using the techniques helped me land a local car wash commercial the previous year. I took one big, deep breath in, let it out, turned, opened my eyes and began.

I remembered my monologue word for word, feeling the emotions of the character radiate through my facial expressions, dramatic pauses, and punch lines. The monologue was about a young girl who was reminiscing about her father. It began with happy memories of early childhood and morphed into her feeling guilty about her teen years because she never gave him the time of day anymore. At the end, the audience realizes that she is speaking from the foot of her father's grave. The character cries as she apologizes to the dirt and lays down a flower. I felt good about my performance. I liked to use method acting, where the actor uses previous experiences to help portray realistic emotions. It's terrible to admit, but I used the death of my mother to help recreate the pain. The tears I cried as the character were very real when looking into my own life. I nailed the performance, but when I looked down at Karen's blank stare, I knew I had it coming to me.

"She has a lot of feedback," I thought. "That's what the kid said."

I prepared myself for this woman to rip me a new one, but still, she said nothing. She wrote a few words down on her paper, looked up at me, and said, "Call back. Next Tuesday at seven o'clock in the evening. Thank you for your time."

What? That was it?

"Thank you," I said, confused as I walked toward the door. I still wondered—why didn't I get any feedback? Before I walked out I turned and asked, "Do you happen to have any feedback?"

She paused for a long time, thinking before responding, which made me regret even asking. "Get rid of your New England accent. Oh, and don't put Pasqualina on your resume. Just use Nina."

"Thank you," I smiled.

I ran out of the audition on cloud nine. That was it? Get rid of my accent? Wait, what accent? People from Connecticut don't speak with an accent. Do we? Ah, who cares, I just went to my first audition, and *nailed* it!

When I got home that night, I could hardly sleep from the excitement. Grace assumed I was possessed, as she always does when I get overly-excited about something, but ordered pizza in celebration anyway. She even paid for it.

"Hey, thanks for the rest of the rent," she said as she slopped greasy pepperoni and cheese onto the side of her plate. She always picked off the good stuff and only ate the bread. Too many calories.

"You're welcome. Sorry about us fighting. Hey, are you going to eat that?" I pointed to her cheese and toppings.

"Nah, it's all yours," she said, forking it over.

We sat cross-legged on the living room floor and were watching *Breakfast at Tiffany's*—Grace's pick, of course—when another travel advertisement for Israel came on.

"Oh! I went on that trip!" Grace exclaimed.

"Wait, you are Jewish?"

"By blood only. I'm agnostic. But hey, it was a free trip, why not?"

"I guess so. Me, too. Sort of. My mom is Jewish."

"If your mom is Jewish, then *you* are Jewish."

"Really?"

"Yep."

"What does aliyah mean?"

"It's the term they use when a Jewish person moves to Israel. It's Hebrew for 'ascending,' or like, 'going home,' or something like that. When you move there, you 'make aliyah.'"

"Why didn't *you* make aliyah?"

"It didn't feel like home there—not to me at least. I mean, like I said, I'm agnostic so, whatever, right? New York felt like home, so I moved here instead."

"Makes sense. Did you ride a camel?"

"Actually, I did!"

"I was kidding. But really, you did? Do you have pictures?"

"Yeah, I have them around here somewhere."

We spent the rest of the night looking at photos and talking about her trip. I considered signing up for the trip myself since apparently I'd be Jewish enough to go. We laughed and ate pizza until I swore I'd never eat another piece again. It was refreshing to have a light-hearted night with Grace. For the first time since I moved in, it felt like we were actually friends.

I woke up the next morning on the couch with pizza sauce still stuck to my cheeks. Grace had already left for work, and put a note in the kitchen for me to "please clean up."

"Yeah, yeah," I grumbled.

I cleaned up the counters and emptied the trash quickly. After "dry cleaning," which consisted of splashing water on my face, putting on deodorant, and brushing my teeth, I looked up where the cheapest walk-in health clinic was.

"Lower East Side," I read off the computer screen. It was far, but I'd have to make the trek.

I puttered around the apartment for a while, adjusting the pictures on the wall and swept the floor. I didn't want to know if I had an STD, and I didn't have a choice about knowing if I was pregnant or not. Eventually I'd find out.

At the end of the day, ignorance definitely wasn't bliss, so I went to the free walk-in clinic, which was attached to a hospital emergency room. The lobby was full of people. Some were homeless, and were there just for warmth and a free sandwich. A five-year-old girl was screaming due to a dislocated shoulder. "She fell out of bed," her mother kept repeating to anyone who would listen. I filled out the paperwork and waited my turn. Two hours of circling the waiting room and staring at the vending machine later, they called my name.

They drew blood and swabbed me with a prickly pipe-cleaner thing, though I'll admit, I'd rather have a pap smear than relive Mr. Strong again any day. They told me the results would be in by Tuesday and sent me off with a handful of condoms and the morning-after pill, suggesting I take it right away. I swallowed it gladly, before I even left the building.

Tuesday rolled around and it was nearly time for my call-back audition. I was getting ready to head out when I got the phone call. Yes, *the* phone call. The call I dreaded. The call I thought about obsessively for three days.

"Hi, is this Miss Panicucci?"

"Speaking."

"I'm calling from the lab with your results from the blood and pap."

"Yes, and?"

"Everything is clear."

"Clear as in—?"

"The blood work shows that you are not pregnant, you do not have herpes or HIV, and don't have gonorrhea or chlamydia. We suggest you come back in six months for another HIV test just to be sure, but all in all, you are one-hundred percent clean. Welcome to the rare twenty percent of people."

"What do you mean rare twenty percent?"

"Well, only about twenty percent of the world's population is totally clean. A lot of people at least have some form of herpes, but you don't even have that. Congrats!"

"Judas priest, thank you."

She laughed. "Well, don't thank me, thank yourself for always staying protected. It's important you know."

"Yeah, well, *now* I know. Thanks."

"You're welcome. Have a good night."

A good night? I was going to have a *great* night thanks to that news. I grabbed my purse and glided to my audition.

I showed up at the same place the auditions were held before. I got there about an hour early, expecting to see another line out the door, but surprisingly, only one other person was there. I walked up to him and leaned against the door frame.

"Hey," I said.

"Hey. I'm Peter"

"Nina."

"Were you here last week?"

"Yeah, were you?"

"Yeah," he said.

Above us I could hear some music playing. Well, music would be putting it nicely. More like organized cacophony. I walked over and read a sign posted to the adjacent door that read, *Band auditions tonight—Seeking guitarist/backup vocals.* I turned to tell Peter what the noise was all about and smacked right into a guy carrying a guitar, causing his instrument, and me, to fall to the ground.

"Holy, what the heck. Geezes, I'm sorry!" The man helped me up off the ground. "Are you OK?"

"Yeah I'm fine." My hand was throbbing from breaking my fall.

"Are you sure?"

"Yes, I'm fine." I looked at Peter, horribly embarrassed, and rubbed my hand.

"Well, OK," the man said. "Have a good night. Again, I'm really sorry."

"It's all good."

The man walked through the door and five minutes later Peter and I heard another guitarist warming up with scales.

He was nice enough not to laugh at my fall, or mention it again. We talked for an entire hour. He was eighteen and had just moved to Brooklyn pursuing—what else? Acting. He had a job working at a restaurant in Times Square and told me they were hiring. I figured I could check it out after the audition if things didn't go over well. They called us in. Altogether there were twenty of us. Karen sat us in the theater with her this time and we watched each other audition. We were assigned a cold reading, and Peter was up first. He stumbled, cracked, fell, and failed.

"Thank you, Peter, you may leave now," Karen called out, cutting Peter off mid-sentence. "Next!"

My turn.

"Good to see you again, Nina." She handed me a side.

I took the script from her hand and realized she had given me a male's part.

"I think you gave me the wrong part."

"It doesn't matter, just do the reading, please," she said, waving her hands in the air.

I had to read the part of a fifty-year-old drunken husband. How the hell does a girl in her twenties play the part of a middle-aged drunk? I spun around and did my normal breathing and relaxation techniques, and then went into it. I stumbled over a few words, naturally, as cold readings aren't exactly the friendliest auditions on the planet, but overall I thought I had done OK. Her face was stagnant.

"Good. Come back and sit down," she said.

I sat in the row behind her. She turned around to me and said, "I thought I said to work on that accent. If we are going to work together, I need you to listen to me."

"Yes, ma'am," I replied.

An hour passed. Actor after actor appeared on stage, was ripped apart by the woman, and sent away. By the end of the night, I was the only one she kept.

"I only had room for one," she said. "Congratulations, you are my pick."

I held myself together, barely, and gladly accepted. It was now official: I had an agent. I was disease free, baby free, and I had an agent! Karen instructed me to come by her office that Friday to sign the contract, though she said she would start sending out my headshot and résumé right away to get me some work. Ecstatic, I smiled, laughed, and clapped my hands the entire way home. People looked at me like I was nuts.

FIVE

"OK, Nina, we signed all of the initial paperwork on Tuesday," Karen said. "Are you having any second thoughts before we break out the big contract? It covers you for two years."

"No, ma'am."

I signed the contract with a huge smile on my face. She explained to me that because I was still nonunion, I was actually in a very good position. She could send me out for both union and non-union projects, which would be good for building up my resume. Once I joined SAG-AFTRA, I could only do union work.

After I signed the contract, Karen stepped out of the room. I stood up and began to look around her office. She had several photos of herself and other celebrities. Some looked to be random meetings at bars and film festivals, but one stood out in particular. There was a large photo of Karen with Emma Simon, a popular child star who kind of fell off the planet once she hit sixteen. It was signed, "Thank you for all you have done. Without you, I wouldn't be me! Love, Emma." Seeing Emma's note intimidated me.

I meandered around the room looking at her paintings and eclectic décor, which definitely reflected Karen's style. My first impression of her was rough and bitchy, but once I started talking to her and getting to know her, I couldn't help but love her. When it came to the entertainment business, she knew what she was talking about, and I felt safe putting my career in her hands. She came back into the room, and her assistant brought us both a coffee.

"If you aren't already a coffee fiend, you will become one," she said. "Sometimes actors get very early call times."

"I'm on it." I took a sip and winced. Apparently, she didn't believe in sugar.

"So it looks as though we might have a job for you if you are interested. A very popular television show is looking for a new stand-in for the female lead."

"What show?" I asked.

"It's called *Blazing Love* and it airs on Wednesday nights."

"Oh yeah, I think I've heard of that."

I played it cool. The reality was that I had obsessed over that show for years. The actors who played the firefighters on the show were hot as hell and inside I was freaking-the-heck-out. Stand-ins are the "B-Team" actors that never appear on the show, rather they stand in the place of the "real" actors while the lighting and camera teams set up. Once everything is set, the B-Team goes back to the craft table to indulge in doughnuts and peanut butter and jelly sandwiches while the A-Team actors deliver their lines.

"They need someone about your height and weight, and you look similar to the actress as it is. I sent your headshot in and they liked your look. They said if you can start tomorrow, they would take you."

"What does a position like this pay?"

"They pay you hourly, but you are contracted for at least eight hours. Even if you work two hours that day, you still get paid for eight, so your minimum payment is around two hundred per day. You will most likely have overtime pay, so a lot of my stand-ins bank around three-fifty per day with that. And of course, I take my cut."

"Wow."

"It was a lot more than I was used to getting paid; I really hoped that it wasn't too good to be true.

⋙

"Karen wasn't kidding," I thought as I woke up to my alarm at five o'clock the next morning and brewed a pot of coffee. Grace was, of course, already up and doing her morning workout routine, which consisted of running like a banshee up and down the Hudson River dodging unattended dog poop bombs. I woke up especially early to curl my hair and apply enough makeup to cover up the bags under my eyes. I was actually going to be on the same set as Declan Long. *The* Declan Long. Super sexy, brown-haired, blue-eyed, rock-solid body Declan Long, who was one of the supporting actors in the show.

When I left, I followed the directions to where the bus was going to pick me up on Central Park South near Columbus Circle. I was standing out on the curb avoiding the panhandling homeless and the ruthless runners for twenty minutes longer than expected, when I had the sudden panicked realization that this actually *was* too good to be true. I was waiting for cameras to come busting out with a TV host screaming, "Gotcha!"

"I'm such a *stupid* idiot," I thought. I put my hands in my pockets and walked back and forth on the sidewalk. "I'm glad I didn't tell Grace about this," I whispered. "I never would have heard the end of it."

Just then, a Lincoln Town Car pulled up next to me, and the window rolled down. An older gentleman who introduced himself as Rudy asked for my name.

"Who are you looking for?" I asked. He was a clean-cut, nice-looking older man, but I was still unsure about him and didn't trust him enough to give my name quite yet.

"I'm looking for Miss Panicucci," he said.

Relieved, I said, "That would be me. Please call me Nina."

"Perfect. Hop in. I'll be your driver to the set this morning."

"I was actually told that a bus was coming to pick me up," I said.

"Karen Picard sent me and told me to tell you that it's a closed set today, and she is sorry for the mix-up."

"OK." I climbed into the back.

"It will be about twenty minutes to Brooklyn."

He was right. Twenty minutes later, he dropped me off and I was met at the door by a production assistant named Tina. We were filming at a location that looked familiar to me. It was the firehouse they used on the show! The actress I was standing in for was just who I thought it would be: Larissa Bane. People frequently told me that I resembled her, and once, a couple of months ago, I had done this celebrity lookalike thing at a bar with Grace portraying Larissa and won fifty bucks. Tina got me set up with my tax forms, a voucher for payment, and brought me to the catering area for breakfast.

The spread was amazing: muffins, fruit, oatmeal, omelets cooked-to-order, more coffee than you would need for a year, doughnuts, bagels, and breakfast tacos.

"One of our actors is from Texas, and he will only eat breakfast tacos in the morning. Try one, they are really good," Tina said before she walked away.

I bit into one of the egg, brisket, cheese and potato tacos, and nearly fell over in amazement. "Man, these *are* good."

"I know, aren't they?" a voice said behind me. I turned around, and there, standing before me, was Declan. "I thought they were the weirdest things when Jack requested them, but after I had one I've been addicted." He reached over me to grab a taco and his arm brushed against mine. "Oh, sorry about that," he said and jogged back to his trailer outside.

I stood, staring out of the door with my mouth open.

"Snap out of it, Nina," I told myself.

I went into the bathroom and splashed my face with water completely forgetting I had put on mascara. I lifted my head up and looked in the mirror. "You have *got* to be freaking kidding me," I complained.

"Oh, don't worry, I've done that before," Larissa said as she walked out of the stall and cranked on the sink next to me. She puckered her lips in the mirror and blinked her eyes repeatedly while soaping up her hands. "Go to hair and makeup; they will fix it for you."

"Good call."

"You are my new stand-in, right?"

"Yeah, my name is Nina."

"Cool. It's great to meet you."

"Yeah, you, too."

That was the extent of our conversation. In fact, for the entire ten months that I worked on the set, that was the most she ever said to me.

Working on *Blazing Love* was one of the best experiences of my life. The director was a light-hearted guy and very easy to work with. The food they served was exquisite. I was making decent money and landed myself a spot in the union. When a horror movie was filming nearby, Karen got me a quick role in it. Of course, I played the screaming idiot who gets killed by a psychopath in the very beginning. I spoke eight words and had three solid minutes of camera time and was paid five thousand dollars. Needless to say, Karen was pretty thrilled. With the money I had after taxes and Karen, I gave Grace two months' rent, then bought myself a shit-ton of designer clothes and a pair of Jimmy Choo shoes. Jimmy Choo was my new shoe designer of choice and it had everything to do with the fact that Declan was also a fan of Choo.

After the taco incident, I avoided Declan for a month. I was too star-struck, and I didn't want to risk acting like an imbecile in front of him. However, one afternoon during a lunch break, talking to him was completely unavoidable. We were filming at a resort in upstate New York that week. I was having a rough day and battling a stomach bug. Instead of eating lunch with everyone else, I headed outside to sit on a park bench and get some fresh air. Five minutes later, Declan came up behind me and asked if he could sit down. There were plenty of other park benches for him to choose from, but he picked mine.

My cheeks immediately became flushed and hot. I felt my hand start to twitch, so I shoved it in my pocket nonchalantly.

"Is this seat taken?" he asked.

"How cliché," I responded.

"Ouch."

"I mean, yeah, you can sit here. Sorry, I'm not feeling well."

"What's wrong?"

"It's just my stomach. Careful, I really do not want to throw up on you. You're too pretty."

He laughed.

"Oh geez, I'm sorry," I said. "You know, I avoided you for a month so I wouldn't say something stupid like that."

"Oh, so that's why I haven't been able to talk to you?"

"Yeah. I guess Pepto-Bismol doubles as a truth drug."

He laughed again. "Nice shoes."

"Thanks," I blushed.

We sat on the bench and talked for a few minutes more. He told me how he liked to play basketball and I told him how baseball is the only sport I can tolerate. We both agreed that Italian food is God's gift to cuisine, and Pepsi is definitely better than Coke. He was called back to set and I stayed on the bench to sit for a while longer. Two minutes later, Lisa came up to me with a plate of bread and some ginger ale. Under the bread was a piece of paper folded up. I opened it to find Declan's phone number.

Later that night I experienced the real FDNY as they kicked in my door. The little stomach bug turned into a huge, giant stomach bug that completely took over my digestive tract. I couldn't get up off of the floor, and when I was finally brought to the hospital, I needed five bags of IV fluids and two bags of anti-nausea medicine just to get me to stop throwing up. They kept me there all night. I wished I could have slept, but they placed me in the emergency room next to a convicted felon who was handcuffed to the bed and complained for three hours about them only having cheese sandwiches to eat. By two in the morning, I was tired, cranky, and wide awake thanks to the piss-head next to me. I took my phone out of the plastic bag they gave me for my belongings and texted the number Declan gave me.

> Me: Hey.
> Him: Hey, who is this?
> Me: Nina, sorry it's so late.
> Him: Oh hey! No prob. R u ok?
> Me: Not really. In the ER.
> Him: What? No way.
> Me: Yeah, I feel like death :(
> Him: I didn't know you were that sick. Hope it wasn't the ginger ale.
> Me: Nah, thanks for that though.
> Him: Do you need anything right now?
> Me: Just someone to talk to.
> Him: I can help with that :)

We texted back and forth all night. By morning I was feeling a lot better. One of the nurses brought me a Gatorade and after chugging it, I felt ready to leave. Declan insisted that he pick me up so I wouldn't have to take the subway home. The firefighters had taken me to a hospital in Queens and it was quite a hike back to Harlem.

When I stepped out of the hospital doors, Declan was there to greet me, standing outside of his black Porsche with a bottle of water and a box of saltines. I melted. I heard a girl come running up behind me, push me out of the way, and snap a photo with her phone.

"It's Declan Long! You are on TV!" she was screaming.

Four other girls on the street ran over to snap photos, and before I knew it, Declan grabbed my hand and quickly put me in his car, slammed the door behind me, and drove us away.

"Go, Guadalupe, go!" he said.

"What?"

"My car's name is Guadalupe."

"Should I even ask?" I laughed.

"Better you don't."

I covered my face with my hands and began laughing uncontrollably. "This is crazy; this is just crazy."

"We are going to be all over Twitter in three . . . two . . ." he said.

I laughed.

"It's alright, I don't care." He reached over and held my hand. "How do you feel?"

"Well-hydrated," I said.

"Great. Want to go to the Burger Pit?"

"Hell no! What, are you trying to kill me? I can't eat fast food right now." I flicked my hair off my shoulder and laughed. "I am hungry though."

"Well, I know just the place, and it happens to have great breakfast tacos, if you are interested," he said.

I smiled so hard my face was sore.

He took me to his apartment in the Upper East Side. I was surprised when I saw his place. I figured he would have a larger apartment, but it was rather normal in size—big for New York City, I guess, and certainly bigger than mine. It was a one-bedroom flat with a beautiful balcony overlooking a small garden in the back, full-sized kitchen appliances, and granite countertops. The place was spotless. He had an American bulldog named Fender, who was fat and cute, and extremely well-behaved. He cooked me some delicious breakfast tacos, and I ate my plate clean, unashamed.

Being on set after that was definitely more fun. Declan and I were together daily and got to know each other quickly. Sometimes, we would sneak away into his trailer for a midday quickie. I will tell you one thing, he was not called "Mr. Long" for nothing! The production assistants were suddenly a lot nicer to me—not that they were ever mean, but now they were just more aware of where I was and what I might need at any given moment.

After three months of dating, he asked me to move in with him. I accepted, but was nervous to break the news to Grace.

"You mean, you're leaving!" Grace yelled. "Just like that, you're up and gone?"

"Grace, relax, please."

"I can't cover the rent by myself. Why didn't you give me more time? I thought we were friends! I thought we were *best* friends."

Whoa. I was friends with Grace and all, but *best* friends? Not really. I mean, I had hardly seen her for the past three months. I'd basically been living at Declan's anyway. I slept there all the time, and half of my wardrobe was there.

"You've got to be kidding me, Grace, it isn't like I'm moving to France! I'll still be in New York."

"But what about the rent? Oh, the *rent!*" she said with the palm of her hand to her forehead.

She was so dramatic.

"Put an ad out online; you'll find someone just as quick as you found me. And I'll leave my furniture so you can sell it. Just keep the cash. Maybe psycho roommate will come back and live here."

My words rang true. Two months after I moved into Declan's, the psycho roommate took her room back over. Grace forgot about me after that.

SIX

My relationship with Declan ambushed me. I didn't think I could have a connection with anyone the way *we* connected. When it came to guys of Declan's caliber, I was usually fucked and chucked, you know? Men took me by my looks and didn't care much about my brain. Once they were done with my body, they stopped calling. I never went to college, but it wasn't like I was stupid. I still had something to offer intellectually, or at least I thought so. I longed for conversation about meaningful things, and Declan fulfilled that desire. After lovemaking, we would talk about constellations, and politics, and literature, so much so that it inspired me to put my library card to use. I'd check out books about music and history—all sorts of topics. I was inspired to learn more about the world around me, and Declan loved that, so he encouraged it. They say chivalry is dead, but, he was a chivalrous knight. A hot, sexy knight dressed in designer clothes.

He took me out to dinner often, and one night we decided to go to the famous Giuseppe's. We were seated against a window on the second floor that overlooked the street below. Halfway through our dinner, I peered out of the window and saw a white Mercedes pull up to the curb. My heart was a speeding bullet. Out of the passenger's seat came a blonde porn-star-looking woman, and out of the driver's side came none other than Marco. Declan was telling a story that I barely heard because I kept replaying my past with Marco in my mind.

"Hey sweetie, is everything OK?" Declan slid his fingertips across my palm.

"No, not really."

I told him about Marco—the short, *Reader's Digest* version—and it infuriated him.

"This prick is *here*?"

"Yeah, actually he is sitting right over there." I pointed to the booth I had sat in with Marco, just two tables away from ours. "I bet he sits in the same booth every time."

Declan removed the napkin from his lap, placed it on the table, and stood up.

"No, Declan, *no*," I insisted, but he didn't listen.

He went over to our waiter and handed him a one-hundred dollar bill, whispering something. The waiter then gave him his pen and a small scrap of paper. Declan wrote for a moment, passed the pen and folded up note back, then returned to the table.

"What did you just do?" I asked.

"Keep an eye on the scumbag's table."

A few moments later, a waiter emerged from the kitchen with an expensive bottle of champagne. Instead of bringing it to our table, which I assumed he would be doing, he brought it over to Marco's table. I heard the waiter say, "Compliments of Mr. Declan Long."

The note was attached to the bottle.

"What does it say?" I wondered.

"She's perfect. Better she's with me and not with you!" Declan smiled and winked at me.

Confused, Marco looked up from his table and spotted us. Declan raised his glass to him just before planting a kiss right on my lips in front of everyone. We finished our dinner, and I walked out of the restaurant in front of Marco and his date like a boss. I gave him a wink, waved to his playmate, and had a good laugh.

We were attached at the hip most of the time, Declan and I, at least in the beginning of our relationship. We frequently visited the Metropolitan Museum of Art and went out clubbing like it was our job. Actually, for Declan it was. Clubs would pay him to make appearances and would go out of the way to make him extra comfortable. Whenever we went out it was usually with the *Blazing Love* crew: Jack, Desi, and Luke, three supporting actors, and whatever girls they were sleeping with at the time. They roped off VIP sections for us and set up tables to mingle around. A bottle of Martini & Rossi Asti was always waiting for me at whatever table Declan requested. He knew I loved sweet champagne, and I would drink the entire bottle until I couldn't feel my face every time we went out. He thought it was the funniest thing to see me drunk, but I would never get quite drunk enough to actually throw up. I wish I could say the same for Declan. He could pound back three or four shots of tequila in a matter of minutes, but if he didn't take time between the marathon shots, he would get terribly sick. I hated when that happened because that meant I definitely was not having sex that night.

We kept our sex life spicy, for the most part. Whenever he was on top of me, he always stopped what he was doing for a brief second, dipped down and kissed me softly, then whispered in my ear, "You are the only girl I ever want to do this with," which immediately made me orgasm every time.

We joined the mile-high club together. Although I don't recommend having sex in an airplane bathroom, everyone must try to experience it at least once for bragging rights. This happened on our impromptu trip to Israel. I saw in a travel magazine the wonders that a soak in the Dead Sea does for your skin, hair, and nails. I mentioned I would like to go there sometime, maybe even sign up for that free trip, but Declan surprised me three days later with plane tickets. He woke me up at four o'clock in the morning and said he had a surprise for me and that I shouldn't ask questions. He had apparently stayed up all night packing our bags and arranged doggie day care for Fender. When the taxi pulled up to Newark airport, I knew right away what he was up to. I flew first class for the first time. Unfortunately, first-class bathrooms are no bigger than coach. We waited until everyone was either asleep or preoccupied with something else. I made my way to the restroom first. He waited three minutes before coming over and knocking five times on the door, which was our secret code. I let him in. I bent over the tiny sink and we joined the club. When we walked out of the bathroom together, a few people noticed, but considering Declan's celebrity status, no one cared. The story did, however, make it into a magazine two days later. I thought it was hysterical, but I prayed my father didn't see it. He never mentioned it so I'm fairly certain that my secret stayed safe.

My father absolutely loved Declan. He only met him once but, of course, the fact that he was on a show about firefighting scored major points. My father was all about anything and everything firefighting. When the studio wrapped the series, Declan sent him the badge he wore on the show for a birthday gift. It was all Papà needed to practically hand me over to him in marriage. Declan talked about proposing all of the time, but would never do it. I was convinced he was going to propose when he whisked me off to the Dead Sea, but it didn't happen.

The Israel vacation was amazing. We spent a week at a spa right on the Dead Sea; I had never experienced anything so unique. The rumors about being able to float in the sea and read a book at the same time were true. The salt and all the minerals only had to touch my skin for a second before they penetrated it, making it feel the softest it had been since birth.

Since we flew into Tel Aviv, we set aside a day for shopping. I had to purchase a separate suitcase after I discovered a popular Israeli store and bought up half their new arrivals. I also bought ten bags of Dead Sea mud, mineral shampoos, soaps, and bath salts. It was the best vacation I had ever taken, invigorating in entertainment, but also spiritually.

I loved spending time at the Dead Sea, but I wanted to explore some of the other areas of the country. After two hours of bugging Declan about it, we signed up for a tour of Jerusalem. The next day, we took a long bus ride from the sea to the city, passing through vast desert and an occasional palm tree. I wasn't caught up in international affairs or current events, so I didn't realize how war-torn the country was. Once we reached the city, we were escorted to the city gate by a man who had a gun that covered half his body.

"An armed guard?" I asked. "For what?"

Declan seemed just as confused as me.

"Maybe we should have researched this a little more?"

"You literally begged me to come here; we're going in," he said with a half playful, half nervous laugh.

The tour we signed up for would be taking us into the Jewish quarter of the city. I wished I could have seen the city as a whole, but the tour made it very clear we would only be in the Jewish section.

I grabbed Declan's hand and squeezed.

"OK, let's go in," I decided.

The tour guide led us through the city and showed us the various sights. The first stop was an excavation site showing the different layers of Jerusalem. The city had been destroyed many times, and rather than clearing the area and rebuilding, the ancestors of the city instead built right on top of the rubble. We walked down the stairs and soon I found myself on a pebble road that had been placed there nearly two thousand years ago. I kneeled down to touch the rocks with my hand. When my fingertips touched the road, an electric shock flowed through my arm. At that moment a loudspeaker started to blare. A man was speaking in a language I didn't understand, and suddenly he began to sing.

"What is that?" I asked.

The tour guide told me that several times a day, the speakers turn on and Muslim prayers ring through the whole city. It was beautifully sung, with musical scales I had never heard before. It was haunting and intriguing.

"The prayer can be heard for miles," the tour guide said.

I stood still, listening and admiring the melodic devotion. When the man finished singing I looked at Declan and raised my eyebrows. Life was very different on the other side of the world. Laws and religion were a married concept, unlike the separation of church and state in America. I yearned to learn more about it.

The woman who led our tour took us through the streets, showed us where to get the best falafel, and pointed out other structures from ancient days. Eventually, we ended up in a beautiful stone courtyard. She lifted her finger to a window and said in her thick accent, "That is upper room."

"The what?" Declan asked.

It clicked in my head what she was saying. "The upper room, with the last supper?"

"Yes!" she replied.

I looked up at the window, and again felt some sort of electric pulsing in my temples. I knew I needed to get inside that room.

"Can we go in?" I asked, expecting her to say no.

"Of course."

I couldn't believe that they would actually let us into a structure that was thousands of years old. I followed the tour guide, and Declan followed close behind me. We climbed the stairs and entered the room, which was incredible. High intricate arches stretched across the ceiling and the stonework was well kept. I ran my hand along the wall and tried to picture Jesus in there with his disciples. I hadn't been to church in years, but I still remembered the stories. The people I read about in the Bible seemed so out of reach, like some fairy tale. Standing in the room where they had actually walked, talked, and ate with each other gave me a different perspective. I pictured Jesus at a table, talking with his followers and breaking bread, when I felt an overwhelming wave of panic. He was captured, tortured, and killed shortly after he was in this room. The more I thought about it, the more the panic set in. Eventually, it welled up so strong that I started to tear up, and soon I was in a full-blown ugly cry, completely catching the poor tour guide off-guard. Declan came up behind me.

"What's wrong?" he asked, puzzled.

"I don't even know!" I cried back.

He placed his hand on my shoulder and the panicked feeling faded. His arms wrapped around me, I took a deep breath in, and exhaled. As the breath left my body all I could think about was how comfortable and relaxed I felt in that moment. I didn't want to move. For the first time, I actually felt grounded, secure, and even in a land filled with turmoil, I felt safe.

After the crying episode, Declan thought it would be best if we cut the tour short and went back to the sea. It was a far drive, and both of us were getting tired. We approached where the shuttles were lined up, and relaxed in the comfortable chairs until the rest of the tour returned. Declan took a nap, but I stayed awake the entire trip back. I was trying to make sense of what had happened in the upper room. It was a strange, supernatural experience.

The only other time I had been outside of the United States was to go to Canada for a crappy family vacation. Going to Israel taught me a new culture. The feeling in the air was obscure. When I first arrived, I wasn't aware of the tension between religions; I never paid much attention to international issues. When I stepped off the plane, the thickness in the air boasted something powerful. It was an intense awakening as I realized maybe there was something out in the universe beyond our comprehension. Maybe some sort of spirit world actually *did* exist. Looking back on it, I wish I had spent more time experiencing this new spirit world.

When we landed back in Newark, I felt disconnected and lost. I returned to the fast-paced life, where everyone buried their cold faces in their cell phones. Coming from the slow-paced vacation life, it was an unwelcome jolt back to the grind.

When we got home, we were on Israeli time and stayed up until three in the morning unpacking, eating lo mein, and reminiscing about the trip.

"I think I want to go to school." I was dumping the clothes from my suitcase into the laundry basket when I had the epiphany.

"Why? Didn't Karen just send out your headshots again?"

"Yeah, but like, I could do it online and still act."

"I guess. What would you study?" Declan was talking with his mouth full, which annoyed me.

"Anthropology, I think."

He started laughing. "And what would you do with an *Anthropology* degree? Nobody cares about that. Just stick to acting, you'll get something."

I shrugged my shoulders and continued unpacking.

After the show wrapped, I didn't have any long-term work lined up. I wanted to take some time off anyway and had a significant amount of money in my savings, which I knew would be enough to cover at least two semesters of school at a local college. Declan paid most of the bills. I truly thought I was going to be with him forever, and didn't see any reason why I would need to have a savings account. We had a deal. I'd keep the place tidy so he wouldn't have to pay a maid anymore, and we split the utilities. I regretted that decision daily when I had to wash the entire sink of dirty dishes he had made every morning just to make a pot of coffee. I ended up buying a K-Cup machine so I could at least save the washing until I had caffeine in my blood.

I took up smoking marijuana with Declan. Every morning, we would "wake and bake" out of his oversize bong, which we nicknamed "Mammoth." Occasionally, Declan would do some harder drugs like cocaine, but I stayed away from that. I still remember my first experience getting high. Declan, the *Blazing Love* crew, and I were all sitting in his living room. It was two or three weeks after we had started dating, and we were getting plastered, watching *Breaking Bad* reruns.

"I swear, I'm inside of the TV right now," I kept repeating.

Declan laughed so hard he almost puked. "I wish I could still get that high."

"No, you don't understand. I'm having an out-of-body experience *right now*. I'm legitimately inside of *Breaking Bad*," I insisted.

The crew just kept laughing.

"You have no idea how jealous I am of you," said Jack. "I have to smoke three joints and drink a bottle of whiskey to get that trashed!"

"You guys are not listening to me at all. I am Walter White. I'm inside of the TV," I insisted firmly.

I pointed to the TV screen in all seriousness, shaking my finger, and they lost it in laughter. I ended up being so high that when I walked out onto the street to go home, I had to immediately turn back and stay the night. Declan wasn't opposed. In fact, he said that was the night he fell in love with me.

I grew very fond of marijuana after that. It gave me the relaxed feeling I felt I needed in a busy and stressful city. Many of our gatherings focused around smoking sessions, drinking, and clubbing.

This one particular time, we happened to be partying in the VIP section at NYC's hottest club with Big A, a famous rapper. I was never really one for rap music but thought it was fun anyway. He came over to our table with his entourage of girls and partied with us for a few hours. One of the girls he brought over had her eyes on Declan for quite some time before she got the courage to go over and talk to him. I didn't care that she was hitting on him because I knew he would never do anything to hurt me. She was a model named Coco. She was very pretty, thin, had nice boobs, an even nicer butt, and a killer outfit, but I wasn't intimidated. She whispered a few things in his ear that I couldn't make out, and he smiled. He pointed over to me and I could make out the words "girlfriend" from his lips.

"That's a good boy," I thought. I walked over to him, grabbed the collar of his shirt and pulled him into me, squeezing myself between them. I dragged my fingernails across the back of his neck, which made his breath on my cheek tremble. Keeping our eyes locked, I led us away from Coco and into the private back room.

Behind the thin door, he pressed his swollen pants against my body and kissed my neck. With a quick unzip of his pants, I rewarded his devotion, took him into my mouth, and for the first time, swallowed.

Coco stuck around for the rest of the night and made a complete fool of herself. She got up on the table with her minidress and six-inch heels, started dancing, and lost her balance. Strings of lights hung from the ceiling for decoration, so she grabbed them to balance herself. Instead, she pulled them straight out of the ceiling and landed flat on her back, legs up in the air. Maybe she shouldn't have worn a thong that day. Maybe she shouldn't have been on her period either. She left shortly after.

Later on, I found out she had slipped her phone number into Declan's pocket, and we had our first real blowout fight.

"If she put it in your pocket, then why is it sitting here in your wallet?" I asked.

"I put it in my wallet because I didn't want you to find it and freak out. I was going to throw it away, I promise."

I had found the number when I went into his wallet to tip the delivery guy who brought us a late night snack.

"Why didn't you throw it out at the club?" I demanded.

"Because I just didn't! I don't have to explain *anything* to you!"

"We've been dating for over a year, and I live with you. I think you should be honest enough to let me know when a girl gives you her number."

"Do me a favor and don't touch my stuff."

"Well, that's kind of hard when we live together, Declan."

"This is stupid. I don't need this shit. I've never been unfaithful to you."

"I know, but I just want you to tell me when things like this happen."

"I didn't see any need to tell you because I wasn't going to call her."

"Then why was it in your wallet, if she put it in your pocket?" I yelled.

The cycle repeated itself until Declan snapped.

"That's it! I'm out of here," he spit.

He packed an overnight bag with clothes and left for the night. I sat on the kitchen floor drunkenly sobbing with Fender in my arms. He could always sense when I was upset and would sit on my lap licking my tears. One time I bit into a jalapeño pepper by accident and my eyes welled up from the heat. He even came to lick those tears, too. He was such a good dog. I cradled him and sobbed until I fell asleep. I have no idea where Declan went that night, but he came back the next morning freshly showered and didn't say a word.

SEVEN

After the phone number incident, things started to go downhill. Declan didn't talk to me the way he used to. He didn't touch me with affection either, which was really starting to screw with my head. When we had sex, it was purely physical. I could tell by the look on his face, if he even took the time to look at me at all, that the emotion was gone. He was always "going out with the crew in Brooklyn," he would tell me. I couldn't go anywhere myself because he would ask me to stay home with Fender. He had fired the dog walker because she apparently "didn't walk him right."

I spent many lonely nights at home with Fender. At first we would binge-watch old *Real Housewives* episodes. I'd sit on the floor and he would plop down on my lap, and we'd zone out to grown-ass women arguing over petty, meaningless things. I'd drink nearly an entire bottle of wine and smoke out of Mammoth until I passed out. I'd have to go for a five-mile run the next morning just to burn it all off, and it got old after a few weeks. One cold night in November, I decided to pull out Declan's beat-up guitar, which was lying around, and started to learn to play. He had received it as a gift from an ex-girlfriend and it supposedly had been owned by Eric Clapton, but I honestly doubt it. Playing it was harder than I thought and killed my fingers, but I looked up some tutorials and tried to figure it out anyway. I managed to learn a few chords and after practicing them for a week, I was better at making the shapes with my fingers.

I tried to avoid tourist locations at all costs, but one afternoon I stopped in at the Guitar Center in Times Square to see about buying my own guitar. A sales associate came over to help me pick one out. He was scruffy-faced, tattooed, and wore a band T-shirt with black skinny jeans. He had ragged brown hair with blond streaks in it and hazel eyes. When he introduced himself, I didn't catch his name because my mind was wandering. He sort of looked familiar to me, but I couldn't put my finger on where I knew him from.

"What can I help you with today?" he asked.

"I'm just looking for a guitar. I'm not sure if I want to buy one, or if I *should* buy one. I mean, I've only been playing for, like, a week."

"Well," he laughed, "I've got seven guitars of my own, but I really only play one of them. My old PRS. Occasionally my strat, but usually the PRS. So for a guy who buys guitars just for the hell of it, you're talking to the wrong person if you are wondering if you *should* buy one, because my answer will always be yes."

I laughed, both because I had no idea what a PRS or a strat were, and also because when he talked his hair would sort of flop down into his eyes and he'd have to flick it to the side or slick it back with his hand. It was so sexy. I suddenly had to remind myself that I was a taken girl.

"Sorry, I have no idea what you are talking about," I admitted.

"Alright, well, let's start there."

He showed me the differences between the types of wood and brands. He explained that PRS is a brand, and "strat" is short for Stratocaster, which is a type of guitar Fender makes. I told him my dog's name was Fender and he joked that it was the best pet name he'd ever heard. The words "my dog" bounced around my mouth. I *wished* he was mine.

"Do you want to play any of them?" he asked.

I wanted to, but I was embarrassed by how bad I was.

"I don't really know how to play anything. Can you play them and then I can just listen?"

"Sure." He grabbed an acoustic off of the wall and started picking at the strings with his fingers, playing a gentle blues song. When he started to sing I damn near kissed him right then and there. His voice was soulful and smooth and raspy all at the same time. I watched his lips as he sang. Good god, it was the sexiest thing I'd seen in a while.

"What song was that?"

"Oh, I wrote that a few years ago for my father."

"You *wrote* that?" I was impressed.

"Yeah. Do you want me to show you a couple things?"

"I don't know, I'm terrible compared to you." I shied away.

"Oh come on, you started a *week* ago. Everyone sucks at first. Let me teach you a couple chords. I'll show you enough so that you can write your own song if you want to." He handed the guitar to me.

I reluctantly agreed and he tenderly started to place my fingers on the frets. I noticed how his eyebrows raised to the middle of his forehead when he was explaining something, and it killed me. When I played an F chord properly for the first time, I smiled and looked up into his compassionate eyes and adorable brows. I had been trying to play an F for weeks with no success.

"It feels good, doesn't it? The strings ringing through the guitar against your body. There's no other feeling like it," he said.

"You are *so* right. Learning to play is kind of addicting." I tucked my hair behind my ear.

"Here we go. This one's a beaut." He took down a guitar down from the wall. "It's a PRS Angelus made from mahogany and rosewood. Check it out."

"Oh my gosh," I said. "This feels really nice. I know I'm a beginner, but I can say that this one feels amazing in my hands. I don't want to put it down."

"Well, when you know, you know," he said.

"Definitely. I'm going to tell my boyfriend about it. My birthday is coming up in a couple of weeks and he said he would take me out shopping for something. I think I'll ask him for this."

"You have a boyfriend?"

Fuck, fuck, fuck. Why did I mention Declan?

"Oh, yeah, I do. Though I haven't been seeing much of him lately."

"Gotcha. Well, I'm glad I could show you around. We work off commission here, so here's my card for when you come back, if you don't mind asking for me again."

"Of course. Thank you—David," I read his card. "David," I said again. "Do I know you from somewhere? I feel like I've seen you before, but I don't remember when."

"Yeah, I know. Actually I wasn't sure if you remembered."

"Remembered what?"

"Well, I sort of plowed you over on the street like a year ago or something. At an audition. Or at least, I'm pretty sure it was you. You're sort of hard to forget."

His statement startled me, and then I remembered.

"You! That was *you*?" I gave his arm a playful punch. "Small world."

"Yeah. I'm still terribly sorry about that. And hey, just call me Dave. Everyone does. What's your name? I probably should have asked you that sooner. Can you tell I'm new to sales?"

"Pasqualina, but call me Nina. And no, you're fine. I mean, you just sold me *that*, anyway." I pointed to the guitar.

"Thanks. Well, I'll see you soon, Nina."

He walked away with the soon-to-be-mine guitar in his hands. I kept the card in my purse so I wouldn't lose it and left. I smiled the entire three-block walk to the subway and didn't realize it until I stepped onto train. I couldn't wait to go back and see Dave again.

"Where were you all day?" Declan asked when I came home.

"Just at the guitar store. I think I'd like to get one for my birthday, actually."

"One of what?"

"A guitar."

"It's your money, you can buy whatever you want."

"Well," I hesitated. "I was hoping this could maybe be your gift to me?"

He stared at me for fifteen straight seconds with no expression on his face, making me feel like an asshole for asking.

"Whatever," he finally said, and turned back to his phone as he scrolled through his text messages. "Oh, I want you to start paying rent."

Hi statement stopped me in my tracks.

"I haven't really been working, Declan, and you know I want to go back to school. I already applied for the spring at Hunter and *I got in*."

"Take out a student loan then."

"Seriously? Come on, what is this about? I know you don't need the money."

He looked up from his phone and back down again. "I just think you should contribute more."

I looked over at the spotless kitchen. "Cleaning up all your crap every day isn't contributing? Walking Fender every time you disappear, and making sure your clothes are clean—dragging them back and forth to the laundromat and folding them just the way you like so they fit in your drawer without wrinkling—*that's* not contributing?"

"Not financially."

I rolled my eyes. "Whatever, Declan. How much do you want?"

"A grand a month."

"Fine." I knew the rent was a little over four thousand a month. At least he wasn't asking for half, because I wouldn't have been able to swing it. I also knew that I wouldn't be able to afford school if I gave him that kind of money, and it was too late to apply for financial aid, so I'd have to wait until the fall. The whole situation sucked.

I sat down next to him and extended an olive branch, asking if he wanted to watch a movie and order take-out that night. He seemed reluctant, but for once he agreed to a night in with me rather than going out with the guys. That night was one of the better ones we had together in a while. We sat close together on the couch and watched a comedy, which wasn't my favorite, but I figured I would do anything to keep him at home for a night. We ordered dumplings from a hole-in-the-wall place down the street, joking and smiling at each other as we ate on the living room floor, putting our rent conversation in the past. I couldn't remember the last time we had laughed like that. Butterflies returned to my stomach as he put his hand on my thigh and kissed me. After the movie, we made love on the couch. At least it felt like love, for a minute.

"I want to cum in you," he said.

After I moved in with Declan, we started having unprotected sex, utilizing the "pull and pray" method. After a year of pulling out and never getting pregnant, we basically had it down to a science.

"You know you can't."

"I want to feel you, please let me." He kept going.

"I'm not on the pill, you know that."

I thought about it for a second as he continued making love.

"Maybe he was coming around?" I thought. I doubted that I'd get pregnant anyway. It was only *one time.* "OK."

He came hard that night, and so did I. I felt so in love, and finally back on track. The next day seemed normal. He made no mention of our sex the night before, but smiled when he asked if I wanted to go pick up the guitar for my birthday.

"Of course!" I said.

We went to Guitar Center that afternoon, and I made sure to ask for Dave.

"Hey, Dave! This is my boyfriend, Declan, I was telling you about."

Declan shook Dave's hand hard and asked where the guitar was. He was being *so* rude, and it was embarrassing.

"I'll grab a new one from the back for you." Dave disappeared into the back room.

"*Now* I know why you were here all day," Declan grumbled.

"What are you talking about?'

"I saw how he looked at you. Did he give you his number?"

"No. Why would you even think that?"

"I know how other guys are, and he's interested in you."

"Well, I never did anything wrong. I wish you would relax," I said as Dave came back with the guitar. He was talking loud and I hoped Dave hadn't heard.

Declan acted like he was my enemy while paying for the guitar. A few people in the store started to recognize him and take photos with their phones, which annoyed him even more. He was texting someone, barely paying any attention to me. I didn't understand. Dave darted his eyes at me, questioning the situation with raised eyebrows, but I turned away.

After he paid, Declan walked out, leaving me with my new guitar.

"Is everything OK?" Dave asked.

"I'll be OK. Thanks for everything."

I caught up with Declan, who was already waiting in his car. "I really wish you would chill out. I didn't do anything but look at guitars, I promise. I love you, Declan. I'd never do anything to hurt you, I promise!"

"Thanks." He softened his face. "What kind of guitar did I just pay for?"

"It's a Paul Reed Smith. Don't worry, I'm not after his balls either."

Declan went back to his texting conversation and snickered.

"Are you smiling because of my joke or because of what you just read?" He didn't respond. "You shouldn't be texting and driving. It's dangerous, not to mention illegal."

"Keep telling me what to do and you are really going to piss me off." He kept glancing at his screen.

"Fine."

We'd had such an amazing time the night before, but it wasn't good enough to change the attitude that had developed over the last month.

"What is wrong with—you know what? Never mind," I finished. It wasn't worth it. All we would do is argue and I didn't want to ruin a good day.

He gave me a kiss goodbye before he left to pregame for a club appearance he had booked with his friends later that night. He once again asked me to stay home with Fender, leaving me hurt and disappointed. I couldn't understand how we could have passionate sex the night before and he was still asking me to stay home. Why couldn't he just rehire the dog walker? Or hire a different one? When he came home at two in the morning, drunk and smelling like perfume, things started to click. His phone buzzed while he was in the bathroom, so I leaned over to see who was texting him, and there on the screen appeared the name "Coco." Although I had pretended to be asleep when he came home, I sat straight up in bed and turned the lights on.

"What's with you?" he asked.

"Why is Coco texting you at two in the morning, Declan?"

"I don't know, she probably wants weed or something."

"I thought you threw her number away?"

"One of my friends gave her my number. She just texts me randomly, but I never respond."

"I've known you long enough to know you are lying."

"You are really crazy, you know that? I'm not lying to you."

"Yes, you are!" I started to get louder.

"Whatever, dude." He grabbed a backpack full of clothes.

"You are cheating on me! I know you are! Just admit it. *Admit* it!"

"Stop." He was emotionless.

"Admit it!"

"Listen," he paused. "I am going to go now. And when I come back, you are not going to be such a lunatic anymore. OK?" He didn't wait for me to respond before he slammed the door.

I couldn't sleep at all that night. Was I making this up in my head? Was I jealous for no reason? No way, he was totally cheating on me, right? Or was

I wrong, and did I just completely screw everything up? Around four in the morning, I decided to take matters into my own hands. I found Coco's profile online and sent her a message. I had a hunch something was going on, and I was determined to figure it out.

> Dear Coco,
> I'm so sorry for e-mailing you randomly here. I'm also sorry if I'm accusing you of something you aren't doing. But Declan has been gone so much lately, and I don't know where he is going. He tells me all of the time that he is going out with his guy friends, but he comes home so late and smells like perfume. We have been fighting a lot lately, and I don't even know why. I want you to know that I love him so much, but I need to know if he is cheating on me with you. I'm really confused, and you texted him so late tonight. I just want to know.
> Thanks,
>   —Nina (Declan's girlfriend)

Five minutes later, I got a response. Sick to my stomach, I read the words on the screen.

> Nina, he's here right now sleeping. I'll message you tomorrow morning after he leaves.
>   —Coco

I screamed at the top of my lungs into a pillow so that the neighbors wouldn't hear me. I went into the bathroom and threw up into the toilet. I sucked in a huge hit from Mammoth, ran a bubble bath, and sat in it with a cup of tea, trying to calm down. By six in the morning, I had moved nearly all of my belongings from the bedroom out into the living room. I sure as hell wasn't going to sleep with him anymore. And screw him for calling me a "lunatic." I knew I was right. At this point, we were definitely going to break up, but I didn't have anywhere to go. Plus, I had just given him November *and* December's rent, and I wasn't going to let that go to waste.

I stayed glued to my laptop waiting for Coco to respond. Finally, a message came through.

> Coco: Hey.
> Me: Hey.

Coco: I'm sorry, but Declan and I have been seeing each other for about two and a half months now. I swear on my life that I had no idea you were in the picture. He said that he broke up with you months ago.

I took a deep breath to keep me from vomiting again.

Me: No, quite the opposite. We are still living together, and still fucking, at that.

Coco: What? When was the last time you slept with him?

Me: Two nights ago.

Coco: Oh my god. What the hell? He's been two-timing me too then.

Me: I guess so. I don't know what to do, and I don't know where to go. My whole life is shredded apart.

Coco: I'm so sorry, I feel like this is partially my fault. I remember you from the club, but I swear, he told me he had broken up with you. I'm just as hurt, trust me.

Me: I believe you. I need to go.

I signed off.

I sat on the couch and started crying into Fender's fur. Not only would I be breaking up with Declan, but I would lose Fender in the process, and that made my heart hurt even worse.

Declan stormed in.

"You are crazy!" He screamed at me as he went into the bedroom and locked the door behind him.

I kept crying. I could hear him through the bedroom room wall talking to Coco on the phone. He was actually trying to get *her* back. What about me? *I* was the one living with him. *I* was the one who had been dating him for over a year. Why wasn't he trying to save *our* relationship? It didn't make any sense! I paced back and forth in the living room, trying to keep myself from crying so that I could hear his conversation.

"No, Coco, you don't understand! She's crazy, like legitimately crazy. I don't know why she contacted you. Yes, we broke up, I promise you, and I'm not lying!" he yelled.

"You *are* lying!" I slammed my hand against the door.

"Did you hear that? She's literally banging herself against my door right now. I'm trying to tell you, she is crazy," he yelled.

After much silence, I heard him slam something hard on the ground. She must have hung up on him. He stayed in our room for hours. I laid down on the couch with Fender, unable to move, unable to eat, unable to do anything, really, but wait on Declan. I realized then that waiting for Declan was all I had been doing this entire relationship. I took a hard look around the room. I saw all of the things we had bought together: paintings from local artists we spotted outside of the Met museum last summer, our colorful caricatures from Central Park, images of us smiling, and memories in picture frames. I replayed our relationship in my mind. I blamed myself for our demise, and my heart just wanted so badly for his eyes to look at me with love again. I yearned for our deep night talks about space exploration, and for our quickies in the trailer. I wanted what we *had* back, but I didn't know what I could do to make that happen.

The reality, I found out later, was that Declan had been cheating on me from the very beginning with several different girls, and I just happened to catch on when Coco came into the picture. Did I honestly think that it would be any different? After all, he was a celebrity. He could have any girl he wanted. Why would he settle for just me? All those times he waved hello to a girl he knew in the coffee shop, or girls he invited out with us, insisting they were only friends, were lies. I felt so stupid.

I went to the bathroom and took out a bottle of Tylenol. I dumped a handful of about fifteen in my hand and started swallowing them down with wine. I wanted to get as fucked up as possible. I sat on the floor for a while, then looked at myself in the mirror, only then realizing what I had just done. I threw the bottle on the floor, as my stomach started cramping in pain. I keeled over and slammed into the bathroom door in the process. I heard Declan emerge from the bedroom to check on me. He opened the door, but I didn't open my eyes to see. I felt him drag my body over to the bathtub and throw water on my head. He stuck his fingers down my throat and got me to vomit several times. All the while he was yelling at me.

"What did you do?" he screamed, and threw the empty pill bottle in the sink. "You are nuts! You're going to try and kill yourself now? Just get the hell out of my life, you've already ruined it enough! I'm calling the cops!"

He shoved his fingers down my throat once more, and I vomited again.

He poured water into my mouth until I swallowed it. When I eventually came around, I told him I was feeling better and begged him not to call the police, so he didn't.

"You are not going to kill yourself because of this," he said.

"I didn't intend to kill myself."

"No, you didn't, you just wanted some stupid fucking attention. What the fuck is wrong with you?" He scooped me up and carried me to the couch. "You can stay here if you want, but Nina, this is insane. This has to end. All of this is too much for me. I'm so pissed off at you." He paced, and put his hands to his head, and then, more calmly, said, "This has to be over."

I looked down and picked at my fingernails. "Why did you cum in me?"

"What?" He looked perplexed.

"If you knew you were done with me, then why did you bother?"

He let out a long drawn out sigh. "I don't know," he paused. "I guess I was hoping that I would feel something for you, but I just didn't. I tried, but I couldn't."

"I just want to know what I did wrong." I said it over and over again. "What did I do wrong? What did I do?"

He covered his ears and went back into the kitchen. "I'm not going to have this conversation," he snapped.

After a few minutes of silence, still feeling groggy, I fell into a deep sleep that washed over me in a wave of numb heat. My body felt good, and my mind experienced a unique ecstasy slipping me away into a euphoric dream. I didn't care if I lived or died. I must have been feeling high from whatever absorbed into my system. Truthfully, I probably should have gone to the hospital, but I didn't want to get evaluated in the psych ward. I wanted all of the pain to go away. I wanted my life to go back to the way it was, being happy with a man who I believed was the love of my life. I had to accept the fact that it was over. Lust consumed our relationship, and it didn't matter how much water my tears produced, we were burning to the ground.

EIGHT

The next six weeks were difficult to get through. The holiday season was in full swing. The tree in Rockefeller Center was lit up, snow was on the ground, and the carolers were scattered throughout Central Park. I was still sleeping on the couch at Declan's, desperately looking for work so I could move out. I had contacted Grace to see about moving back in. It turned out that Grace and psycho roommate, whose name was Samantha—Grace insisted I call her by her "real name" from now on—had a romantic connection and were sleeping in the same room these days. Now I understood why Grace took it so hard when I moved out. She must have had deeper feelings for me than I had for her. My former room had been empty for some time, but was rented out to someone else in the last month. Grace sympathized and said she would let me know if anything changed.

Declan was a little nicer to me now that we were officially broken up, although I was treated strictly like a roommate. For two weeks he showed a little more concern for my well-being, hoping at the same time I wasn't pregnant, but that ended when I got my period. We spent Thanksgiving together with the *Blazing Love* crew, pretending everything was fine. There were moments when he would open a door for me, or offer to grab dinner for us. Those were the moments I cherished. At the same time, there were nights where he wouldn't come home. I knew he was out with some "girl of the week," and it killed me. I pictured him being intimate with another woman and it churned my stomach. He had bought a box of condoms and kept them in his bedside table. Sometimes I would go in there and count them, figuring out how many times he had slept with other girls, but the more I did that, the more upset I became. I lost twenty-five pounds in six weeks, bringing me from a size two to a double zero.

I had to break the news to my father that Declan and I were no longer together, and that really sucked because I knew how much he liked him. We played phone tag for a little while. A lot of our conversations had been delayed lately because we always seemed to pick the wrong time to call one another. Four days in a row he called me while I was going to the bathroom. Two minutes later I'd call him back and it would go straight to voicemail. Finally I got ahold of him. I don't know why, but I felt like I had to protect Declan, so I just told my father we parted ways amicably and didn't say much else. He asked what my plans were, but I didn't have an answer for him.

"You should always have a backup plan," he reiterated to me for the one-hundredth time in my life.

He was right. I couldn't stay with Declan forever, and the nights I spent in the apartment by myself felt like I was repeatedly picking off a scab. I began to hate him, and the hate grew every time he went out all night. I needed to get out of the situation, and fast. I called up Karen and asked her if she had anything for me. She said she didn't have anything currently, but would let me know if anything changed.

I spoke to Papà again two weeks before Christmas. He said he had seen me in a tabloid at the grocery store after the split. It was the last taste of lime-light I had before the media forgot about me. They had snapped a picture of me walking out of Whole Foods. Of course, they caught me on the one day I decided to leave the apartment wearing sweatpants, six-year-old torn Uggs, and no makeup. "Broken Up and Forgotten: Former Girlfriend of Declan Long Drops 40 Pounds, Almost Hospitalized," the headline read.

"They are so dramatic," I said to my father.

"Well, I just wanted to call and let you know I love you."

"Thanks, Papà."

"I hope you are eating," he said. "Even if it's just a little bit of chocolate, any kind of calories in your body is better than nothing. Remember, you used to say that to Mom when she was going through chemo?"

"Yeah, I guess so."

"What was it you would always get her?"

"Nutella," I recalled. "She was obsessed with that stuff."

We talked for a few more minutes, and I told him I had opened a post office box since I didn't know how much longer I would be at Declan's. A week later a package came. It was an oversize jar of Nutella with a little note attached saying, "Some calories for you."

I brought the jar back to Declan's and cracked it open. I didn't even bother to put it on anything. I plunged a cold spoon right to the chocolatey goop and ate it with a tall glass of milk, just the way my mom use to eat it.

I pulled up my online banking account. Just under two-thousand dollars was all I had left to my name, which I knew wouldn't last long. My phone rang, and it was a Connecticut number that I didn't recognize.

"Hello?" I answered.

"Hey, Nina?"

"Yes, speaking."

"Yo, what's going on? It's Jacob. I got your number from your pops."

"What!" I exclaimed. "Jake freaking O'Malley."

Jake was one of my best friends from high school. We had gone on a couple of dates our junior year, but we realized we were much better off staying friends. He was one of the few football players that actually still talked to me after I quit cheerleading, and it had been quite a while since I had seen him last, so I was surprised to hear from him.

"Yeah, dude! I'm coming down to New York City tonight with a couple of my buddies for a bachelor party. It's just a bunch of guys, but figured I'd call you to meet up if you aren't doing anything."

"I can pretty much guarantee you that I'm not doing anything," I said. "Where are you going?"

"We're supposed to go to Downtown Bay."

"I've heard of that. It can get pretty crazy over there!"

Downtown Bay was a bar that was notorious for girls dancing on the counters and people doing the craziest things for a free shot of watered-down alcohol.

"Yeah, that's why we picked it," he said.

"Great, well, I have your number now. Send me a text when you get there and I'll take the subway over."

"Cool. Can't wait to see you. It's been too long."

"I know! See you soon, man."

Jake always knew how to put a smile on my face. In theory, he would have been a good boyfriend, but I hated how he always referred to women as "broads," and he drank just a little too much for my taste. So, friends we were, and friends we remained. A night out with him would be fun, needed, but most of all, harmless.

When Declan came home late that afternoon, he walked in to see me hunched over my guitar writing a song. This was something I did often. I knew about six chords, but it was enough to write a catchy progression and work out some of my frustrations.

"Hey, before you leave again I just wanted—"

"Why do you assume that I'm leaving?" he cut me off.

"Well, it's Saturday night. You always go out on Saturday night for your club appearances or whatever."

"Point?"

Clearly, he was in "jerk mode" again. Ever since we had broken up, I'd been slowly seeing how cocky Declan could be. There were times I couldn't believe that I actually had the patience to date someone like him for so long. I had been so wrapped up in the celebrity life that I never took a moment to see who he really was.

"Stop being so difficult," I said. "I'm just trying to tell you that I can't watch the dog tonight, so call your old dog walker or something."

"Where are you going?" he asked.

"Out to a bachelor party, actually. A friend from high school invited me."

"What the hell are *you* going to be doing at a bachelor party? Are you their stripper?" He laughed. "They know you don't have any tits, right?"

He continued laughing.

"You are such an asshole," I snapped. "It's none of your business what I'm doing. I'm just telling you that I won't be home tonight. That's it."

"Cool. See you tomorrow." He locked himself in his bedroom.

Declan didn't go out that night. He was sitting on the couch when I got out of the shower. Just to drive him crazy, I dropped my towel and walked into the living room completely naked, sporting my new spray tan. I actually surprised myself at how good I looked, despite the fact that I was skin and bones. I took the skimpiest black lace thong I had out and put it on with a matching bra. I walked around in my underwear for a few minutes trying to get a reaction out of him, but his face was stone solid. As I zipped my new skin-tight tube-top dress up and strapped my high heels to my feet, he crept up behind me and put his hands on my waist.

"I know you still want me. We could have a quickie before you go," he said.

"No thanks." I swung my hips and walked away. "You can sit in the apartment and suffer. Go jerk off or something."

A text from Jake had come through saying they were at the bar, so I grabbed my purse and left.

Typically I would have called a cab, but I had started taking the subway to save money. I needed to hold onto every penny I had for as long as I could, which meant that I had to get used to longer commutes again.

Downtown Bay was just as crazy as the rumors I had heard about it. When I walked in there were four girls dancing on the bar pouring shots into people's mouths. I managed to find Jake and his friends in the shoulder-to-shoulder crowd. I had forgotten what it was like to party like a "normal" person. The bar didn't even have a VIP section. Even so, I wouldn't have been allowed into it anyway.

"Hey, buddy!" Jake yelled.

I gave him a long hug and he lifted me up over his head while I laughed and screamed for him to put me down, pulling at my dress so no one saw my ass hanging out. Jake towered over me at six foot three, and thought it was funny to playfully throw me around. I remember once, in high school, while we were out one night, he picked me up and put me on top of a Hummer SUV in a Taco Bell parking lot. He laughed at me for five minutes straight before he helped me get down—and just in time before its owner walked out. He rested me on his broad shoulder, which gave the bartender an idea. She yelled out, "Put a girl on your shoulders and you get a free shot!"

Jake treked over to the bar and the cute girl poured a shot into each of our mouths. Hard alcohol wasn't something I was used to, but it felt warm going down, and with the way things had been lately, this would be a good way to escape my mind for a bit.

"What was that?" I yelled down to Jake.

"Whiskey," he yelled back as he put my feet back on the ground.

"Not bad!"

"Yeah? Let me buy you another," he yelled as he signaled the bartender.

He came back with drinks all around, and we pounded them back.

The bartender yelled out again, pointing out the groom-to-be.

"The first ten girls to give this bachelor a kiss get a shot for a buck!"

I leaned over and gave him a kiss on the cheek, collecting another shot.

The night continued, and shots kept getting passed around. I was dancing with Jake when it occurred to me that the room around me was pulsating to the sound of the music. I was drunk beyond any other time I have ever been drunk. Jake definitely had his share of alcohol, as well.

"I need to get going," I yelled into Jake's ear.

"No, stay," he yelled back as he kept dancing.

"Nah, man, I'm done drinking tonight. I need to go home. It was awesome seeing you!"

"Do you want me to walk you out?"

"No, that's OK!"

"All right, take care of yourself! It was good to see you!"

I started to make my way to the door when my legs began to buckle so I held on to the wall and found the exit. I spilled out onto the sidewalk and took a moment to collect myself. I really wished I hadn't worn high heels. Balancing in them while shit-faced was tough. Where was Declan to hold me up? I reached my hand out, searching for Declan's arm and then remembered he was home. I turned the corner and felt like I was in a fun house. People were staring at me and making comments under their breath. I heard a man ask me if I was OK. I turned around and continued to try and find the subway through my blurred vision.

As I walked, I heard a loud electric blues riff sounding from one of the bars nearby as someone opened the door to leave. I peered into the window and there, on the stage, was Dave from the guitar store playing an intricate solo. He was incredible. His fingers danced over the guitar, and the strings sang beautifully. The lights on the stage blurred and bounced in my hazy vision. I looked into the bar and it was mostly empty. I couldn't understand why; he was phenomenal. Why wasn't anyone there to listen? He lifted his head for a moment and our eyes fixed. I was too embarrassed to stay in my current condition so I turned my head and stumbled away, holding onto the glass.

I managed to find the subway, and hobbled down the stairs, ripping a hole in one of my stockings in the process. I disappeared into the tunnels below, where the air was heavy and the only life I saw were cat-sized rats running in and out of holes in the wall. I looked around and didn't see anyone. I sat on a graffiti-covered bench and waited for half an hour by myself. Marco was right, it was very difficult to catch a train late at night. A train finally came, and I felt my way into the empty car. Just before the doors closed, a large, burly man walked in. He was no doubt over six feet tall, and at least three hundred pounds. He wore a coat with a hood that covered his head and a scarf wrapped around his face. He didn't look well kept, and had gloves on that were caked with dirt. Of all the open seats on the train, he walked over and sat next to me. My heart pounded. I was drunk, on the verge of passing out, and a giant man I didn't know was sitting next to me on an empty freaking train. My eyes attempted to focus on the walls whisking past the windows as the train picked up speed. The lights flickered and I felt the man move closer to me. I kept repeating the same sentences over and over in my head.

"Check your purse. There is your purse. Do not pass out. Check your purse. There is your purse. Do not pass out. Check your purse. There is your purse—"

Ding.

The subway halted and the door opened to my stop. I got up and walked out onto the platform. The man got out and walked behind me. The tunnel was still empty. I walked up to the dark, deserted street with the man close behind, and raised my hand up to catch a cab. To my luck, one came zipping over. As I got into the car, the man rubbed against my back and walked away. He looked back for a second, and I gave him the finger.

I slapped myself down into the cab and shivered. It never occurred to me how dangerous the city could be. Over the past year, any time I went out I was always with Declan. I realized I would have to survive this city on my own, and with the way things were at home, that time would be soon. I slumped in the back of the cab and cradled my throbbing head in my hands. All I wanted to do was go up into my apartment, open the door to the bedroom, and quietly slip into bed with Declan. Maybe his offer for sex was still up for grabs. Even if it wasn't, maybe just for tonight he would allow me to sleep close to him. Snow had started to fall and the cold winds were picking up. Maybe we could have one last romantic night. It was the seventh night of Hanukkah and Christmas was in a few days. Weren't the holidays supposed to be cheerful?

I walked up to the apartment and had made up my mind; I was going to sleep in the room with Declan tonight. I unlocked the door and pushed it open. All of the lights were out. I took a few steps in, and suddenly I was on the ground. My hands hit the floor hard as I caught myself, and my keys dropped with a loud *clank*. I stood up and flicked the light on to see what I had tripped over. My numb skin tingled as the hairs on my arms stood up. There on the floor lay a chic pair of red high heels that did not belong to me.

NINE

My breath stopped. I gasped for air, but I couldn't feel my body. Goosebumps coated my arms, and my heart was racing too fast for me to balance myself. I hugged the walls and walked back down to the street. By now it was three o'clock in the morning, and I assumed Declan's whore for the night would be leaving in a few hours. My face was hot and red, but I refused to cry. I walked around the corner to the neighborhood diner and sat for five hours drinking unhealthy amounts of coffee, obsessing over who the girl was. I scrolled through all of social media, digging to figure it out. Finally, as the sun warmed the cracked concrete sidewalks, I walked back to the apartment. As I approached my door, I saw a female I didn't recognize leaving my brownstone wearing the same red heels. I pulled my hood up over my head and put on sunglasses. She turned toward me and that's when I saw her face. Coco. It took every ounce of energy not to run down the street and rip all the hairs out of her head.

I ran up the steps and tore into the apartment like a lion protecting her young. I kicked open the bedroom door and started screaming at him with red bloodshot eyes.

"What the hell is wrong with you? Why would you bring a girl back here! You knew I was coming home, why would you do that to me!"

I was frustrated. My mind was too cloudy to know what else to say, so I just started screaming at the top of my lungs, saying nothing in particular.

Declan didn't quit without a fight.

"Don't you ever come in here and yell like that again. Stop screaming, the neighbors are going to hear you! You are crazy!"

"Stop calling me crazy! I'm not crazy, you are making me crazy! I was fine until I met you! You are making me insane!"

I started grabbing his pillows and throwing them. I grabbed the blanket he was wrapped in and yanked on it until he fell out onto the floor.

"What are you doing?"

"I'm sending these to the cleaners to get Coco's disgusting perfume out of them."

"Stop, Nina, stop it!"

I didn't stop. I took the pillowcase off of the pillow so hard that it ripped the seam open and feathers sprinkled on the floor.

"You are damaging my property! Stop it!"

He stood up and grabbed my arms from behind. He held my body close to his, and I let loose, crying until tears and snot were running in a full stream down my chin.

"Stop," he said as he hushed me and placed his forehead on the back of my head.

"Why are you doing this to me?" I cried.

"I'm not doing anything. I'm just trying to live my life!"

"Why can't you live your life with me? What is wrong with that?"

"I don't want to have this conversation."

"You *always* say that. You used to trust me with your deepest secrets. Why can't you trust me with your feelings anymore?"

He let me go and walked over to his nightstand. "Here." He handed me a tissue. "You look like hell. Go wash your face and I'll clean up this mess. Then we'll talk, OK?"

"OK."

I put on a new shirt and walked into the bathroom. I splashed warm water on my face, put on some deodorant, and brushed my teeth. I caught the wastebasket out of the corner of my eye as I walked out and saw two condom wrappers in the garbage.

"Twice?" I screamed. "You had sex *twice?*"

He didn't respond.

Suddenly images of him having sex with Coco in the bed that used to be ours were flashing in my head. I put my shoes and coat on, and walked out without saying anything. I didn't know where to go, but thought I would make my way to Guitar Center to keep my mind occupied. Maybe I would see Dave and he could show me that chord again. I had washed all of my makeup off and I was still semi-drunk, but I didn't care.

When I got to Times Square it was only nine in the morning, and the store didn't open until eleven. I was wandering around looking for a place to eat breakfast when I heard the faint sound of a choir. Intrigued, I followed my ears to where the sound was coming from. The closer I got, the more powerful the voices became. I found the door where the voices were coming from and looked up at the marquee to see where I was.

"Community Church of Times Square," it read.

Just then the door opened and a gentleman in a light blue sport coat stood before me.

"Would you like to come in?" he asked.

"The choir sounds really beautiful," I responded.

"It is our Christmas concert. The show is free, and everyone is welcome here."

"Sure, OK."

I had two hours to kill so I found a seat in the back of the auditorium, which was packed solid with at least two thousand people. The church was an old theater in the heart of the Theater District. I looked up and saw intricate paintings of angels, cherubs, and clouds. A giant golden chandelier hung from the middle of the ceiling. The walls were covered with large red velvet drapes. A full band, complete with drums, guitars, trumpets, keyboards, and saxophones, was on the side of the stage. Front and center was a large choir made up of about seventy people. The conductor raised his baton, and they began singing the Christmas carol "O Holy Night." The voices were powerful. I could feel the sopranos vibrating the walls and the bass shaking the floor as they sang the famous chorus.

My head began to nod to the music and I felt warm despite the snow outside. I was captivated enough to stay for the entire performance. After the final song, a minister went to the pulpit for some closing words.

"Thank you, everyone, for coming out to our Christmas concert. The choir starts preparing for this in October, and they blow me away every year with their talent. I wanted to say some closing words before we part ways," he said.

I checked to see where the nearest exit was.

"Have you ever felt like you were alone in the world? No matter what you do, things just don't work out the way you planned?" he asked. "Perhaps relationships always fail you."

I stopped looking for an escape route and focused back on the platform. It was like he had a magnifying glass and was pointing it straight into my life. *Yes*, I thought, *Actually, my relationships* do *suck, and I* do *feel alone.* I rolled my eyes.

"I am here to bring you the good news that no matter where you are in life, God is with you, and you are never alone. Christmas is in a few short days. We will have another concert on Christmas Eve at seven in the evening followed by a small reception. If you don't have a family to celebrate with, come be a part of our spiritual family. Have a great afternoon, and God bless." He walked off of the stage and the band played "Silent Night" as the people got up to leave.

I hadn't really thought about where I would go for Christmas. With everything going on with Declan, especially last night and this morning, Christmas was not a priority. We hadn't set up a Christmas tree or pulled out any of our decorations. My father had decided to spend Christmas in Italy with his new girlfriend, but he sent me a card before he left, which I opened early. He gave me $300 and I put in my savings account rather than spending it at Bloomingdale's. He would be proud. I supposed I could have flown to Italy, but the plane tickets were astronomical at that point and I was trying to conserve.

The people cleared out of the church, but I stayed in my seat and drifted off into a daydream. I pictured myself on stage playing my guitar and singing sad breakup songs to thousands of people. My dream was abruptly interrupted.

"Hello."

I looked up and there was Dave.

"Hey," I said, shocked. "What are you doing here?"

"I go to church here. I usually walk to work after."

"Oh, I didn't know that. Are you working today? I was actually heading there this morning, but I was early so I came here."

"Yeah, my shift starts in about twenty minutes." He stopped and smiled at me for a beat. "You look really nice today. Have you been here before?"

"First time." I smoothed my hair down and slicked it back into a ponytail. I knew I looked like hell, but it was nice of him to try and boost my ego.

"It's nice here and I like that it's nondenominational. Even a couple of Jewish people attend."

"Interesting."

"Well, I've got to go. Time to make the 'big man' some money."

"Wait up, I'll walk with you," I said, shuffling to get my coat.

We walked back to his store and grabbed a coffee along the way. I had already consumed enough coffee for a week, but he offered, and I couldn't refuse. When we arrived, I bought some strings and he rang me up.

"You should really come to the reception on Christmas Eve. It's usually a lot of fun, and you will meet a bunch of people. Plus, I'll be there. My mom is on some weird yoga trip thing in Thailand, so I'm sticking around."

"Yeah, I guess. My father is traveling too. Sucks."

"Yeah, it does. You can bring your boyfriend if you want."

"Oh, yeah. Declan and I broke up. But I'm still living in the apartment with him until I can find work and a place of my own."

"How's that working out?"

"Last night he brought a girl back to our apartment and slept with her. *Twice*," I said as my eyes started swelling.

He looked flustered and searched for something to say. "Geez, that's rough." He walked from behind the counter and even though there were customers around, he gently touched the back of my neck and pulled me into his chest for a hug. "That's really awful. You've got to get out of there."

I barely knew him, but his arms were comfortable and he was making me feel kind of better.

"It's been really hard." I snorted up a glob of boogers.

"Come to the reception then. Trust me, it will take your mind off of everything. It's a lot of fun."

"Yeah, I guess."

When I got home that night, there was a note from Declan saying that he and Fender would be out of town visiting his family. He'd be back a week or so after the new year. He felt like he needed some space. Quite frankly, I was happy that he was gone. I had inner peace for the first time in months. I missed Fender though.

When Christmas Eve rolled around, I walked down to the Christmas tree lot outside of the subway stop. All of the trees go on sale on Christmas Eve. I spotted a small one at the end of the lot that was bursting with strong green branches. It was perfect. I paid the man and dragged it back to the apartment. I had no idea how to set it up, but I knew Declan had a stand under his bed. Eventually, after watching a couple of YouTube videos, I figured it out. I didn't have any ornaments except for a photo-framed ornament from last year, which had a picture of Declan and me with the words "Our first Christmas." I threw it in the trash on top of the used condoms, which he neglected to empty. Since Fender wasn't around, I spent the better part of the afternoon popping corn and trying to thread it on a string I had bought at the corner bodega, then draping the garland on the tree.

I blasted holiday music trying to be happy. I took a shower and started getting ready for the second concert and reception at the church. I always felt really uncomfortable in churches. My father dragged me to church so often growing up that eventually I grew to detest it. When I turned eighteen, I made it perfectly clear that going to church three times a week was something I was *not* going to do any longer. Yet, here I was going through outfits getting ready to go.

The concert was great. It was the same concert the choir had performed that Sunday, but since I had missed the first half, it was nice to see it from the beginning. They sang all of the timeless carols, such as "The Christmas Song" and "Silver Bells." At one point a beautiful Spanish woman who looked to be about seven months pregnant got up and did a solo of the Yiddish song "Lech Lamidbar," and it surprised the heck out of me. She slowed down the tempo a little and turned it into a lullaby, and I'd never heard anything so beautiful. I can't deny that it made me cry a little. It made me think of my mom and I started to miss her immensely.

I didn't see Dave when I arrived, so I ended up sitting by myself next to a gentleman who introduced himself as Jordan. As much as I enjoyed the show, I could have done without Jordan's game of twenty questions, and commentary after every song. He was nice, but annoying.

"Hey, are you going to the reception?" he asked.

I wanted to lie and tell him "no," but I didn't know where the "attic" room was, and I had a hunch he could lead me there.

"Yeah," I responded.

I walked up to the room with Jordan blabbering away about video games, and I kept a lookout for Dave.

"Can I get you some punch?" Jordan asked.

"What?"

"Punch. I'm going to grab some, can I get you a glass?"

"Sure."

I used the opportunity to sift through the crowd of people to find Dave. Finally, our eyes met. He squeezed through the crowd and gave me a hug.

"You're here." He seemed surprised.

He wore a green buffalo-checked, button-down, flannel shirt with black skinny jeans and black boots. He looked like a rock star. A gentle, kind, church-going, best-hug-in-the-world-giving rock star. I felt my cheeks turn pink. I wanted to tell him how good he looked. I wanted to tell him how nice I thought he was. I wanted to talk to him all night long, take him back to my apartment, and make crazy love to him. I opened my mouth to say something and then a hand stuck out from behind me.

"Hi! I'm Jordan," he said, extending his hand toward Dave. "Here's your drink, Nina," he said as he handed me a glass of punch.

Dave's face stood frozen as he shook hands with Jordan.

"Are you having a good time?" Jordan asked me.

"Yes," I said with a hard stare.

"Well, it was great seeing you," Dave said. "We'll catch up later." He turned his back and walked away.

He ended up talking with a girl all night. It looked like it was someone he knew, because she greeted him with a kiss on the cheek sort of close to his mouth. I tried to approach him a few times, but Jordan followed me around like a puppy. I regretted the fact that I sat next to him in the first place, but I was trying to be nice.

I called it a night early and went back to the apartment. I was disappointed that I didn't get to spend any time with Dave, and even more disappointed that he was talking to another girl the whole time—probably his girlfriend now that I thought about it. It was nearly nine o'clock, and I sat on the couch staring at my Christmas tree; nothing but empty space was beneath. I took out the jar of Nutella, put on *It's a Wonderful Life*, and watched until I fell asleep.

When I woke up in the morning it was snowing. Thankfully, it wasn't a blizzard, which was something we New Yorkers were becoming very accustomed to that particular winter. I walked down to the deli and got myself a strong cup of coffee and a few pastries. I sat at the lunch counter and scrolled through the e-mails on my phone. It had been a while since I had checked it. I had an e-mail from Karen dated December 22 so I opened it up.

Nina,
I have some work for you if you are interested. A small role in a film out in Oregon. Let me know.
Regards, Karen Picard

"Yes!" I screamed.

I didn't care that it was across the country, and I didn't care that everyone in the deli thought I was crazy. I wrote back:

Karen,
I'll take it. Merry Christmas!
—Nina

I hit send and said "shit," at the same time. Karen is Buddhist. Ohh well. My dad rang me while I was typing and I forwarded his call by accident. When I called back it went straight to voicemail. No surprise there. I decided to call him later and walked back to the apartment to look for hotels in Oregon. As I was scrolled through the listings, an ad popped up in the sidebar.

"Meet Christian Singles in Oregon. Click here for a free trial!"

"Already? Jesus, Google, slow your roll."

I actually had seen a bunch of ads on TV for various online dating sites, but never one specifically for Christians. Would dating a church guy be better than a non-church guy? All I knew was that I wanted the exact opposite ⌐Declan. Maybe if a guy believed in God, he wouldn't cheat on me or treat garbage. Dave was a churchy person and he was awesome. Taken, ʾut awesome. Then again, Jordan was a churchy person and he ɔle. I tossed a coin.

"Heads, I sign up for this bullshit, and tails, I pass it up."

Heads.

I placed the cursor over the ad and clicked. I typed in all of my information and chose one of my headshots as a cover photo. I selected New York City and Oregon as my locations. Why not? I'd be out there for a few months, at least, anyway.

I had to pick a screen name. I wrote "CoffeeGirl."

I started typing my introduction:

"I am an actress, and I don't go to church but I believe in God. Just looking for someone to hang out with and get to know. I like to have fun, but I'm not looking to be played. No cheaters. No liars."

It was true, I *did* believe in God. I was raised to believe in God, but after my mom died I was pretty pissed off at him for a while. Jerusalem sort of jump-started my belief, but I didn't pray every day or read the Torah or Bible or anything. I clicked out of my profile and went back to hotel hunting. Ten minutes later, my e-mail made my phone buzz nearly off the coffee-table.

I opened it up, and to my surprise, I already had seven e-mails from the website and they were still rolling in. Most of them were from men in their late fifties wanting to chat, or people my age, who I'm sure had great personalities but were too short, too hairy, or too pimply. I turned off my notifications and started scrolling Airbnb.

That evening I ordered Chinese from one of the only restaurants in Manhattan that didn't have an overly priced prix-fixe menu. I had spent most of my Christmas on a couch by myself and really wanted someone to talk to, so I tried calling my dad back. After a few tries, he finally picked up. I totally forgot he was on Italy time and it was two in the morning there. We had a quick chat and said "*buon Natale,*" but he was groggy so I let him go back to his dreams. I wished I had Dave's phone number, but figured he was probably with the girl he spent so much time with at the party. Plus, I'd be off to Oregon soon anyway, and what would be the point of starting something now? I figured I could always track him down when I came back to town and was ready to settle somewhere permanently. I didn't realize that I had been sitting in the dark when the Chinese deliveryman came. I flicked on the light and picked up my phone.

Twenty-four unread messages.

Since I was bored and alone, and it was Christmas, I decided why the hell not? There were other people in the same boat as me. Why be alone on Christmas, when I can talk to—

"Herman Snuzzlebrough," I said, before I started laughing hysterically.

"How the hell do you even pronounce that?" I asked myself. "What a name."

"Oh God, this one is worse. Last name: Ballicks. 'Nina Ballicks.' Nope, couldn't marry this one. I don't need any more name issues, thanks!"

Alto. OK, that's normal. I can work with Ezra Alto. Very "biblical."

He hadn't sent me a real message, rather a "nudge," which was a button you clicked on if you wanted to get to know a person but didn't want to put yourself out there by saying too much. I opened up his profile and to my surprise, he was very attractive. He was six foot one, had light brown hair, big green eyes, and olive skin. His "About Me" section read:

"I'm a down-to-earth, happy, fun-loving guy. I have a great relationship with my family. I am hot as hell! (Get it?) I believe that God leads me through life, and guides me spiritually. I like music, golf, hanging out, and drinking Coca-Cola. I'm looking for a Proverbs 31 woman."

"Proverbs 31," I thought. I knew that referred to a book in the Bible, but I didn't know what it said or what it meant. I decided to look it up. I still had my little pocket NIV translation Bible, which my dad gave me when I was baptized as a kid. I found it in one of the boxes I had stacked up in the living room. I flipped through the stiff pages and found the passage Ezra was referring to. It read:

> 10 A wife of noble character who can find? She is worth far more than rubies. 11 Her husband has full confidence in her and lacks nothing of value.

"Aw, that's so sweet," I thought.

> 12 She brings him good, not harm, all the days of her life. 13 She selects wool and flax and works with eager hands. 14 She is like the merchant ships, bringing her food from afar. 15 She gets up while it is still night; she provides food for her family and portions for her female servants.

Up before dawn? Servants? This is obviously outdated unless you are, like, Kate Middleton or something.

16 She considers a field and buys it; out of her earnings she plants a vineyard.

Hmm. A vineyard. OK, OK, I can get down with that—I love wine.

17 She sets about her work vigorously; her arms are strong for her tasks. 18 She sees that her trading is profitable, and her lamp does not go out at night. 19 In her hand she holds the distaff and grasps the spindle with her fingers. 20 She opens her arms to the poor and extends her hands to the needy.

I help the needy sometimes. I volunteered at the children's hospital for a whole year after Mom died, reading and playing games with the terminally ill kids. It really helped the mourning process, until some of them started dying, and I just couldn't handle the pain of it anymore. They weren't poor, but they needed fun, and I was able to give them that.

21 When it snows, she has no fear for her household; for all of them are clothed in scarlet.

Red is totally my color.

22 She makes coverings for her bed; she is clothed in fine linen and purple.

Wait, I thought I was supposed to wear red?

23 Her husband is respected at the city gate, where he takes his seat among the elders of the land. 24 She makes linen garments and sells them, and supplies the merchants with sashes.

Hold up, what about the vineyard?

25 She is clothed with strength and dignity; she can laugh at the days to come. 26 She speaks with wisdom, and faithful instruction is on her tongue. 27 She watches over the affairs of her household and does not eat the bread of idleness.

What the heck is "bread of idleness"? So many questions!"

28 Her children arise and call her blessed; her husband also, and he praises her: 29 "Many women do noble things, but you surpass them

all." 30 Charm is deceptive, and beauty is fleeting; but a woman who fears the Lord is to be praised.

"Well, that doesn't sound too bad. I mean, basically this woman is an 'I-don't-need-no-man' feminist who does everything for herself in life, yet I have absolutely no control over *my* life," I laughed.

One part of me felt that I was some of what this woman could be, but I certainly didn't bring "food from afar" or "spindle" all night. I wanted to talk to the guy and I figured this would a good topic to ask him about. I sent him a message:

> Hey! My name is Nina. I noticed that you sent me a nudge. I checked out your profile and you seem really cool and laid back. Your picture looks great too—yes, definitely 'hot as hell.' Where are you from? What kind of things do you like to do besides watch movies and listen to music? Have you ever heard of the show *Blazing Love*? I worked on that set for almost a year behind the scenes. Anyway, what is this stuff about a 'Proverbs 31 woman?' I looked up the passage but I don't get it. Talk to you soon, I hope.
> —Nina

I read through the message eleven times, making sure I didn't sound stupid or spell anything wrong. Finally, I sent it and immediately tried to hit the back button.

"He's going to think I'm so dumb," I thought. "Why would I go on a Christian dating site, and not even know a Bible verse?"

I stared at my computer screen for an hour waiting for a reply and skimmed through my message four more times.

I didn't get a reply so I started putzing around. I surfed through a few more apartment listings and checked my e-mail again. To my surprise, I had an e-mail from Guitar Center.

"That's weird," I thought.

When I opened it, I saw that it was an e-mail from Dave.

"Hey, Nina! I'm sorry, I took your info from the database. (Please don't rat me out!) I wanted to reach out and just say hi. I didn't get to talk to you much at the Christmas party. It's cool that you brought Jordan. I hope everything is going well. See you in the store, hopefully."

He polished off the e-mail with his name and phone number. "Epic timing," I thought. If he gave it to me yesterday, I would have considered shooting him a text, but again, why would I bother now that I know I'm leaving? I was unsure about his relationship status anyway. I bet hot guys work at guitar stores in Oregon, too.

I figured I would at least text him to let him know that I did not, in fact, bring Jordan to that party, but I got distracted when a message came through on the dating site from Ezra.

TEN

December 25

Nina,

Hey! Thanks for the compliments, right back 'atcha! So you are an actress? That's great. *Blazing Love* . . . I have seen a few episodes. Why did your profile pop up for Oregon? I saw that you are in New York City, but I was looking through the profiles in my area, and couldn't seem to find anyone I might connect with. I prayed about it and felt that maybe I should expand my horizons until you came up as a new user. Sort of odd, eh? The whole Proverbs 31 thing . . . yeah, it is definitely outdated. The part I really focus on is, 'A wife of noble character who can find? She is worth far more than rubies.' I have had a lot of bad luck with women. It seems that I fall in love, and wear my heart on my sleeve, and then get cheated on. I was engaged once, but she cheated on me too. She left me basically at the altar and I never saw her again. Then I dated a girl for about a year, but she was sleeping with our neighbor. I guess I just have a lot of bad luck. I'm hoping you might bring some good?

—Ezra

December 25

Ezra,

Wow, that is crazy. I'm so sorry to hear about your experiences. I wish mine were better, but they aren't. I was dating a cast member of the show, and he was cheating on me basically the whole time we were together. What is it with cheaters? We are still living together, but I sleep on the couch in the living room. It's hard, especially when he brings girls here. And yeah, that is sort of odd. I put my profile in Oregon because I'll be coming out there for a few months to film. I don't have the details yet, but I'm sure my agent will tell me soon since it's a holiday and all. What is Oregon like? The only thing I know about Oregon is that it is very rainy, and I don't mix well with rain! Regardless, I'm looking forward to getting out of this apartment and starting fresh. The Proverbs 31 thing—that's good because I definitely don't make linen garments, and I certainly don't sell them either! Anyway, what kind of music do you listen to?

—Nina

December 26

Nina,

Well, I listen to all styles of music, but mainly Christian stuff. Actually, I own a Christian radio station here in Oregon! It does really well. We have a ton of sponsors and listeners. So you're coming out for a few months to film? What movie? I'm sad it's only for a few months. You should come out and live here instead, ha-ha. Just kidding (sort of). I live in Fairview and it's really beautiful! It's about a forty-five minute drive to Multnomah Falls, the most gorgeous place. I'll have to take you there when you come out. Oregon was listed in *Smile Guide Magazine*'s list of top places in the country to move to because of our scenic hiking spots and growing economy. Just something to think about! And you would already have one friend here! Or heck, you can just come and work at the radio station. So many options, and none include a cheating ex-boyfriend, ha-ha. Anyway, I saw that you uploaded more pictures to your profile. Dang. You are so gorgeous it kills me. You are literally the perfect girl. I hope I'm not coming on too strong. You're just absolutely beautiful. God did a great job when he made you!

—Ezra

December 27

Ezra,

You are so sweet. No, you aren't coming on too strong. I haven't been told I was beautiful in a while. Thank you for that. Fairview, that sounds amazing. It's also really great about the economy, but I don't know how much work they would have readily available for an actress long-term. Working for a radio station would be cool though. How did you come to own the radio station? As far as moving goes, I wouldn't say that I've never considered moving out of New York. I always dreamed of living here my entire life, but lately, I just feel so crappy. I don't have many friends, since they are all buddies with my ex, and my family life is complicated. So, not to say that I'd move there specifically, but I have definitely considered moving out in general. I've been wanting to go to college to study anthropology and I enrolled here at Hunter, but now with the film, and a couple other things that have happened, it just doesn't look likely for the spring. Maybe I'll look at schools in Oregon. Just for fun. Anyway have you ever been to NYC?

—Nina

PS: Just heard from my agent. She said the movie starts filming in February. It looks like it's going to be about six weeks before I make my way out there. I'm not sure what I'm allowed to leak, but it's a film based on a book.

December 28

Nina,

Nope! Never been to NYC. I've wanted to go there though. I grew up in Oregon, lived in Texas for a while, but moved back here to Oregon a few years ago to be closer to my parents. You should come out for a visit in January then. I'd love to meet you in person sooner than later. I feel like you and I have a connection of sorts. I mean, it's crazy . . . out of all the people in the country, I landed on your profile, and you just happened to message me. The radio station: It is a very cool story. I had been working in radio as a DJ for six months before I moved here so I had a little bit of experience. After I moved, I took a job working as a corporate window washer and felt disconnected to what I love the most, which was radio. I fell off a ladder one day and got knocked out. When I woke up a few minutes later, the first thing I saw when I opened my eyes was a vision of the station. I knew the idea came from God, so I got to work on it. Now we are huge! And on the topic of God, I also felt like he pushed me to create this online profile. I'm starting to realize why. Have a good night, beautiful Nina. Talk to you soon.

—Ezra

PS: You should really consider visiting the Pacific Northwest next month.

December 29

Ezra,

I would love to visit Oregon next month, but I'm going to wait until February because I'd rather go out on the studio's dime instead of mine. *You* should totally come to NYC in January! I could show you everything. Times Square, the Statue of Liberty, we could do it all! Think about it! So, tell me more about yourself. What nationality are you? I'm 100% Italian. My real name is Pasqualina, so you can see why I have people call me Nina. Growing up in school, teachers always got my name wrong. What kinds of food do you like to eat? When did you become a Christian? I would ask what your dreams and aspirations are, but it seems like you are already living the dream! I want to know more about you. I think you are really great.

—Nina

PS: I'm serious. Come visit.

December 30

Beautiful Nina,

I would like to get to know you more as well. I really think you are something special. My family is from Portugal. I grew up in a Christian family, so I've always believed in God. I think that's why I have such a strong connection to my religion. My family and I are really tight. I like to eat out a lot, specifically Italian(s) (get it?). Haha, kidding. I actually really do like Italian food a lot, but I'm a horrible cook, so I usually order from this family-owned Italian place down the street. They have fresh-made pasta and meatballs that are amazing. See? Another reason why you should move here! My mom cooks a big dinner every Sunday so I will head there, usually. Of course, her specialty is Portuguese food. What else do you want to know about me? (cyber kiss goodnight).

—Ezra

December 30

Ezra,

Cyber kiss accepted! Though I wish I could get a real one at midnight tomorrow. My ex is still out of the house, thank God. I was going to go out, but I think a night in is probably best. I worked on a soap opera today. It was a quick job my agent scraped up for me to hold me over until the film starts. I'm so exhausted, it was a long day. Funny joke about Italians, sir. Way to make me blush! You sound like you have a really great life. Hmm, what else do I want to know? Well, everything. What else do you like to do in your free time? What are you doing for New Year's Eve?

—Nina

December 31

Nina,

I'm glad you caught my joke. You have a sense of humor! Good. As I said in my profile, I like playing golf. It's a thing my family likes to do together. We are all so busy, it's nice to just zone out at a driving range. I also own a motorcycle, so on nice days, I take it out. You wouldn't believe the scenery here, and it's even better on a bike. If you come out here, I'd love to take you for a ride. (More than one meaning to that sentence!) Sorry, bad joke. And what am I doing for New Year's Eve? I'm taking you out for dinner. Meet me at the Westin near Grand Central at nine o'clock at night. I'll be there. I promise. I'm already en route.

—Ezra

ELEVEN

Are-you-freaking-kidding-me? He's here? He can't be *here*.

It was six o'clock when the message came through. I had sent my e-mail to him the day before, but he must have been planning the trip this entire time. Maybe? This was absolutely crazy! How much faith did he *have*? I could have lied on my profile and said I lived in New York when I really lived in Tennessee for all he knew! We had only been chatting online for all of one week, and all in all I didn't know the man well. He could be a man of faith, but he could also be a serial killer or a rapist. His spur-of-the-moment nature reminded me of the romantic Dead Sea trip Declan took me on. I meditated visions of us skating in Rockefeller, kissing under the tree, and rolling through Central Park in a horse-drawn carriage.

Dave briefly interrupted those dreams. I wondered what he would be doing to ring in the new year. Probably a church thing or whatever, and sorry, but I was not about to go through another night of Jordan just to watch Dave talk to another girl again. Another girl who *kissed* him nonetheless. No, thanks.

I started going through my boxes looking for the particular black dress I had worn last New Year's Eve. It was classy, tea length, and had three-quarter sleeves. It dipped down in the back but came up higher in the front, leaving no cleavage at all and plenty to the imagination. I thought it would be appropriate for a meeting with a nice "Christian" man. I finally found it and slipped it on. It was a bit loose because of all the weight I had lost, but luckily, with a few safety pins, I made it look good.

I had just enough time to throw my hair in a bun and spread some color across my eyelids and lips. I grabbed my coat and headed for the Westin. It was the perfect night to be out. That winter was not only chock-full of blizzards but also happened to be one of the coldest winters New York had seen since the 1800s. The air was different that night. The breeze was still. There was no wind chill at all, and having gone through periods of below-zero temperatures, the brisk thirty-nine-degree air felt like spring was on the way. I grabbed a cab to be sure I would get there on time. It was only when the cab started pulling up to the hotel that I had second thoughts.

This man could be totally crazy, I thought. *Maybe I should have brought someone with me, or at least told someone that I was going out.*

I pulled out my phone to text Declan, half because I sort of wondered how he was doing and half because I wanted to throw my date in his face.

"Hey, Declan. I'm only texting because I'm going out on a semi-blind date tonight. I met him off the Internet. Save your jokes. Anyway, check in later, please."

He didn't respond, but my phone told me the message went through, and that was good enough for me. If I ended up dead in a ditch somewhere, I felt like Declan would at least have the common decency to send out a search party.

The cab dropped me off, and I stood outside the hotel looking for Ezra. It was 7:52 pm.

"Eight minutes," I sighed.

A moment later, I felt a hand take mine and spin me around. There stood Ezra. My eyes traced the outline of his eyes, down through his jawbone, and continued down to his feet. He was a lot shorter in person, about five foot seven, although his online profile said otherwise. I guess I couldn't judge him on one tiny little white lie. After all, he was still taller than *me*. His profile picture did not do him any justice at all. He was *way* more attractive in real life, and that was a huge relief.

"Hi," he said as a big goofy smile stretched across his face. "You look like you are in shock," he chuckled.

"I think I am!"

He leaned in and kissed my cheek, then smothered me in a warm hug. "I was looking up places to go for a New Year's Eve dinner, but most of them had to be booked in advance, so I figured we would go to a diner I found down the street. Are you cool with that?" he asked.

"Yeah, sure," I said, looking down at what I was wearing and suddenly feeling extremely overdressed.

We walked into the diner and were seated right away. Instead of sitting across from me, he sat next to me.

"Well, it's nice to not wait an hour for a table," I said, reflecting on the positive side of things, as a diner wasn't exactly the type of atmosphere I was expecting.

"Selfie!" he said, holding up his phone and putting his arm around me.

I pushed closer to him in the booth and he snapped a photo. He smelled amazing. I could pinpoint his scent right away, too. It was familiar cologne, the one my ex from Connecticut used to wear, which also happened to be my absolute favorite "manly" smell.

He shared the photo and tagged me with the caption, "We decided to ditch the fancy restaurant idea and get some burgers at a diner. She's awesome."

I thought it was a little strange, because a fancy dinner was never on the table, and I hadn't even ordered yet. Why did he assume I would get a burger?

"I'm going to tag the radio station, too. All of the listeners know I'm in New York City. Have you had a chance to listen to the station? You know, you can stream it online too."

"No, I haven't, but I'll check it out."

The date was off to an awkward start but, after all, he *was* really cute and he *did* travel all this way to meet with me. He didn't seem like the kidnapping-murdering-rapist type, so I was at least comfortable with that.

"Here, I can actually stream it on my phone. I'll set it up and we can listen to it right here in the booth." He propped his phone up with a menu.

There weren't many people in the diner, and it didn't seem to bother the ones that were there since we were seated in the corner. I started to listen to his station, and to my surprise, it was actually really good! No wonder this man had so much confidence. He was actually quite talented. Not only did he own the station, but also he was the main radio personality. He spoke very highly and fondly of it, but after an hour of listening to him talk shop, barely taking a moment for a breath, I was beginning to get bored. He must have sensed it because he finally asked, "How is your food?"

I had ordered meatloaf, mashed potatoes, and a salad. It truly was delicious. I ate about half of it, but even so, it looked like I barely touched my plate since the portions were so large.

"It's really good. How's yours?" I asked, kicking myself that I had thrown the invisible microphone back to him.

"It's delicious. This has got to be the best burger I've had in a while, actually. And, of course, the company I have is really nice, too." He reached down to hold my hand.

He started asking me more questions about my life and upbringing. The night was starting to get better. The bill came and he paid cash, but asked me to leave a tip. I thought it was kind of weird because no one had ever asked me to do that before. Maybe it was an Oregon thing. I didn't hold it against him. I left a tip, and we were on our way to the next activity. He had asked me to take him to the tree in Rockefeller Plaza.

"I want to do all the typical tourist things," he said. "I've never been here before, so show me everything!"

"Well, I can take you to Rockefeller, but Times Square might have to wait until tomorrow. It's kind of filled with millions of people right now," I laughed. "How long are you here for?"

"Four days," he said. "I fly out on the fourth."

"How did you get a flight last minute?"

"It was actually cheaper to fly on New Year's Eve. Isn't that crazy? The prices were jacked up for yesterday, but if I flew today, it was only $200. Also, my parents let me use their miles to buy the ticket, so it was free!"

"Wow, that's awesome!"

"Yeah, and I found the hotel on Groupon for half price. I didn't think they would honor it for tonight, but they did."

"That's amazing. Seriously, I've never heard of that happening before."

And it was true. Hotels usually raised their prices significantly on holidays, especially on New Year's Eve.

"I feel like this was meant to happen. Everything just fell into place."

"I guess so," I said. And I believed it.

We went to Rockefeller Plaza, and it was packed with people. Most were trying to make their way into Times Square unsuccessfully. We decided to go ice-skating, talking nonstop, getting to know each other, and laughing hysterically. He was actually a fun and charming guy! After two hours of waiting in line, we finally hit the ice for our twenty-minute session, which he paid for—in full this time. It was the ultimate romantic experience. He held my hand tight and helped me up when I fell. We eventually decided to skate near the wall so that I could hold on to it. Just before our skate time was up, he took both of my hands, pulled me close to him, and kissed me. It was beautiful, magical, and perfectly sloppy.

Alright, so he's not the greatest kisser, I thought. *Who cares? This is still amazing.*

When we started kissing, a few people around us started clapping and cheering. We thought it was for us, so we really started going at it, but then we quickly realized it was because a marriage proposal was happening three feet away. We turned to see the commotion and joined in with the shouts and cheers. Ezra and I locked eyes, and he gave me a smile emitting a thousand words, or possibly, only three.

"I love," he paused, "This."

"Me, too." My eyes squinted from my gargantuan smile. "This is the best night I've had in a very long time."

He kissed me on the forehead. We left the rink and sat on a bench to take our skates off. I looked at my watch and it was nearly 11:30 p.m. already. I wondered if he was going to go back to his hotel at this point, or if he wanted to stay out with me. When he left briefly to return the skates, I pulled out my phone and saw that I had a text from Declan.

DECLAN: You alive?

ME: Alive and kissin'

I put the phone away before Ezra came back.

"So what's next?" I asked.

"Well, you are the tour guide, aren't you?"

"Yes, so you must do *everything* I say!" I joked.

"Ah, so you like to be the dominant one, huh?" He grabbed my waist, thrust my hips into his and bit his bottom lip.

I thought it was a bit straightforward, and slightly awkward, but I kissed him anyway.

"Maybe," I said, giving him my best "I'm-awkwardly-trying-to-be-sexy" stare.

"Can you give me a tour of your apartment?" he asked.

I knew what he wanted, but it had been a good four months since I'd had sex, and furthermore, I didn't have time to shave my lady parts while getting ready. Those two factors alone led me to say, "Maybe not tonight."

"Oh." He lowered his eyelids. "Sorry, I just thought we were having a good time, and, I'm sorry. I'm so embarrassed."

I didn't know what to say back other than "OK" in as kind a voice as I could muster in such an uncomfortable moment. We walked down the street, and he was a full step behind me. When I turned around to see if he was OK, he looked like a six-year-old that just got his candy bar taken away.

"Are you upset that I said no?" I asked. "I didn't mean to upset you. I'm actually having a lot of fun tonight."

"No, it's not you. It's me, really. I got ahead of myself. I was in the moment, but I feel like God is slowing me down a bit. I tend to jump into things, and then I end up getting hurt. This is probably God saving me from that."

"What do you mean? I wasn't planning on hurting you. I was having a lot of fun with you. I think you're great."

"I know, I guess it's just my past creeping up on me. I'm sorry. I'm sure you are a great girl."

I felt an overwhelming pressure to prove to him that I was a good person and not just another girl who was going to stomp all over his heart.

"Look, it's my ex-boyfriend's apartment. I'm still sleeping in the living room and it's not the greatest setup. I didn't have time to clean either, but we can go and hang out there if you want. We can put a movie on or something. Declan won't be back for another few days so we have the place to ourselves."

His eyes lit up, and he was back to being his usual, overconfident self. He walked up next to me, and I raised my arm to grab a cab. The cab ride back to the apartment was short but necessary as my feet were killing me in my high-heeled boots.

"I really need to stop wearing heels in this city," I mentioned, rubbing my calves.

When we pulled up to the apartment, I reached over to pay the driver, but Ezra insisted that he pay the eight-dollar fare. I wasn't going to argue. We went inside and I immediately changed my clothes, putting on something more comfortable. By that I mean I put on my grey sweatpants, a long-sleeved cotton T-shirt and my fuzzy slippers. Ezra excused himself and said that he was going to run down the street for a minute, and that he would be right back. He was gone for a little under ten minutes, and when he came back he was equipped with a bottle of red wine and two paper New Year's Eve hats he had bought from the corner bodega. He placed a hat on my head.

"You are so funny. Thank you," I smiled.

"Do you know what time it is?"

I looked at the clock. Midnight. He put the wine on the counter and started kissing me. His tongue was all over the place, half of the time spitting drool out of the corner of my mouth. I pulled away slightly, but he kept kissing. I pulled away harder and gave him a little smile so that I didn't seem too pushy. He pulled me back in and started kissing again. It was too sloppy, and I just needed a break so that I could wipe my chin off.

"OK, OK," I said as I officially pulled away.

"What's the matter?" he asked.

"Nothing, it's just that I only met you today, you know? You just got off the plane, and, it's not that I don't like kissing, it's just—a lot."

"Oh, sorry." He seemed genuine. "Do you not like the wine and hats too?"

"No, it's not like that. I like them. I just wanted to talk a little more, or watch a movie or something."

The night was starting to turn awkward again. We both sat on the couch not saying much. I cleared off the mess I had made when I went through my boxes earlier, and we decided to pick out a film.

"How about *Lord of the Rings*?" I asked.

"I've never seen it before."

"What? No way, you have to see it!" I exclaimed with a smile on my face. "The trilogy is one of my favorites!"

"Sounds good to me." He let out a long dramatic sigh and crossed his arms.

I was still fairly full from dinner but made some Orville Redenbacher to accompany the wine he opened.

Halfway through the movie, I was drunk off two glasses of wine and in a food coma. He was also feeling the effects of the alcohol. He leaned over, put himself on top of me and started to kiss me again. At first, I welcomed it, but then it became too wet again, and after making out for a time, I needed some air, so I pulled away.

"You know what?" he said loudly. "This is stupid, why are you pulling away? Do you like me or not? I flew all the way out here. I just want to show you that I love you, and this is the best way I know how to do that."

"Hold on. You *love* me?"

"Yeah, I think I do." He lowered his voice. "The whole flight here, I prayed for you, and for this trip. I have the Lord's blessing with this, I know it. I'm sorry I raised my voice, and I'm sorry if I'm coming on too strong. I just feel from God that you might be the one for me, and I was trying to impress you. Will you forgive me?"

I crossed my arms and rubbed them. It was refreshing to have someone admit a wrong and apologize. There were times when I thought he was really awesome, and times when I thought he was a little weird, but at the end of the day, he was sitting on my couch offering his love and trying to be affectionate. I couldn't remember the last time I was with a man who showed me this kind of attention. Maybe he was right? Maybe this was a sign from God that we could end up being together? I gave him one last shot to finish the night on a positive note, and I was glad I did. We snuggled and when the movie ended, Ezra was faintly snoring. I didn't want to wake him up, so I left him on the couch and slept in Declan's bed. Tomorrow would be the day I showed him I was a decent girl and worth his visit.

"Good night," I whispered before I turned out the lights.

The next morning I woke up to Ezra struggling to make a cup of coffee.

"Sorry, I have an espresso machine at home. Crazy I can work one of those, but not this." He laughed at himself.

"No worries, I got it." I took over. "An espresso machine, that's fancy."

"Yeah, my mom bought it for me like four years ago and it is still kicking. I love the thing."

"Do you use the word 'love' often?" I asked. "Just kidding," I said quickly.

"Ha—ha," he said sarcastically. "No, I don't use it often. In fact, I've only ever said it to one other person. My ex-fiancé."

"Wait, you dated that other girl for a year and never said, 'I love you' to her?" I filled the machine with water and popped in a K-Cup.

"Nope. I just didn't feel it. I knew it wasn't right, and God made it very clear, especially toward the end."

"Wow."

"So, what are your plans today? Can we make up for last night?" he asked.

"Ezra—"

"Call me Ez. My whole family does," he said abruptly.

"Aw, only your family?"

"Yeah."

He leaned in, giving me a kiss on the cheek. I grabbed his face and kissed back on his lips. When I pulled away, he was smiling.

"The only thing I had planned today was to go to the library. My book is already overdue, so I just wanted to drop it off. I also have the perfect place I want to take you to. It's not really a tourist thing, more something that the locals do. Is that OK?" I asked.

"Yeah, that sounds great."

We stepped out into the winter sun and it was yet another warm day. The thermometer read forty-three degrees.

"It hasn't been this warm since September."

"I'm telling you, God is blessing this time we are having together. Look at all the signs. I love you."

I paused and reflected on his statement. A week ago I stumbled into a church, saw a choir, decided to go on a random Christian dating website, and a man from Oregon was now here, holding my hand and telling me he loved me on a beautiful and sunny forty-three-degree day in the middle of the coldest winter in over a hundred years. Maybe this *was* God? I started to believe it.

"I think I'm falling for you, too."

"Falling in love?" he asked.

"Maybe."

We stopped in at the library, but I totally forgot that it was closed on New Year's Day.

"Looks like I'll owe another dollar or so," I said, shaking my head. "Oh well. It was a good book anyway. Worth it." I shoved the book back into my bag. "Want to stop and grab a quick bite? There's a little bookstore down the street that serves pastries and stuff. Best biscotti you'll ever have."

"Sure, that sounds like fun."

We walked to the store and plopped ourselves down at a bistro table near the front window so we could people watch as we ate. We both ordered chocolate-chip biscotti and cappuccinos.

"So what is that book about?" he asked, pointing to my bag.

"Oh, actually some pretty weird stuff. It's a nonfiction book about the existence of aliens. Do you believe in aliens?"

"That would be a negative. It sort of goes against my religion."

"Well, the book touches base on that. It suggests that aliens are possible, and maybe God just didn't think it was important enough to tell us about it, which is why it wasn't talked about in the Torah."

"The Torah?"

"Yeah, I mean, the Torah or the Bible—it's basically the same thing except for the New Testament. Didn't I tell you I was half Jewish? I guess I forgot."

"Hm, OK. But you *do* believe in Jesus right?"

"I think so, yeah. I like celebrating Christmas, and I was raised Catholic. But there's something about the Jewish traditions I really enjoy, too. I only got to celebrate Hanukkah a few times, but it was really a lot of fun, and my mom let me light the menorah and everything. She would cook us these donut things and latkes. Oh my god, it was so delicious. I don't know why we didn't do it every year."

"Well, maybe that's something we can explore together?" he asked.

"I'd really like that."

"What's that necklace all about?" he asked. I had been twirling it with my fingers.

"Oh this? It was my mother's. It's a hamsa."

"It's that symbol that keeps away the evil eye, right?"

"Yeah, something like that."

"You know that's demonic, don't you?"

"What?" Was he serious? Demonic? "I think you are mistaken."

"You should look it up. I think it originated in ancient Iraq. I'm not completely sure of the history, I just know it's demonic."

"I'm not sure that's correct. I mean, sorry to ruin a good talk here, but I really just don't think it's true. My mom wouldn't give me something *demonic*."

He sat quiet for a moment, then took my hand.

"You're right. I'm sorry. I shouldn't have said that. I bet it's fine. It's probably something else I'm thinking of. I just want to have a good time, so tell me more about those aliens."

The mood lightened and I took the book out of my bag. I scanned through the pages and showed him all of the alien "evidence." We both agreed to disagree when it came to aliens, but it was actually a really fun conversation. After a couple hours of talking, we cleared our table and started walking to our next destination. Along the way, he stopped at a bodega and bought us an Oh Henry! candy bar.

"You can't find these anywhere in Oregon!" He was excited to share. "Here, have a bite—this is the best candy bar ever. I'm telling you, just give it a try."

I didn't want to tell him that I've had many Oh Henry! bars before. In fact, it was *my* favorite candy bar, too.

"Oh yeah, super delicious," I said with a mouth full of gooey chocolate.

I ended up taking him to the Roosevelt Island Tramway, which is a cable car connected to the 59th Street Bridge that flies over the East River. It is simply a way for commuters to get on and off of the island as an alternative to the subway, but it also brings its passengers up high and the views of the city skyline are vast. I had occasionally taken the tram for a slice of stillness when Declan brought a girl home. I'd walk the path along the river and chain smoke.

"This is amazing." Ezra came up behind me and put his arms around my shoulders, looking out at the view. "I've never seen anything like this before."

"Welcome to New York, my—love?" I still wasn't sure about the word "love," but I knew the more I used it, the more comfortable I would feel saying it to a man I'd only known for a total of eighteen hours.

When we got to the boardwalk, I did my usual routine of lighting up a cigarette.

"Ew, you smoke?" he asked.

"Yeah, it's a horrible habit. I've been meaning to quit. At least I don't smoke pot anymore."

"You smoked *pot?*"

"Yeah, sometimes."

"You should quit that."

"Yeah, I know," I said as I took a deep drag. I looked at the cigarette and studied it. "I lived kind of a crazy life before." I gave my pack of cigarettes to him. "Here. Do whatever you want with them, but I'm finishing *this* one."

He threw them into the East River, which was cliché and predictable. I had paid ten dollars for them, but I could always buy more. Plus, there were only three left anyway.

"See? You are already making better decisions being with me," he said.

"I feel healthier already." I really wanted my damn cigarettes back.

We talked as we walked down the boardwalk to the lighthouse at the end of Roosevelt Island.

"So what do you mean by a crazy life?" he asked. "What did you do?"

"I don't know. I just partied a lot."

"Like, drugs, alcohol, sleep around a lot?"

"All of the above I guess."

"How many guys you been with?" he asked. I had never really counted, so it took me a few minutes to figure it out. "Never mind. If you have to think that hard, I don't want to know."

"Are you mad?" I asked.

"No, you've just been with a lot more than me, and now I feel like I'm not experienced enough."

"How many people have *you* been with?"

"Just one. My ex-fiancée."

"So you lived with a girl for a year, never said 'I love you' to her, and never had sex with her?"

"Nope. She went down on me a few times, but I was always so embarrassed that I would cover myself with a blanket and she would have to be under it to finish me off. It was too weird for me. I just couldn't get it up for someone I didn't love. I'm sorry, that's probably more information than you wanted."

"No, it's fine. I asked. So—you've only been with one girl?"

"Yes."

I felt dirty. My number was so much higher than his. However, if he and I were to have sex, I knew I would completely blow his mind, and that made me feel like a goddess.

"Well, that's fine. Do you want to go back to your hotel and change?" I asked.

"Actually, yes. I feel disgusting," he said.

When we got to his hotel room, he took a shower while I messed around with the TV. I couldn't find anything to watch so I sat in silence and reflected on our talk at the island.

I haven't had sex in four months, I thought. *And, if I have sex with him, I would show him the best time he's probably ever had. I'm attracted to him, and I love him, I think. Plus, if God is blessing this, why not? Maybe we'll get married one day and then it won't matter.* I dug through my purse and found an old condom, checking the expiration date. It was still good. When he walked out of the bathroom in a towel to grab some clothes I stopped him. I placed my hands on his hairy chest and kissed his neck. I moved my hands down. He was a bit smaller than I had hoped, but I played with him until his appetite thickened and he became stiff with desire.

"Well, that's a good sign," I said.

"I told you, I love you."

I led him to the bed and he tossed himself back onto the lumpy mattress, rolling the latex over his erection like a seasoned professional. I slipped my underwear from under my dress and started sweet and slow. I felt him flip me to my back. He thrust hard into me. I felt the condom shift, and it felt strange, but I didn't stop him. He felt it too and pulled out, revealing it was busted.

"Do you have another one?"

"No." He was lucky I had *that* one. "It's OK, just pull out." I mean, I did it with Declan enough times and it was always fine.

He entered my warmth and forcefully continued.

"OK?" he asked.

"Better than you thought," I lied.

I wanted to be on top again so I could control where he was hitting, but every time I tried he just went harder and kept me stuck to the mattress. It took him twenty minutes. A bit extreme since he hadn't had a woman for so long, but I didn't question it. I didn't fake it that time, but he didn't *ask* me if I came either, so I was off the hook. At least he pulled out in time, leaving his seed on my stomach. Declan always kind enough to use a wad of tissues or something, so I was kind of grossed out when I had to clean it all up. We lay on the bed naked and Ezra stroked my hair. I missed Declan and his sweetness, which got me every time.

"Why don't you move to Oregon?" he asked.

"Are you being serious?"

"Yes, one hundred percent serious. I love you."

"I love you, too," I said, still uncomfortable about it. "Why don't you move to New York? This city is really cool, and we can get a place together."

"No, I can't do that." He sat up. "I can't move the radio station." He sat me up and took my hands. "I'm serious. Please move to Oregon with me. You are coming out anyway and what's the big deal if you come out a few weeks sooner? Don't worry about the money—just charge it and I'll help you pay it off later. Don't make me beg. I prayed about this in the shower. I asked God for a sign. I think what we just did here was it."

"You think God told me to have sex with you?"

"Call me crazy, but I *did* ask Him for a sign, and five minutes later, this randomly happened. Yes, I do."

"I thought premarital sex was bad for Christians."

"God works in mysterious ways!"

He was smiling. I racked my brain thinking about Declan, the movie in Oregon, and my current living situation. I knew that I had to get out of that apartment, and the sooner the better. This seemed to be a way out.

"Then—yes," I said.

"Yes— you will move to Oregon?"

"Yeah, why not? What's there to lose?"

TWELVE

We spent Ezra's last day in the city taping up most of my boxes and walking them down to the post office, where I mailed them all to his address in
Oregon. By the time I was done, I had a small suitcase of clothes, a hair dryer,
makeup, and my purse left. We also looked for plane tickets to the West
Coast for me. I decided that I would take the train up to visit my father before
I moved the farthest away from him I have ever lived. He was more than
overjoyed when I told him I was coming for a visit, and told me he bought a
pull-out sofa for such an occasion. I left out the part about me permanently
moving across the country with a guy I just met. I figured I would tell him
in person.

When I bought the tickets, I had to pay for them using my credit card.
Since it was last minute, the ticket cost me nearly eight hundred dollars. I was
doing fine with money, but after paying for all the postage, which was over
five hundred dollars, it drained my account. I hated using my credit card and
only used it in emergency situations. Even then, I would pay it off immediately to avoid interest charges.

The fact that I was now in debt, and had less than a thousand dollars to
my name, was a little nerve-racking, but Ezra assured me everything would
be OK.

I called up Karen and left her a detailed message about how I had met a
wonderful man, and he was moving me out to Oregon to be with him. I told
her how grateful I was to have met her and enjoyed working with her. I then

explained that I would be staying in Oregon after the film wrapped and since I was still under contract with her, I assured her that I wouldn't take up any acting work in Oregon unless it was through her. When I hung up the phone, I had a gut feeling that I had made a terrible mistake, until Ezra put his arm around me and started crying.

"Don't cry," I said as I wiped away his tears. "I'll see you soon, I'm flying out in like a week!"

We were standing outside his terminal and his flight was due to board in ten minutes.

"Promise you are going to come?" he asked.

"Of course I promise. I already bought the plane ticket."

"I know, but you bought the 'refundable' one. You're going to cancel it, you won't come, and I'm going to be completely crushed," he cried. "I know it."

"Are you being serious? I just mailed *all* of my possessions to you. Trust me, I'm coming."

He stopped crying and took my hands.

"When you come out to Oregon, I'm going to make you my bride."

The intercom interrupted and called his row to board the plane. We shared one last parting kiss, and he was gone.

When I returned home from the airport, I cleaned up the living room, as I knew Declan would be home in a few days, and he hated clutter. I picked up my phone and saw I had six unread e-mails and a missed call from Karen. One of the e-mails was from the agency.

> Nina,
> I just want to reach out to make sure this is what you really want to do. I'm concerned you might be making a hasty decision. I've enjoyed working with you, and I feel like you are just getting your career started. I'd hate to see you throw it away. If you ever come back to NY, please call me. I'd love to continue working with you.
> —Karen

When I opened the e-mail I was expecting her to be suing me for breach of contract, but she was actually taking a more motherly approach. After reading it, I felt like maybe I *was* rushing all of this. Couldn't it wait? The only problem was that I had already sent all my stuff out there. And I had spent all of my money on tickets. If I turned back now, I'd lose it all. I called Ezra when he landed, and he put my mind at ease. He was being really sweet to me and it got my heart back on track.

"I prayed for this." "It's meant to be." "God told me." These were all things Ez repeatedly told me. He would know much better than I would, since I've only been in a church a handful of times in years and never actually "heard from God." I just had to put my faith in him and trust him. I also kept going back to the fact that he traveled across the country to visit me, even if the plane ticket was free and the hotel was half price. The thing that gave me the most strength to move away was the idea that I might finally have a place I could call home, and *feel* at home. Ever since I'd been sleeping in the living room, I'd felt out of place. I knew I didn't belong in Declan's apartment anymore, and he made it very clear on a daily basis. If I moved to Oregon, I would live with Ezra, and we would probably get married, and live out our "happily ever after." I wouldn't have to live life in limbo anymore. My feet would be grounded. As Grace put it so long ago—I would be "making aliyah." *My* aliyah—a journey home. These thoughts kept me hanging on to the insane idea of living across the country with someone I barely knew. But after all, it *was* God, wasn't it?

The next day, Declan came home.

"Fender!" I yelled out as the dog came pouncing toward me and nearly knocked me over in excitement.

"Hey, how's it going," Declan said.

"Good," I said. "Really good."

"What's that, are you *smiling*?"

"I guess I'm just happy. How's your family? I really miss them."

"Yeah, no kidding. My mom asked about you like fifty times this week."

"Didn't you tell her we broke up?

"Not exactly. She saw your Whole Foods tabloid story and told me I was an idiot. That was about it."

"I will always love your mom."

"Whatever. Anyway, are you feeling better and not psycho now?"

"Seriously, Declan, we were actually somewhat getting along here. Why do you have to be a jerk?"

"Sorry."

He put his luggage away and sat next to me on the couch with a can of diet soda.

"Listen," he started. "I thought about it, and I really am sorry about the other night. I didn't think you would be back. I thought you were going to be out all night, like on a date with someone. It kind of pissed me off a little bit, so I had Coco over. You weren't supposed to know."

"Right. But Declan, that's the point. You are always doing things behind my back. The whole time we dated, you did *so* many things behind my back. I probably don't even know about half of them. But whatever, it doesn't matter. I don't even care anymore."

"Yes you do, Nina. I *know* you still care. I'm just telling you that I'm not going to do it again. As long as you are still living here, I'll keep the girls out of the apartment. I don't want another breakdown like that."

"Well, you don't have to worry about that, because I'm moving out tomorrow."

"What?"

"Yeah."

"Where? Brooklyn?"

"No, a little farther West."

"Hoboken?"

"Oregon."

"No way. There is no way that you are moving to Oregon *tomorrow*." He let out a loud belch.

"Actually, you are right. I'm visiting Papà for a week first, then I'm moving to Oregon."

"Shit. You're not kidding?"

"Nope. That guy I met online lives out there. I'm moving in with him."

"Whoa," he said as he set his can down on the table. "Are you insane? How long have you known him?"

"I don't know. Why are you so concerned? I'm out of your space. You should be happy."

Declan stood up and started pacing in the room. "No. No, I'm not happy. Nina, that is crazy, you don't even know this guy."

"Well, I moved in with you after a couple of months and we were fine until *you* fucked it up."

"Yeah, that's my point! How do you know he isn't going to be a total jerk? What if he decides he doesn't like you anymore once you get there? Then you are stuck, and you've changed your entire life for nothing."

"Where else am I supposed to go, Declan? I can't keep sleeping in your living room!"

"I told you that you could stay as long as you need to."

"Yeah, I know you *said* that, but look how you are treating me. You are constantly going out and fucking other girls, bringing them back here. You cheated on me so many times, and you don't even care."

Declan sat down on the couch and put his head in his hands. He sat there for a long time saying nothing. My mind began to trail off in the silence, picturing what the Pacific Northwest must look like.

"I bet it's really pretty out there," I said, breaking the silence.

He still said nothing.

"I'm moving to Fairview. It's going to be gorgeous. Apparently, the sun stays out for ten hours a day in the summer. Isn't that crazy?"

He remained silent.

"I still don't know why you are upset. I really thought you would be happy."

He lifted his head and looked at me. His eyes were swollen and wet.

"Take care of yourself," he finally said as he stood up and kissed me on the forehead.

A few minutes later Declan walked out the door and, aside from a few tabloid photos with a different girl on his arm each time, that was the last I ever saw or spoke to him.

The next morning, I got myself ready, grabbed my belongings, and stood in the doorway of a place I once called home. It felt foreign to me now. The photos of happy times with Declan were out of their frames and in a landfill somewhere. Any trace of a woman once living there was gone. Before I walked out the door, I heard Fender whimpering. I turned and saw him looking at me from his dog bed in the corner of the kitchen. I threw my bags down and laid myself beside him, hugging him hard. He licked my face as tears spilled down my cheeks. Leaving him was the hardest part of leaving New York City. Fender was the only one I found comfort in after all of those months of emotional torture. I gave him one last hug, kissed the top of his furry head, and left.

THIRTEEN

My father greeted me at the train station with a hug and a latte, knowing full well that my caffeine addiction had corrupted my bloodstream.

"My flower! It's been a long time!" His accent sounded thicker than usual.

"Papà!" I threw my arms around his neck.

That night the two of us went out for dinner at a pizzeria. I had been feeling queasy since I woke up, so I picked at my food and didn't eat much. Ezra texted me the entire time, asking if I had told my dad yet, and if I did, what he thought about the idea.

"Maybe it's best you don't tell him," he suggested.

"I'm going to tell him, and I am doing it tonight," I responded.

After dinner we went to the local bakery for chocolate-chip cannoli. This was something my father and I had in common—our love for anything chocolate, and good fresh-made cannoli. We were sitting at a bistro table licking our fingers clean, and I thought this would be the perfect opportunity to tell my father my plans.

"So Papà, I have some big news to tell you," I began.

"Oh yeah? What's that?"

"I'm moving out of New York. I have an opportunity in Oregon, so I'm taking it."

"What kind of opportunity? A job?"

"Well, yes, and another opportunity as well," I smiled.

"Pasqualina, no—don't tell me you are doing this because of a boy."

I never had to tell him. He *always* knew.

"He's not a boy, he's a man, and yes. He's a great guy, Papà, you would really like him."

"For how long do you know him?" His hands waved in the air.

"It doesn't matter, what matters is that I love him, and he is a Christian!" We started to get louder.

I knew that throwing the word "Christian" around would win my dad over, and for the moment it worked.

"A *Christian*?"

"I know, I decided to be with a Christian man for a change, and maybe start going back to church. I'm moving out there to be with him. He is going to ask me to marry him. He said that he heard from God that I'm the one for him."

"Pasqualina, are you *sure* about this?" He squinted his eyes.

"Yes, absolutely."

"But what about Declan?"

Of course, he had to bring up Declan. Even though he knew Declan and I were over, he was still hopeful that the bastard would smarten up and we'd get back together.

"Papà, you know Declan and I are done. We've been done. I wish you'd stop asking me about it, it's annoying."

He slapped his hand on the table. "I can never tell you what to do, I know that. You won't listen to me anyway. But if this is what you are deciding to do, then fine. I just ask one thing, OK?"

"OK?"

"Please don't get married right away. In the Bible, God uses the number forty as a waiting period. Forty years in the desert. Forty days of Nineveh. Just wait forty days, please."

I let out a long, hard sigh and rolled my eyes.

"Pasqualina, I'm serious," he said. "You've been dreaming of your wedding day your entire life. Don't gyp yourself. Promise me. Forty days." He waved his finger at me.

He was right. I dreamed of my wedding as a little girl. Even now I was picturing it in my head. Selling myself short and not having a wedding would be devastating.

"OK, I promise."

That night, after my father had gone to his room, I went outside on the back patio to call Ez.

"Hey, Ninaroni," he answered.

"What?—Hey."

"Do you like your nickname? I figured it would suit you since you're Italian. You know, like macaroni."

"You're funny." Ugh, I hated it.

"So, Ninaroni, how was your day? What did your dad say when you talked to him?"

"My day was fine. He took it pretty well, I guess."

"What did you tell him?"

"Just that I was moving out there, and I told him you are a Christian."

"What did he say back?"

"Well, he's obviously worried about me."

"Why would he be worried? Didn't you tell him that this is a *God-ordained* move? I'm going to marry you. When we were in New York City, I wanted to take you ring shopping."

"I didn't know that. But Ez, do you think," I spoke carefully, "this might be moving too fast?"

"No way. I love you and I want to be with you. Don't you love me, too? Or were you lying to me like every other girl I've dated."

"What? No, I'm not lying to you, I just think that maybe we can be engaged for a little while before we get married. Like, maybe a year or two. How do you feel about that?"

"No, absolutely not. I want to get married the day you move out here. We will have a romantic courthouse wedding. You'll see, it's going to be so perfect."

"Why do you want to get married so fast?"

"If my listeners at the station know that I am living in sin—having a woman live in my home and sleep in my bed who is not my wife—I look really bad. I might lose the station because of it. And after all, the Bible says, '*But if they cannot control themselves, they should marry, for it is better to marry than to burn with passion.*' You can find that in Corinthians. I don't know why I have to keep convincing you that this is what God wants us to do. But, if

God's own words in the Bible can't convince you, then maybe you just aren't as serious as you make yourself out to be. Honestly, do you even *believe* in God? I need to know now, are you *in* or *out*? Because I am all in."

I sat on the phone, silent, completely shocked that he was speaking to me in such a manner.

"Do you have anything to say?" he asked.

"Why are you being so rude to me?"

"I'm not being rude, I'm being passionate. There is a difference. That is one thing you will learn about me. I'm very passionate and I put myself out there. I wear my heart on my sleeve. That's why I get hurt so much. If you marry me, I know that you promise to honor me, and respect me, and be a loving Christian wife to me, and then I will trust you."

"I guess I didn't see it that way. I'm glad you are passionate," I said. " I just wish your passion would come out in a better way, that's all."

"I'm sorry," he said. "You're right. You know, yesterday I was helping my father out at his company and he noticed that I was on edge. He told me that it is because I'm so far away from you. He said that's how he knows I am truly in love. I turn into Mr. Hyde without my Ninaroni!" He started laughing.

"OK, well, I just have one thing I have to tell you about what my dad said."

"What's that?"

"He wants us to wait forty days before we get married. He said forty is a number of waiting in the Bible, and he would like us to wait."

"That is absolutely ridiculous. Yes, forty is a number of waiting, but why are we waiting when the Bible clearly says that it is better to be married than to lust? Lusting is a sin, and why would God want us to lust and sin for forty days? It doesn't make any sense."

"Um," I paused, "I also kind of want to have a wedding. Or, at least a wedding dress."

"Don't worry about any of that, it will all be taken care of."

"I still think it's a good idea to wait."

He paused to think, then lashed out. "Your dad thinks he knows the Bible so well? Even the devil can quote scripture. Would you listen to the devil if he told you to do something?"

"I don't know. Probably not," I said.

"Call me crazy, but I think the devil doesn't want us to get married. I heard a sermon once, and the pastor said when the devil tries to stop you from God's will, then that means God has some really big and awesome plans for you. It's just something to think about."

"I can see how that makes sense," I said.

"See? I knew you would come around. I think that the next step is for you to just come out to Oregon now. I don't think you should be around your dad anymore. It just doesn't feel right to me. Aren't you getting an uneasy feeling right now?"

He was right. I did feel very uneasy.

"Yeah, a little."

"That's God pushing you to get out of there. See? You can hear from God too, if you just listen hard enough."

"That's God?"

"Yup. Pretty cool isn't it."

"Yeah, but, I'm supposed to be here for a week."

"You got the refundable ticket, didn't you? Why don't you call the airlines and ask them to change the date to a sooner flight? Plus, I have such a cool surprise for you. But you'll have to come out here sooner if you want it."

"I just got here, though. Don't you think I should stay for at least a little while longer? What's the surprise anyway?"

"No. Nina, as your future husband, it is my duty to look out for you, and I really just don't feel like you are safe there. Not spiritually at least. And trust me, it's something you will love. I wanted to keep it a surprise, but—I'm taking you out for dinner with an astronaut. Apparently he has real footage that proves aliens exist. You know I think it's a hoax, but I knew you'd love it. I couldn't believe it when I saw the tickets. It's a dinner and a seminar at the Hilton. It's going to be so much fun, and I don't want you to miss out on it. I was going to ask you to change your flight anyway so we could go, but now with this going on, I *really* think it is for the best."

It was so enticing. He remembered that book I had read, and he was so sweet to get us tickets.

"When is it?"

"Three days from now, but you should still come early and get settled."

"OK. I'll call the airline in the morning."

"You should call them now."

"Now? It's eleven o'clock at night!"

"The sooner the better. Please, I am your family now—trust me. Plus, I just really want to kiss you. I miss you so much."

Even though I felt unsure about the situation, I kept going through with our plans. Ez had a way of making sense of everything, and that put my mind at ease. For the first time in my life, I had a man who was willing to spend the rest of his life with me. He was going to shelter me, and protect me, right? I hung up with Ezra and called the airline. They had a flight out to Oregon leaving the following night, so I decided to take it.

The next morning, I informed my father about the flight change. He was devastated and tried to get me to stay, but I had to pay an extra $500 to change my flight, even though it was supposedly refundable, and there was no way I was canceling it. After I booked the flight, I called Ezra back and told him about the extra charge, and that I had to put it on my credit card.

"Your debt is now my debt. Like I've said, I'll help you pay it off."

When I told my dad about my recent credit card purchases he turned into a crazed Italian, throwing his hands up in the air.

"Nina, stop putting yourself into debt for this man! How are you going to pay this off? You don't even have a degree! What kind of work are you going to do out there? McDonald's wages won't pay off a $2,000 credit card bill! Have you thought about any of this?"

"It's fine, Papà! I talked to Ez about it and he has repeatedly told me he will help me pay everything off. Maybe I will go back to school or something. Have some faith in me! He's going to take care of me. I'll be OK. Plus, I'm working on the film for a whole month. I'll have plenty of cash once I start working. I'll pay off the credit card and save the rest. Squirrel it away, just like you say."

"This boy sounds like a controlling idiot, and I don't trust him at all."

"Papà, most of the time you are right. But this time, I'm telling you, he's fine. He's a great guy."

He leaned forward onto the kitchen table and took a few deep breaths.

"If he makes you happy, then all I can do is tell you how I feel. In the end, you are an adult and you make your own decisions. What time do you have to be at the airport?"

"My flight leaves at nine o'clock. It's an overnight flight."

"Jesus, so soon?"

He took me to dinner and a movie that day. It was a silly kid's comedy that he had wanted to see, but I didn't care. Being around my dad felt good and made me realize how much I missed him. I was still feeling sick to my stomach, so I picked at the popcorn and only had a few sips of soda. It bothered me that Ezra said the devil was speaking through my father because there wasn't an ounce of evil in him.

That night my father slipped me fifty for the trip.

"You know I love you and I am always here for you. No matter what."

"I know, Papà."

"Don't ever hesitate to call me if you need anything."

"I won't. I love you Papà."

"I love you, too. Let me know your wedding plans so I can fly out for it. I don't care if I hate the guy, I'm walking my girl down the aisle."

"I will let you know."

"Ciao, my flower," he said with one last hug.

"Ciao, Papà."

I walked into the airport and found my terminal, grabbing a cup of coffee along the way. I sat at my gate, and one whiff of the steaming coffee made my stomach churn. I tried to take a sip, but the thought of drinking it made me want to vomit. I started to gag and ran for the bathroom, tossing the untouched coffee in the trash on the way. Panic struck me as I lost my dinner in the toilet. When I finished, I found a small convenience store two terminals over and bought a test. I walked back to the bathroom, unzipped, and peed on the stick. Five minutes later I flipped it over, dropped to my knees, and whispered, "Fuck."

FOURTEEN

I landed in Oregon in the early morning and Ezra met me at the airport with a bouquet of flowers.

"I hope you like them. I know they are kind of crappy flowers, but the florist was out of the way, so I got them from the gas station. I didn't want to be late."

I took the bundle of wilted flowers and smelled a half-dead daisy.

"It's the thought that counts. Thank you, Ez."

We kissed, and he held my hand to lead me out into the fresh air where I would begin my new life. I wasn't sure when I should tell him about the pregnancy, so I kept it to myself. He stopped me in front of a beat-up silver car from the early 1980s. Well, silver isn't exactly the right word to describe the color, as most of the car was rusted out and more of a copper color encased it.

"OK, hop in."

I started laughing. I honestly thought that he was kidding.

"What's so funny? Get in," he said.

"I thought you had a motorcycle?"

"No."

"You told me you had one."

"No, I didn't."

"Yes, I'm pretty sure you did."

"Not me, must have been another guy you were talking to."

"I wasn't talking to anyone else, I swear. You said that."

"I don't have a motorcycle and I never told you I had one either. Would you just drop it?"

"OK, OK. Fine. So, this is really your car?" I continued laughing.

"Yes." He looked confused. "Why are you laughing at my car?"

"I'm sorry. I didn't mean to laugh. I really thought that you were kidding. I figured the owner of a successful radio station would drive, I don't know, probably something newer."

He gave me a hard blank stare and got into the car, so I kept quiet during our ride home. He pulled into the parking lot of a beautiful apartment complex.

"I may not have a nice car, but I do have a nice apartment."

I remained silent as we got all of my belongings out of the car and brought them into his home. The sun was just rising. Once I was settled in, we sat outside on his porch. I was feeling out of sorts because of the long flight and two layovers, and also because I couldn't read Ez's feelings. I didn't know if I had made him mad, or what. Just then, he pulled a small black velvet box out of his pocket.

"If this is still something you want to do," he said, "Then you can have this ring."

My mom once said that a man really knows you when he can pick out jewelry you actually like. When he opened the box, I was expecting to see the ring of my dreams. A white gold solitaire ring, any carat diamond, of course. But when the box opened, he displayed a tacky, cheap-looking 10-karat, yellow gold-filled ring with a few diamond chips on it. My heart dropped. It was the ugliest ring I had ever seen, and now I had to wear it every day for the rest of my life and pretend to love it. I gasped and told him that it was beautiful. He slipped it on my finger. At least it fit.

He told me that he wanted to go to the courthouse straight away and after quoting a slew of Scripture to me, interpreting each one basically to say "Jesus wants us to get married immediately," I gave up and told him that I would go to the courthouse. I mean, why not, I was pregnant anyway. Once we got there, the universe saved me.

"I'm sorry, sir, but you can't just walk up in here and expect to get married," the town clerk said with an attitude as she flicked her long braids off her shoulder. "You need to fill out a marriage license form. You can get those in room 201B, on the second floor. There is a five-day waiting period."

I turned to Ezra and quietly suggested, "Maybe *this* is a sign from God that we should wait?"

His face turned red and he snapped his head toward me.

"If you really want to wait, then fine. But you better not cheat on me before our wedding."

"What the hell are you even talking about?" I raised my voice. "How can I cheat on you? I don't know one single person in the state of Oregon, but you!"

His face lightened.

"You're right. I'm sorry, I shouldn't have said that. Why don't we find you a wedding dress?

"What—a dress? What are you talking about?" I was confused because he went from freaking out to calm and relaxed in about half a second. "Does that mean we can have a wedding, then?"

"Of course," he said, changing his demeanor as the clerk looked on. "Anything for my bride." He tucked my hair behind my ear. "Let's not wait the forty days, though," he whispered. "I don't think I can let myself lust that long. It just isn't healthy and I don't want to live in sin anymore. Why don't we get married in, say, two weeks?" he suggested.

I thought it over. I'd fit better in a wedding gown if I didn't wait, and I could also pass off the pregnancy as legitimate if we rushed the nuptials.

"That's a good compromise. Two weeks then." We smiled at each other. "Oh, hey, I wanted to ask you, when is that astronaut thing you were talking about? You haven't mentioned it since I got here."

"Oh. Yeah. About that. You see, I was *going* to buy tickets, but I wanted to wait because I wasn't sure you would come. I wanted to make sure you would actually be here for it. Anyway, by the time you came it was sold out. I wish you'd have gotten here sooner, but oh well."

I was perplexed. It sounded like he was trying to blame the fact that he didn't buy tickets on me, but it was supposed to be a surprise. The whole thing seemed unfair.

"Well, I guess it is the thought that counts." I said it to ease the tension. I found myself saying it to him a lot, but truthfully, it is never the thought that counts. The person who coined that phrase was an idiot who didn't know anything about relationships. Thoughts don't count, only actions do. At least, that's what Papà always says, and I completely agree.

Over the next two weeks, the dynamics between Ezra and I were very strange. He took me dress shopping, but would not let me choose my own dress.

"No way, that one is *way* too slutty," he said when I put on the dress that caught my eye the most. I couldn't understand why, as it was a simple and classic strapless A-line dress. He ended up picking out a long satin gown with a high neckline made of lace. It was pretty, but not what I pictured myself in.

Next came the location. He insisted we get married in his parents' barn. I didn't have any opposition to that.

When he took me to his parent's home for the first time to meet them, I assumed they might have their reservations about me since we hadn't known each other very long and I was marrying their only son. When we approached his family's home, I saw that it was a well-maintained property with a gorgeous barn lit up with Edison bulbs and sparkling in the snow.

"This is very beautiful," I gasped.

"I told you so."

We walked into his home, and without batting an eye, his mother circled around me with a completely blank face. She was a large woman, nearly three hundred pounds, with a short choppy haircut and big hoop earrings. Her look pierced my eye, and with a half-smile she said, "She's perfect."

His father sat lurking in the corner of the room, not saying anything until dinner was on the table. He then began telling a story about his day. Halfway through his story his wife slapped him upside the head and said, "Would you *please* stop talking? All you do is talk about pointless stuff. It's so annoying."

His father's face dropped and he quietly apologized. My eyes widened in disbelief. Ezra quickly changed the subject.

"So, as you both know, I met Nina online and surprised her in New York City for a visit! We fell in love, and now we are getting married." He reached under the table and held my hand. "We'd like to do the ceremony here."

His mother started to cry and thanked him profusely for choosing her home.

"Don't you worry 'bout a thing, honey. I will take care of everything," she said, patting my shoulder.

What I didn't realize at the time was that she really meant she was going to take complete control of my wedding, from the dollar store decorations to the bouquet of fake flowers. In fact, I didn't have the opportunity to pick out one thing for my wedding.

After dinner, we ate scoops of ice cream for dessert, still seated around the table. It was silent until Ezra leaned over and loudly asked me for money.

"Nina, since you live with me now, I need a favor."

"What's that?"

"I need you to pay next month's rent. I spent all of my money coming out to visit you."

"Wait, I thought you got a really good deal. Wasn't your plane ticket free from your parents' miles?"

"What are you talking about? I had to pay nearly $700 for that plane ticket."

His parents sat listening to us in silence. I looked to them for guidance, but their stares demanded an answer.

"Oh. I could have sworn you said the ticket was free." I looked around the room, feeling surrounded. "How much is the rent?" I asked.

"$1,100."

"I only have $800 right now."

"Then tomorrow, let's open a joint bank account. That way, when I get paid from the station, what's mine is yours and what's yours is mine. Sound good?"

I felt on the spot.

"Honey, if you are going to be married, you should have a joint bank account for situations such as this," his mother chimed in.

"OK."

⚓

Two weeks later, we were married. My father flew out for the wedding and walked me down the aisle as he promised. I could tell that he didn't agree with my decision to marry Ezra, but he never said anything. He knew I wouldn't listen anyway. I was hell-bent on the fact that God was telling me to marry him. Ezra would wake up every morning and remind me of that.

Ezra wrote the wedding ceremony himself, and he had a local pastor from the church he attended perform it. Even though I had been in town for two weeks, he hadn't taken me to his church yet, so the ceremony was the first time I actually met the pastor.

Only his parents and my father attended. It was too last minute for me to invite my friends, and I was shocked that Ezra didn't invite any of his. In fact, I wasn't sure he *had* friends.

Before the ceremony, my father took me to get my hair done. It's something my mom should have been there for, but he was a good sport about it. My hands clenched my necklace as the stylist did my hair, making me feel closer to my mom. Wherever she was in the universe, I hoped she was watching. After I was all done up, Papà took me to a sandwich shop for a bite to eat, but I figured I should probably get back to Ez's parents' house to start getting ready. I took my sandwich to go, and my father dropped me off at the house. I walked in and plopped down at their dining room table to start eating. I was actually starving instead of queasy, for once. I took one bite before his mother walked in and glanced at my food.

"Where is mine?" she asked.

"Your what?"

"My sandwich?"

I felt really awkward.

"Um, I didn't—this is the only one I have."

"You went out to eat and you didn't bring anything back for me?" She waddled her large frame over to the table and put her hands on her hips. "Why not?"

"Um, I didn't realize you wanted me to?"

I was shocked that she was interrogating me like this *on my wedding day.* What fucking nerve, lady.

"That is so rude!" she exclaimed. "But whatever, *I* didn't raise you." She walked to the refrigerator and her husband walked in. "Hey, honey, are you hungry? Do you want me to make you a sandwich?" she asked him, and glared at me.

"Excuse me?" I was starting to get pissed off. First she attacked me, and now she was attacking my parents? Especially my dead mother, whom she'd never even met? My face grew hot with anger.

"What?" she retorted.

"What did you mean by '*I* didn't raise you?'"

She closed the fridge and got up close in my face.

"What I mean is, I raised my son to put others before himself. I don't see that quality in you. And I swear if you don't put my son first I will beat the selfishness out of you myself. Next time, call. Ask us if we want a sandwich. Think about someone else for a change."

I couldn't believe the way she was talking to me. I pulled out my phone and started texting Ezra about what his mother had just said to me. I wrapped up my sandwich and took it in the bathroom. I could hear his mother loudly answer the phone, saying, "Oh hi! It's the world's best son!"

Fuck, she got to him first. I didn't even care to listen to the conversation. I sat on the toilet seat, unfolded the paper around my sandwich and wolfed it down. Five minutes later my phone rang. It was Ezra.

"Hey—"

"Why are you yelling at my mother?" he cut me off.

"What? I wasn't. She was yelling at me!"

"Listen to me. She is your elder. I don't care what is going on, you need to talk to her with respect. I want you to apologize to her immediately."

"Are you kidding me? She got in *my* face because my dad bought me a sandwich! Are you serious?"

"Nina. Go apologize to her right now or I swear I will not marry you. I'm sitting with your dad right now and even he is shaking his head yes."

How did my dad get back to Ez's apartment so fast? There was no way my dad was there yet, and I found out later that Ezra was, in fact, lying. Why did his mother have to say anything at all? *On my fucking wedding day.* I didn't want to deal with it anymore, and I knew if I apologized it would all go away, so I reluctantly agreed.

"Fine."

"Thank you. I'll see you soon."

I walked out of the bathroom and tossed the empty sandwich bag in the garbage. Both his mother and father were eating chips and salsa at the table.

"I'm sorry I didn't bring you a sandwich," I said. "Next time I'll call and ask."

"Good girl," his mother said without even looking at me. "You should probably go get ready now."

I was pretty bummed out at the whole ordeal. I felt like my wedding day was ruined, but I turned and walked back down the hall to the bathroom and started putting some makeup on. The more I thought about it, the more I realized that Ezra's mother was probably the reason Ez was so on edge all of the time. If she treated *me* like this—someone she just met—I can't imagine how she treated *him* growing up. And who was she to get mad about a sandwich when she was over there hitting her husband at the dinner table two weeks prior? I felt bad for both of them. That woman was a real wench.

Two hours later, Ezra and I stood in the cleaned-out barn before our three guests, and the ceremony began. I wore the dress he picked out. The lace neckline covered my mom's necklace, but it was OK. It was still there, underneath all of the white fabric, snug and close to my heart. We exchanged traditional vows and one ring. Because my engagement ring had a few diamond chips on it, Ezra didn't see any reason for me to have a wedding band. It was "flashy enough," he said. He picked out an expensive platinum wedding band for himself and charged it to my credit card.

"The bride is supposed to buy the groom's ring," he told me. "I bought *yours*, and it's tradition for you to buy mine."

I didn't argue it, but I did wish he had picked out something cheaper.

The pastor had us exchange traditional vows, and before the ceremony was finished, he read the Scripture Ezra had picked out.

> 1. [...] wives, be submissive to your own husbands so that even if any of them are disobedient to the word, they may be won without a word by the behavior of their wives, 6. just as Sarah obeyed Abraham, calling him lord.

"This comes from 1 Peter 3:1-5."

Obeyed? Really? Obeyed? And excuse me, but no way would I ever call him *lord*. I felt disrespected by the verse. My father glared at me, but I smiled at Ezra, and we shared our first kiss as husband and wife. I planned to address the verse later, but was never given the opportunity.

Though the wedding was small, his mother had asked a friend of hers to make us a wedding cake, which I thought was very kind. Despite the fact that she had completely taken over the wedding planning, and had acted like a complete jerk all day, I was actually fairly pleased with the cake she picked out. After all, vanilla on vanilla *was* my favorite. We took hold of the knife and cut a slice while our parents clapped and cheered. I looked over at the large piece Ezra was going to feed me and jokingly said, "I can't fit that in my mouth!"

I started to giggle and smile, until Ezra responded under his breath, "Shut up. Stop being difficult."

My smile faded and I said nothing as we fed each other cake. Ezra joked and laughed with his parents for the rest of the evening, giving my father and me some quality alone time.

"Nina, if you ever need anything, you know you can always ask," he reiterated.

I didn't want to talk about it. I had sworn to him that Ezra was a great guy, and I had to stick to my story. Things would be better now that we were married, and in a few weeks I could announce that I was pregnant. I still hadn't told Ez. I felt that a lot of the stresses we were feeling were due to wedding planning itself, and now that it was over, we could be happy.

"I'm just a phone call away," he continued.

Little did he know that Ezra had taken my phone away from me the day we joined bank accounts. I couldn't say anything because I knew my father would cause a scene.

"We can share one phone just like we share one bed," Ezra told me. He kept my phone active and zipped up in his coat pocket at all times. I wasn't allowed to use it, but he did give it back to me just before the wedding, when my dad was in town. As soon as we left for the honeymoon, I noticed it was missing from my purse again. I also had to surrender all of my credit cards and checkbooks to him.

"It just isn't right to have the woman pay for things when we go out. I will hold on to all of the cards, so when you pay for things it looks like *I'm* paying for it," he claimed.

I didn't know how I could pay for anything anyway. All of the money I had was gone and our bank account was constantly overdrawn and slammed with fees. I was wondering when he would get his next paycheck from his radio station, which I still had yet to see. I kept asking him if Karen messaged me about my start date and call time for the movie, but he told me my phone never rang. I had no way of checking my e-mail, and social media was off limits. He caught me looking at my messages one night and flipped out that I was talking to Jake, so he made a rule—"No social media past nine o'clock"—which lasted all of one day because I thought the rule was fucking ridiculous. He took my computer away and locked it up at the radio station. He said he would give it back after the wedding, making me feel pretty shitty for betraying his trust.

He decided that he would drive me to Portland for a honeymoon. By the time we checked into the hotel it was one in the morning. I was exhausted and already half asleep when my head hit the pillow.

"It's our wedding night, wake up," he said, shaking me.

I asked him if we could have sex in the morning instead, hoping the innocence in my voice would sway him.

"Come on, don't you want me? I'm your husband now!"

He didn't wait for me to respond. He rolled me to my stomach, moved my hair from my neck and kissed it. I immediately thought about the baby and thought maybe I shouldn't be on my stomach, but I still hadn't mentioned it. He pulled down my underwear, which read "Bride" across the butt. Grace had sent them to me as a gift.

"Those are cute," he said. He kissed me from my neck down my back. I *really* wanted to mention the pregnancy.

"You didn't put a condom on." I thought that might steer the conversation in the right direction.

"We don't need protection anymore, we're married. If God wants us to have a baby, then we will."

I kept wanting to say something, but he already began. He grunted and kissed and pushed his dick into me for about three minutes before cumming. Maybe it was longer. I wasn't sure since I was only thinking about the baby the whole time. After he finished, I laid on the bed in his stink. He cleaned himself up in the bathroom, came back, and sat down next to me.

"See, wasn't it worth it? We are officially hitched," he laughed.

"I guess so. Ez—" I hesitated. "Are—are you making all of this up?"

"What are you talking about?"

"All of this God stuff. Are you making it up?"

I couldn't believe I had the balls to ask him that, but it was something I had been thinking about.

"Honestly, Nina, how can you even ask me that? Is this your way of telling me you don't want to be married? You *are* cheating on me, aren't you? I had a dream that you slept with our neighbor, just like my ex. I saw how you stared at him the other day when we were in the parking lot. You are such a fucking whore!"

"Whoa, whoa!" I said. "Calm down! I'm not cheating on you! What the hell is going on? I asked you about all this 'God' stuff, and suddenly I'm cheating on you? What the fuck is wrong with you?"

He gasped.

"I can't believe you would talk to me like that."

He put some clothes on, took his phone, and went out onto our hotel balcony. I heard him calling his mother. I couldn't make out everything he was saying, but it seemed like he was discussing me. I took the opportunity to clean myself and put clothes on. I was confused, tired, sore, and annoyed. He had flown off the handle and all I did was ask a simple question—was he making it up? I walked out of the bathroom and heard him yelling.

"She literally cursed at me, Mom. I think she might be bipolar."

I walked over to the glass door and opened it.

"Are you kidding me?" I said. "Why don't you tell your mom what you said to *me*? You are upset that I said 'fuck?' How about the fact that you called me a—"

Suddenly the phone was to my ear.

"She wants to talk to you."

I didn't get a chance to say anything before she started screaming at me over the phone.

"You are supposed to submit to your husband! Don't you ever curse at *my son* again! You need to watch your mouth! This isn't a game of house, grow the fuck up!"

"Oh yeah, OK, so *I* can't say 'fuck,' but it is perfectly OK for you to scream it at me? Whatever!" I yelled back.

I didn't care to hear the rest of what she was saying, so I hung up the phone and threw it on the table. Ezra picked it up and went back to bed to continue texting with his mother—all night. I didn't want to sleep near him, so I took a blanket and went out onto the balcony. I was already extremely tired when we arrived at the hotel, but now I was suffering from exhaustion.

I sat on the porch with my winter coat and boots on, wrapped up in a fluffy hotel blanket, nodding off every so often. After an hour I figured sleeping on the floor was at least better than sleeping outside in the cold. I tried to open the door but it was stuck. I tried again, and it still wouldn't open. I peeked through the window and saw that it was actually locked.

"He locked me out?" I said through clenched teeth. I banged on the glass and saw him sleeping on the bed. When I banged harder, he stirred a bit, and then rolled over to face the other direction.

I climbed down the fire escape and went to the lobby for a spare key. After I got into the room, I laid in the corner, still wrapped up in the same blanket, for the rest of the night. As I dozed off, I remembered that Ezra never answered my question. Was he making all of this up? He changed the subject so fast.

He had seemed like a happy-go-lucky, spontaneous, and confident man when I met him in New York, but now something definitely wasn't right. I felt like he had two personalities. Sometimes he was really sweet to me, but with the flick of a switch, he turned into a total wacko. Now his family thought I was abusing him, but who was really the abusive one? I touched my belly and realized I had made a mistake. A horrible, terrifying mistake.

FIFTEEN

"Why don't you have a fucking job yet?!"

It was six in the morning and I was kneeling over the toilet, vomiting. I had told him about my pregnancy on the second day of our honeymoon. He was actually pretty thrilled and it changed the whole mood of our trip. He went back to being "nice Ezra," for a day or two.

"Our account is overdrawn *again*. Get yourself a fucking job."

"Ez, how am I supposed to know that our account is overdrawn? What are you spending all of our money on?"

"Oh, hmm, let's see: Our lifestyle? Taking care of *you*? It's your goddamn fault. You've been here for *months* already and you haven't even had an interview yet. You are a lazy fucking slut."

I continued to dry heave.

"This is all your fault. We have no money, and we are two months behind on rent. I was fine before you came here. You are ruining my life."

"But I haven't bought anything. None of my clothes fit anymore. You won't even let me buy a pair of pants or prenatal vitamins. Where's all my money?"

"Your money? *Your* money?" he repeated.

"*Our* money. Where is it?"

"You don't even know the extent of what you did."

"How is any of this my fault?" I reached for the toilet bowl again. "I thought I was working that movie, but Karen just ghosted. That's not my fault."

He sat on the edge of the bathtub and put his head in his hands.

"I had a job working third shift at a gas station before I visited you in New York. But because my trip to visit you was so last minute, I couldn't get anyone to cover my shift and they ended up firing me."

"Again, how is that my fault?"

"Well, if I didn't meet you in the first place then I would still have that job, wouldn't I?" he yelled.

"Sure, but you said it yourself that this was God's plan, right? Maybe God has something better for you?"

"I doubt it."

"What about your radio station?" I asked.

He hesitated.

"You are so fucking stupid, you know that? You don't know anything about running a business. I can't even handle it sometimes with you. You really fooled me, you know? 'Oh, let's go to the library, let's read,'" he said in a condescending voice. "Yeah, right. You are such a moron—you probably just went to the library to find another guy to fuck."

"That's not true—"

"Shut up! Jesus, your whining is so annoying. I'll show you the station today and I'll explain how it works, OK?"

Finally, he was willing to shed a ray of light on his secretive radio station. After the fetus was done playing dodgeball with my stomach lining, I pulled on a pair of Ez's sweatpants and one of his long-sleeved shirts to cover my growing body. A week prior, I was getting ready for church and put on the loosest fitting dress I owned, but it tugged and stretched at my hips and Ez wouldn't let me leave the house without insulting me. "Slut," "Bitch," "Whore," "Stupid," "Useless," were all my names now. He scolded me for flaunting my pregnancy with tight clothing and said I would attract all sorts of kinky men who would be chomping at the bit to have sex with a pregnant slut. When we got home, I searched his drawers for clothes I could wear. I settled on one pair of sweatpants and a shirt that I had worn every day since, washing them when I could. At least they were comfortable.

The sun was still asleep when we pulled up to his father's computer repair shop.

"Come on, let's go." He slammed the car door.

We went into the shop, and he opened the door to a closet in the corner, which revealed a small desk with a computer and a few electronic devices I didn't recognize.

"This is the station."

"Wow. It's a lot smaller than I thought it would be." I immediately regretted my reaction, but surprisingly, he didn't get upset.

"Want some coffee?" he asked.

"Sure. Decaf."

Getting out of the house and drinking something other than water was a treat. Every day Ezra would leave me in the apartment by myself, locked in with the alarm set. If I so much as touched a windowpane or the doorknob, an alert would get sent to his phone, and to the local police department.

He brought back two cups of coffee and we sat at his desk. He showed me how he picked songs to play, and even let me sit and watch while he recorded a talk show. After he was done, he clicked on a second screen that had a bunch of statistics on it. He pointed to a number that appeared in a small box in the upper right-hand corner of the screen.

"Seven? What's that mean?"

"I have seven listeners right now."

"Oh, I'm sorry to hear that. Why only seven?"

"Actually, that's a lot. I usually have three."

"Only three? But what about your Instagram page? People are always commenting on it and you have thousands of likes!"

"It's all about the image. Most of those profiles are me. I spend a lot of my time logging onto fake profiles and commenting on my page so it appears bigger than it actually is. It's a business strategy that you wouldn't understand even if I tried to explain it to you."

"I *understand* what you mean. But how do you make any money off of this if only three—"

"Seven" he corrected.

"If only seven people are listening?"

"I don't."

"You don't—what?

"I don't make any money off of the radio station, alright! God, you are so stupid, what the hell do you think I was trying to tell you by bringing you here? What, like this is some field trip or something? We are in the red, Nina, and it's your goddamn fault. I don't even know what the fuck is wrong with that head of yours. Are your wires disconnected upstairs or something?" He pointed sharply at his head. "Too difficult for you to process in that idiot brain of yours? God, why do you have to be so dumb?"

He stormed out of the shop, slammed the car door, and sped away. I heard footsteps approaching and wiped my eyes with my sleeve. His father had heard the arguing and was walking toward the closet.

"Where's Ez?" he asked.

"He left. He was upset about the station, I think."

"Wouldn't be the first time. That's decaf, right?"

"Yeah."

"Good girl. Don't worry, he'll be back." He patted me on the shoulder and walked back to his office.

I felt bad for Ezra's father. He was a soft-spoken man who had a lot to say but could never seem to get more than a couple words out before his wife ripped his dignity to shreds. They had been married for thirty-five years, and after a certain point, he probably figured it was better not to say anything at all.

I sat in the closet for twenty minutes, taking small sips of coffee, wondering when Ezra would be back. His father was already out of sight, and Ezra had left his computer unlocked. I hadn't been able to access the Internet since I came to Oregon, and without my phone, I was completely disconnected from the world. Ezra had created a bubble for me, and made it clear I was to stay inside at all costs. I looked around for my own computer, but it wasn't in plain sight and all of the desk drawers were locked. I stared at his computer for a few moments. I reached my hand over to the mouse, but hesitated when I heard his father come out of the office for a coffee refill. When he returned to his desk, I seized the opportunity. I clicked the mouse, continuously looking over my shoulder to make sure Ez wasn't back yet. When the browser opened, Ezra's e-mail popped up. I hesitated again. Should I look? Was his dad gone? Were there cameras in there? I searched the ceiling, scanning every little nook I could find, and it looked clear. I opened an e-mail from our bank. It was another notification for an overdraft fee. We now had a negative balance of $3,629.36. I scribbled down the number to the bank on a sticky note, as well as our account number, so that I could call to remove my name from the account whenever I got ahold of a phone. I didn't want to be responsible for debt I didn't incur.

The next tab I clicked on was from my credit card company. Ezra had insisted that I open a card in his name under my account when I first moved in, "for emergencies." I checked the balance and nearly fell out of the chair. I came to Oregon with only the airline debt on my credit card, but now I was in debt over seventeen thousand dollars. "What the hell did he buy?" I whispered. I clicked off the tab and slammed my fingers on the keyboard, accidentally opening another e-mail, and when I looked at the screen, a lump in my throat threw itself down deep into my stomach. I read the words six or seven times before I actually realized what I was reading. I didn't know how to process the information, how to react, or what my next moves would be. My fingers trembled while I scrolled down through a conversation that began with a "personals" ad. Someone had e-mailed Ezra in response to an "m4m" ad that he had put out three days prior. *What is "m4m?"* I thought. It seemed like they were exchanging dirty pictures of each other, but when I saw the photos, all I could see was a bunch of dicks. Nothing made sense. I looked up the original ad, and it all came together.

"Straight Acting Top Looking For Clean Bottom".

It took a moment for the words to settle in and make sense.

"Oh my god. *Oh my god!*"

I grabbed my mouth and pressed firmly so I wouldn't make too much noise. I discovered *m4m* meant "male for male." Ezra was gay. What the heck was he doing married to *me?* This explained a lot. It explained why he made me do weird sex shit, like shoving my fingers and small dildos up his ass. I didn't have much of a choice because if I didn't do exactly what he asked, the repercussions were far worse. I would get screamed at, and sometimes left for a day or two in an alarmed apartment in the middle of nowhere, with no car, no phone, and oftentimes minimal food. Luckily, there was a large bag of rice in the cabinet, which I bought when I first moved in. I would cook the rice and eat it for breakfast, lunch, and dinner during the day, when he was gone. Sometimes he would come back with his mother, who would scream at me, tell me what a low life piece of shit I was, and threaten to take away my unborn child if I "*kept up the crap*" and didn't start "*submitting to her son.*" My wrongdoing usually was not having enough sex with him, but he would lie to her and constantly told her I was abusing him. One time it was because the labels on the spice rack weren't all facing the same direction and the towels in the kitchen weren't folded the right way. "I told you to clean this place!" he yelled. That was another quirk about him. He had extreme OCD.

Given my history with Ezra over the past few months, I found myself in a predicament. Should I tell him that I knew about his sexual escapades with other men? Should I run away? Should I stay and deal with it? I decided I would take it a minute at a time. Maybe I could catch the "good" Ezra for once, and actually have a conversation with him, rather than constantly being bombarded with the "evil" Ezra. His two-toned charade worsened daily.

Just then, I heard the front door swing open. I quickly clicked out of his e-mail and opened up the Google tab, typed in "Oregon job listings," and clicked on the first page I found. Ezra calmly came into the room and placed his hands on my shoulders.

"I'm just looking for a job like you told me to," I blurted out.

"I see," he muttered.

I scrolled through the job listings one by one as he breathed down my neck, saying nothing. By then it was one o'clock in the afternoon and I was scheduled for an OB appointment within the hour.

"We should probably get going soon. Thanks for coming back."

"Sure," he said.

He was eerily quiet. He bent down and kissed me on my cheek. He smelled funny, like a mixture of bad cologne and french fries. My mind immediately jumped to thinking he had met up with the guy from the e-mails. I never found out for sure, but all signs pointed to yes. His father called him out of the room for a moment, so I quickly deleted the history and closed out of the browser.

We left his father's shop and went to the hospital. I tried to be seen by the doctor alone, thinking it would be a good opportunity to spill my guts and get someone to help me the hell out of Oregon, but Ezra wouldn't let me out of his sight. He stayed glued to me and listened carefully to every word I spoke and every facial expression I made, so I could not give away any clue to the doctor that I was practically being held captive. Everything with the baby looked good, and she gave me a prescription for the intense migraine headaches I had been recently experiencing.

After the appointment, Ezra drove me back to his wanna-be radio station and made me open boxes of DJ equipment that had just been delivered. We moved it to a space in the back room, which his father had cleared for the station's "expansion." I found a receipt in one of the boxes. He snatched it out of my hands before I could get a good look at it, but I grabbed a glimpse of the total. It was over fifteen thousand dollars worth of equipment. I knew he had charged this to my credit card. I called him out on it.

"Ez, give me that receipt," I said.

"It's none of your business."

"Give me the receipt *right now*!" I yelled.

"Don't give me lip or I swear, Nina, I will—"

"You swear what? That you'll take all my money? Take my phone away? Leave me for three days? What's new? Give me the damn receipt right now!"

I lunged at him and grabbed it from his hands. He threw me off of him and into the wall, but I already had the paper in my hands. I knew it. He had charged all of the equipment to my credit card.

"You used *my* credit card!" I screamed.

By then his father was in the doorway, watching everything unfold.

"She attacked me!" he yelled.

"He stole fifteen thousand dollars from me!"

"Call the police!" Ezra demanded.

His father called, and the police came shortly after. I sat in the waiting room as both he and Ezra talked to the cop. I rubbed my elbow, which at that point was purple from hitting the wall so hard.

Ezra and the cop walked over to me.

"Ma'am, I'm under the impression that you attacked your husband today. Can you please inform me as to what the issue is?" I stared at him hard without saying a word. "Ma'am, are you going to make a statement?"

I looked at Ezra looming over the officer's shoulder, and held my elbow. The officer took my arm and saw the bruise, which now also had a bead of blood falling down from a slight split in my skin. I hadn't noticed that it was bleeding until now.

"This looks fresh," the cop said curiously. "I'm going to have to ask you to step outside with me."

I started to follow him and Ez traveled close behind. When we got to the door, the officer stopped him. "I'm going to talk to your wife in private." He kept Ezra back in the building with his hand.

I walked outside with the officer and told him my side of the story. I didn't leave out any details, telling him about the e-mails, our bank account, and about all of the equipment Ezra bought using my credit card.

"I just freaked out," I told him. "I didn't mean to grab at him, but I wanted to see the receipt."

"Back up a minute here," the cop said. "You're telling me that this guy is cheating on you with other guys, and charged fifteen thousand dollars to your credit card? Why are you still with him?"

I tilted my head down and thought about how I could generate a reasonable response to a completely legitimate question.

"I don't think I really have a choice. I'm pregnant. I mean, I just moved here. I don't know anyone."

"Listen. If you were my daughter, I would break this guy's neck. But I can't do that and keep my job, so I'm just going to give you some advice. You've got to ditch this guy, and the sooner the better."

The cop went back in the building and explained to Ezra that his story didn't match mine. Ezra claimed self-defense, which I guess was kind of true since I *did* attack him first. I felt like shit, and I just wanted to go home.

I didn't even know what the word "home" meant anymore. It made me think back to that conversation I had with Grace so long ago in New York City about "making aliyah." I started daydreaming about Declan, and my trip to Israel, and the feeling I got in that upper room. I started to think back to my apartment in New York, and that church I had gone to. Then I started to think about Dave. I wondered what he was doing. I figured he was probably getting ready for a gig or something, since it was about six o'clock in the evening on the East Coast. The more I thought about Dave, the more upset I got. He was such a kind person, and I always felt safe around him. I hadn't felt like I was in a safe place since I had stepped off the plane in Portland. Next time I had Internet access I would try to contact him, but how? How would I do that without Ez catching me?

"The library?" I said out loud. The cop was walking to his patrol car, so I shuffled over to him. "Excuse me, can I ask where the closest library is?"

"It's about a mile from here. See the main road over there? Take that and walk down about six lights. It's across from city hall. See that green sign?

"Yeah, I see it."

"It's right there. Do you need a ride?"

If I took the ride, Ez would flip out even more, so I thanked him and declined. He asked me about twenty times if I was sure, and I repeatedly told him that everything was fine and that I'd be OK. He gave me his card and wrote the police report number at the top, in case I ever needed it.

After the officer left, I knew I would have to go in and face Ezra and his father, and I wasn't exactly looking forward to it. My arm was still bleeding, and I figured I would go in and ask for a Band-Aid to change the subject. I took a few deep breaths and tried to collect some level of zen first. I placed my hand on the handle and pulled. The door was sealed solid. I tugged and pulled a few times, and it wouldn't budge. I saw Ezra through the glass window and knocked on the door. He wouldn't even so much as look up at me to acknowledge my presence. How predictable.

I started banging on the glass as hard as I could, and again, he wouldn't look up. Eventually, he just walked away. My patience was running thin.

"Open the door, Ez! I'm bleeding! I need a Band-Aid. Ez, open the door!" I screamed as I pounded my hands on the glass.

His father came out of his office and walked toward me, then stopped and turned to Ezra. What I could make out was muffled, but I imagine Ezra instructed his dad not to let me in. Now not only was my arm bleeding, but my the palms of my hands were bruised.

I grit my teeth together and stared him down through the door. He stared back, and the more he stared, the more pissed off I got. I gave him the finger and walked away. I figured I would just walk to the library and get a Band-Aid there. Where else was I going to go? I sure wasn't going to sit outside the door and wait for my so-called husband to mock me from indoors. As I walked away I heard the door unlatch.

"Where are you going?" he yelled.

At this point, I was about fifty feet from the door.

"None of your business," I shouted without looking back.

I could hear him running after me.

"I said, where the fuck are you going?" He grabbed my bloody arm and spun me around. He wouldn't let go of my limb, and the longer I waited to answer him, the harder he squeezed. He shook me, and again demanded to know where I was going. I remained silent. I didn't want to mention the library because I knew he would immediately figure out that I was going there for more than just a Band-Aid.

"You locked me out *again*," I muttered, but he wanted a deeper explanation. "I was going to walk home," I finally said.

"Walk home? Walk *home*? Do you have any idea where you are right now? It would take you hours to get there. Just when I thought you couldn't get any more stupid, you decide you are going to *walk* home. Jesus Christ, you are so dumb!"

"I thought saying Jesus's name in vain was bad. Isn't *that* in the Bible?" I snapped back.

That was the final straw for him. His face turned maroon, and his eyes darkened. I swear, two devil horns could have popped out of his head. He turned around and dragged me by my arms over to his car. My walk turned into a jog trying to keep up with him. He opened the back door and told me to get in.

"Sit down and shut up. I don't want to hear one word from you. You better be sitting here when I come back or I'm going to fucking kill you, do you understand?"

I froze. That was the first time he—or anyone, for that matter—had actually threatened my life. I knew he was nuts, but I never knew he was capable of threatening me like that. He slammed the door and I stared hard at his back as he walked back in the shop and locked the door behind him. For the rest of the evening, he let customers in one by one, and locked the door behind them. He probably made up some bullshit story that there was an attempted robbery or something.

I sat in the car by myself for about two hours, debating the entire time if I should scoot out and attempt the library again. My arm eventually stopped bleeding, but not before it stained his shirt. I knew he would be pissed about it, and although it was technically his fault, he wouldn't see it that way. Every time I thought I could get out of the car and make a run for it, he would come over to the door and look at me through the glass. I thought about the e-mails I read in his account, and played with the cuticles on my nails. I wondered why he had married me if he was gay. Maybe he was bisexual? It really seemed like he just wanted to be with men, though. I mean, he wasn't exactly turned on by me. The fact that he would disappear into the bathroom several times a day and blame it on a sudden "Crohn's" condition gave me enough hints that I wasn't enough for him. I had once found a bottle of some goo called "Masturbate Pro" shoved behind our toilet at home in a little box. It was obviously masturbation cream. I didn't even know that sort of stuff existed until I saw it.

I realized his "Crohn's" condition was completely made up because I was crazy enough to note how the box was placed every time I went into the bathroom. I would go in after every "Crohn's" episode, and noticed that the air wasn't tainted as it should have been if Crohn's was truly the culprit. Of course, every time this happened, the box had been moved. He was masturbating several times a day, and insisted we have sex every other day, at a minimum, to keep our marriage "healthy." If I didn't comply I would have to listen to him lecture for *hours* about how terrible of a wife I was. It was easier to give him the five minutes he needed to get off. He was a sex fiend even with his urges being met outside the home, too.

I decided that I would just keep my mouth shut and try to figure a way out. I thought about my unborn child. I still didn't know if it was a boy or a girl, but would find out at my next appointment, scheduled four weeks out. Ezra was the one that impregnated me, but I couldn't consider the child his. The child was mine, solely mine. It may have his DNA but I knew there was no way I could keep a baby around him and live with myself. Furthermore, I knew I wouldn't be able to raise the child around his family either. Ezra's mother was pure evil, and I knew that she would try to take my kid away from me. She threatened me with it weekly. The more I thought about it, the more my heart raced in a panic. There was absolutely no way that I could stay with him. I didn't care that I was pregnant, broke, and caged like a rabid dog. I would come up with a plan and get the hell out of there. That was my main mission, if not for my sake, for my unborn child's.

SIXTEEN

He didn't speak to me while we drove home. When we got back to the apartment he was five steps ahead of me and let the door slam before I could get to it. Convinced he would lock me out again I quickly turned the handle, but when I entered he was already in the bathroom. I went into the kitchen, took my shirt off and rinsed the blood out as best I could. When Ez finally emerged, I got some peroxide from the bathroom cabinet. I noticed that the box behind the toilet, once again, had been moved. My sleeve was still soiled, so I doused the shirt with peroxide until the blood stains came out. I had forgotten about my arm still crusted over with dried blood.

"Can you iron these pants for me? I'm going to a meeting tonight," he said.

"What kind of meeting?"

"It's none of your business, iron the pants."

He opened the refrigerator and cracked a beer. He never had the money to buy me prenatal vitamins, but he certainly found the cash to buy a case of beer from the local brewery once a week.

"Fine."

He threw his pants over the arm of the couch and unwrapped a steak sandwich he had left over from his french fry rendezvous. Saliva formed in the corners of my mouth as it turned in the microwave. I looked in the cabinet, and all we had was rice and some tomato paste. Where was his mom now to yell at him for not bringing *me* a sandwich? There was a little bit of milk left in the fridge which I poured into a glass and swallowed with one of my new migraine pills.

Neither of us said a word. My stomach started to gurgle so I put on a pot of water to cook up some rice. He wolfed down his sandwich and went into the bedroom with a beer. I dumped some rice into the water when suddenly a tingling sensation began to creep into my fingertips. I was trying to pick up a wooden spoon to stir my dinner when my hand fell limp. Both of my arms began to tingle, and suddenly my chest began to tighten. I thought I was having a heart attack, so I yelled for Ezra to come in. I sat down on the couch to try and catch my breath.

"I can't feel my arms, and my chest hurts," I managed to squeal.

"What's wrong?"

"I don't know!"

My throat began to swell and my breathing became labored.

"I think I need to go to the hospital."

"You *think* you need to go, or you definitely have to go?"

"I think I should go."

"You keep saying you *think*. Do you have to go or not?!"

"Stop being an asshole, just take me to the hospital!"

I collapsed back on the couch, but within seconds, my head flew forward and I tumbled to my knees. He had hit me.

"You are obviously faking it," he said as he grabbed his beer off of the coffee table. "I'm not going to forget what you did to me this afternoon." He went back into the bedroom, sat on our bed, and began to read a book.

I crawled to the bathroom and dug in the medicine cabinet. My arms were still numb and my throat was tight, so I knew it was an allergic reaction. I dug through the small basket of medicine remnants he had and found a box of allergy relief. I split open the pills and dumped the sour white powder under my tongue. My chest began to loosen. I sat on the bathroom floor and rested for a while, smelling the rice still cooking on the stove. I couldn't believe he hit me like that; what kind of *Christian* husband hits his pregnant wife? While I recovered, Ezra emerged from the room with different clothes on. His pants hugged his legs so tight that the seams were stretching.

"I told you to iron my pants," he said, holding the khakis from the couch up in front of the bathroom door. "Now I have to go out looking like *this*."

"I'm sorry," I snapped sarcastically.

"You were too busy faking a heart attack so you wouldn't have to iron them. Look at you, you're fine. You are such a joke of a wife, you know that? *One* simple task. I asked *one* simple thing and you couldn't even handle that."

"I'm having an *allergic reaction!*"

"Don't raise your voice at me, or I swear to God, Nina."

"And hitting your pregnant wife? You're a lunatic!"

"You better watch your mouth when you talk to me—"

"No! You are a fucked-up piece of crap, you know that? You made yourself out to be a nice guy, but *you* are a joke. I don't even care anymore. What are you going to do?! Hit me again? Go ahead, hit me again! Go for it! Hit your wife, then go out to your 'meeting' with your 'clean bottom' you'd like to 'bend over once in a while.'" I quoted exactly what he had said in his solicitation. "Yeah, that's right, I read it, you sicko!"

Another blow struck down on my ear and adrenaline pumped hard through my veins.

"Shut up, you slut!" he yelled. "You want to see me bend someone over? Here we go then!" I felt a clump of hair rip from my head as I flipped over onto the floor. My face pressed into the tile and I heard his zipper come undone. He pulled down the sweatpants I had on and tore off my half soaked shirt. I tried to hit back but he anchored me down with his knees on the back of my legs. I heard him hack and then felt a warm wet glob fall onto my butt cheek. He was spitting on me.

"Get the hell off of me!"

My head jerked up as he pulled me over to the bathroom and slammed the door shut, nearly catching my clawing fingers. My face smashed into the floor again and my mother's hamsa necklace clinked to the floor. He yanked up my hips and jammed the tip of his dick inside of me. I never had anal sex before. I tried to clench my butt together so he couldn't penetrate any further, but he smacked me so hard on the side of my hip that my grip loosened and he continued to jam himself into me, alternating more spit between thrusts. I stared at the floor, struggling to get my head free, wondering if it would hurt more to keep fighting or give in. The more I fought and tensed up, the more pain I felt, so I took a few deep breaths and tried to meditate. He got himself into a rhythm. He dipped further into me, and my stretching flesh pulsated in pain. His thrust was rough, and I felt something pop. My flesh had been ripped open. He began to glide easier, making obnoxious grunting noises and saying things like "That's a good wife" in a low whisper. I shifted my forehead to the floor and looked between my legs. Drops of blood began forming a small messy pool on the white floor. I squeezed my mouth shut as tears hit the tile.

I closed my eyes, and let myself sob only for a moment, focusing back into a quiet and meditative state. The more noise I made, the tighter he pulled my hair and the harder he slammed into me.

"Take a deep breath, let it out, and everything is fine." The words of a gentleman who taught a hot yoga class Declan and I often attended in New York City came to mind. "Everything is fine," I repeated in my head. I could hear his slow, smooth drawl as he repeated the phrase to the imaginary class in my mind. I took a deep breath and stretched my neck forward into a mudra. Ezra's grunting matched the rhythm of his hips, which grew stronger and faster, so I knew he was close to cumming. He pulled out quickly and he slammed me on my back. Stroking and air humping, his white milky cum came dripping out onto my face and with one last shot, he shoved my head into his crotch and pushed his weapon into my mouth. I was tempted to bite down, but the vibrations from his hand slapping my face simultaneously sent him flying out before I got the chance. My shoulder was pinned down with his knee, but thankfully my stomach was sheltered. He stood up, stared at me panting, zipped his pants, and walked out.

Throbbing pain chopped through my body like an ax and I started vomiting cum into the toilet. I pulled myself off of my purple knees, locked the door, and ran a hot bath. My arms shook and my skin was scorched as I slowly lowered myself into the steaming water. I kept my head low. Behind me, the water turned a pale pink. I wanted to get him off of me: his skin, his cum, his stench. The only soap we had was half a bottle of men's Old Spice, since he never felt it necessary to get my own soap. I refused to smell like him. My fingernails scratched up and down my legs, gouging out any trace of him still on my skin. I clawed at my cheeks and plunged my head underwater until I couldn't hold my breath anymore. The hot water stung my salty eyes.

After my bath, I wrapped myself up in a towel and scrubbed the tainted floor until it sparkled pure white again. I kept listening, trying to determine if he was still home or not. I crept over and put the side of my head up to the door, but my numb ears deceived me. When I emerged, Ez was in the living room, resting on his knees. He looked up at me and scowled.

"Put some clothes on, then get back out here."

I said nothing.

I went into the bedroom and slowly put on a pair of baggy pajamas; I didn't want anything touching my flesh. After dragging the time out as much as I could, I emerged and stood next to him.

"Get on your knees and repent."

Staring at him with indignant eyes, I delicately kneeled.

"Repeat after me," he said. "Father God."

"Father God."

"Please forgive me for my sins."

"Please forgive me for my sins."

"I know I do wrong, but please cleanse me white as snow."

I continued repeating.

"I am only human, and I cannot control my urges."

"Please forgive my human sin-filled nature and make me whole again."

"In Jesus' name we pray, amen."

"Amen," I finished.

He stood up and turned on a playlist he had of some church music, and lifted his hands into the air. He started to sway back and forth and spin around the room, yelling, "Devil, get out in the name of Jesus!" and "Holy Spirit, come and fill the room!" Then he closed his eyes and began to hum along to the music. When the chorus began, he started crying and shouting "Thanks be to God! Glory to God above! Thank you, Jesus, thank you, *Jesus*!"

I had absolutely no idea what he was doing. My arms tingled again as the fine hair that covered them stood straight up. When he was done shouting, he turned the music down and took me by my hand, leading me back to the couch. He patted the cushion, but I stood still. His eyebrows curled down deep into his eyelids.

"Sit down."

Pain was immediately distributed throughout my lower limbs as I obeyed.

"We need to talk," he said.

His voice softened as moisture formed under his eyes.

"I'm sorry," he kept repeating.

I didn't know how to react. I wanted to chop off his balls and console him at the same time.

"Those e-mails, it's true," he continued. "The Devil is attacking me, making me like other men. The Devil is making me gay. It's not normal, and it's disgusting. I am disgusting. I begged God to send me a woman that I was so attracted to that I wouldn't look at men anymore, and he sent you. You are my savior."

"Ezra, a long time ago I asked you how many people you have had sex with, and you told me one. Your ex-girlfriend. Is that true?"

He sat silent for a moment. "No."

"How many people have you been with?"

He started to count in his head, just as I had done that day on the island in New York City. "Fourteen."

"And how many of them were men?"

He counted in his head again. "Eleven."

I remained silent, completely flabbergasted as to what to say in return.

"The Devil is torturing me." He stood up and quickly removed a tiny vial of oil from a cabinet. "I have to anoint the apartment!" He started praying loudly and finger painting oil crosses above every door and window in the apartment. I leaned over onto my side and watched him march around the room. After five minutes of him angrily shouting at the Devil and anointing every wood panel in the place, he crouched down in front of me and started to pet my head. My eyes widened as anxiety shortened my breath.

"God has forgiven me, and you should, too," he said sincerely. "It's your wifely duty." He paused. "It's in the Bible." He paused again, waiting for a reply. "It's what Jesus would do."

I didn't respond.

"Say you forgive me," he demanded.

"I—don't. No, I don't! Screw you, and screw your 'Jesus!'"

His eyes narrowed and his stare pierced through my pupils.

"A good Christian wife forgives her husband. I guess you are just a piece of trash then. I bet you liked that, you disgusting slut. It's that necklace! I told you that thing is demonic and it's possessing you. Take it off, take it off now!"

He reached for my necklace to rip it off and I threw myself to the ground to keep him from taking it.

"No! I'm not taking it off. I won't take it off." I started to cry. "Please. Please don't take it from me, it's all I have from her. Please." I begged. "I'll hide it. I'll keep it under my clothes, just please, please don't take it." I wept with my face down in the carpet.

He placed his hand on the back of my head.

"Jesus!" He yelled. "I pray that you extract this spirit of lust out of my wife and make her wholesome again! Devil! In the name of Jesus, leave my wife *now!*"

He started pushing on my skull until my head jerked back and forth.

"Stop it!" I yelled.

"Spirit! Leave my wife in the name of Jesus!" The pushing continued.

The more I tried to get him off of me, the harder he shook and the louder he shouted for the spirit of lust to get out of my body.

"The spirit of lust has left my body!" I yelled.

The shaking stopped. He removed his hand and looked into my eyes for an eternity, then kissed my forehead.

"Good girl," he said softly and smiled. "Now say thank you to Jesus."

"Thank you, Jesus."

"Louder!" he demanded.

"Thank you, Jesus."

"Shout it! He has set you free!" He yelled.

"Thank you, Jesus!" I screamed.

My scream was a final attempt to get him away from me before I attacked him. I wanted to smack him across the face, but I refrained. I still didn't understand what was going on, but I knew that for me to survive the rest of the night I had to play along.

"Good," he said. "Now why—the hell—were you—in my e-mail?" His voice lowered, and his eyes grew dark again.

I struggled with what to say, but I knew it had to be something witty or I might get slapped again.

"Jesus told me to do it." I spit out. "So—that I could save you," I mumbled.

Ez sucked his teeth and had a pensive look on his face for a minute, then stood up, turned off all of the lights, and locked himself in the bedroom.

"I guess he isn't going to his meeting," I thought.

I walked back into the kitchen to find most of the rice overcooked and sticking to the bottom of the pot. I scooped out what I could, mixed in a teaspoon of tomato paste for flavor, and stood at the kitchen counter to eat it.

I was glad he admitted he was gay—that was a start. But what did the Devil have to do with any of it? Ez was a disturbed person, more than I initially thought. There was no way I could stay there anymore, and I realized that if I waited any longer to come up with a plan to get out, I may not ever have the chance to leave.

SEVENTEEN

I woke up to the orange sun flashing beams through the sheer curtains onto my eyelids. My crooked neck was sore from the overused couch cushions. I put on a pot of water to boil, got myself a glass of water, and went back to the window in the living room. The sun was a nice change of pace from the grey cumulonimbus that had plagued the March skies for the last two weeks. The pavement below was dark and wet from an overnight shower, but the rest of the day seemed to have a bright outlook. I went back to the kitchen and stirred some rice into the boiling water for breakfast.

The windows were closed. The door was locked and the alarm was set, but it really didn't matter much considering I had made up my mind that this was the day I would leave.

After breakfast I went into the bathroom, avoiding the large chipped mirror on the wall. I took some dish soap with me and scrubbed in the hot shower for over an hour. When I got out, I stood in front of the steaming mirror and wiped the fog off with the corner of my towel. For the first time since last night, I looked at myself. The side of my face was painted with red lines from the grout on the tiles. Both of my knees were bruised, and I had two black marks on the back of my legs.

I stared at my body for a while, thinking about the past few months.

"You are not that girl," I said to my reflection. "You are not a girl that gets pushed around by a jackass," I commanded. "You are not that girl!" I yelled.

I brushed my teeth and stuffed my backpack with underwear, socks, my toothbrush, and the leftover rice. Within a half an hour I was dressed in Ezra's clothes, and ready to go. I stood in the middle of the living room for a while, contemplating if I should open the door or not. As soon as I turned the handle, I wouldn't have much time to get away, and I didn't have much of a plan once I was out either. The nearest business was a gas station about two miles away, but I knew Ezra would catch me walking along the road before I could make it there. I had to find a way to get there without being seen.

I was just about to turn the handle when someone started banging on the door. I jumped back, nearly knocking the wind out of myself.

"Police! Open up!"

"What? I haven't even touched the door yet!" I said, turning the handle. I remembered my damaged face, so I swept my hair to the side, covering the marks. I realized if they showed, the matter would go into the state's hands and the courts would get involved. I didn't want to stay in Oregon any longer, not for any reason. I kept my head facing down when I opened the door.

"Are you Pasqualina Panicucci?" the officer asked. He botched my name, of course. I hadn't legally changed my last name to Alto, and was happy I didn't.

"Yes," I said. "Why?"

"We got a call from someone named Ezra who claims he is your husband?"

"Yeah?"

"He called us stating that you were at risk for killing yourself, ma'am. He said you were suicidal last night. He claims you were trying to jump off of the roof here, and he had to physically restrain you."

"Are you fucking kidding me?" I said under my breath.

"Excuse me, ma'am?" the officer said.

"Nothing. No, I'm not suicidal, and no, I did not try to jump off of the roof. Trust me, if I wanted to kill myself that would not be the way I would do it." I remembered back to when I swallowed all of those pills in Declan's bathroom.

"Yeah, I'm sorry, but we don't really have any kind of proof for that. When we get a call like this, there are certain protocols we need to follow. I'm going to need you to call this suicide hotline and talk to a counselor. Are you willing to comply?" he asked.

"Of course I'll comply, because I'm not suicidal."

The officer pulled out his cell phone and dialed the number he had on a tiny business card. When someone answered he explained the situation, then handed the phone to me. I kept my back turned and my hair across my face. The woman on the other end of the line asked me all sorts of questions that usually resulted in me saying things like, "No, actually, that's not what happened, that's just what my husband *told* you."

"Ma'am, I have reason to believe that your husband is trying to control you," she said.

"Hey! Wow! Winner, winner, chicken dinner!" I barked.

"Ma'am, there is no need to get smart with me on the phone, I'm here to help you."

"Well, you know what, *lady*? I was actually going to leave him today, but you police officers blowing in here like this really put a damper on my plan."

Just then, I saw Ezra approach the front door.

"Fuck."

"Excuse me, ma'am?"

"He's here."

I gave the phone back to the police officer just as he began talking to Ezra. "Sir, can we talk outside please?"

"Wait!" I said. "Talk to this lady first."

The officer took the phone and listened to the woman talk. He kept saying things like "mm-hmm" and "sure" and "I understand."

When he hung up the phone, he insisted that Ezra talk to him outside in the parking lot. They were gone for about fifteen minutes and the officer came back alone.

"Ma'am, you and your husband are clearly having a domestic issue here and to make sure matters stay civil, I recommended that he leave and stay somewhere else tonight."

"Thank you," I said.

"Ma'am, before I go, I need to ask you: Has your husband ever physically hit you?"

"No," I said.

"Then ma'am, where did that mark on your head come from?"

Fuck. I thought I was doing a decent job of keeping it covered. The officer came over and gently brushed my hair aside. I looked away.

"I fell down on the sidewalk and didn't catch myself in time. It's nothing," I replied.

"If he is hitting you, I need you to tell me the truth so we can handle this matter. Just tell me the truth, dear. You can trust me."

"There is no matter to handle. I'm fine."

"Alright," he sighed. "But if you need assistance, call the number on this card. Your report number is at the top." He slipped the card into my palm and closed my fingers over it. "Please call us at any time."

I had yet another business card from a police officer, and yet another "report number" attached to my name. When he departed, I was left in the middle of the living room again contemplating where I should go, replaying what had just taken place in my mind. A moment passed and Ezra showed up again. He burst into the apartment, grabbed me by the neck, and threw me out on the front stoop. He took my backpack and unzipped it, looking through its contents.

"You are already stealing my clothes, and I want to make sure you aren't stealing anything else."

I resisted my urge to lunge after him and grab the bag because it occurred to me that he might be letting me go.

"This is *my* container."

"Yeah, but I need that food," I begged.

"It's *mine!*" He yelled back as he took the rice out and threw the bag at me.

"You want to leave me? Leave. Here." He pulled out his wallet and threw a five dollar bill at me. "Take this. Go ahead. See how far you get before you come crawling back. You want to go? Then go. Get out of here. Go kill yourself for all I care. You worthless piece of—"

I stood up and slammed the door in his face. I didn't want to hear another word of it. I placed my bag on my shoulder and began to walk away. The door swung open and he started screaming more profanities at me, but I kept on walking without looking back.

An hour later, I approached a gas station and bought some snacks with the five dollars I had. I tried to stretch my money as far as it would go, buying a few pop-top cans of peas, a gallon of water, a loaf of bread, and some peanut butter. I took a plastic knife and spoon from the prepared food section and went up to pay. The total came to $5.60.

"I don't have sixty cents," I told the cashier. I took a can of peas and turned to walk it back to the shelf.

"Hold on," the cashier said. "Take a penny leave a penny." He pointed to a little cup on the counter. I counted out six dimes from the cup and he put the peas into the paper bag.

"Just pay it forward when you can." His smile had a hole where his front tooth should have been.

"Sure."

When I stepped outside, the sun warmed my face. I knew where I wanted to go, but also knew it was far and it might take the entire day to get there. It didn't matter, the trip would be worth every step. With one foot in front of the other, I started walking to the library.

I only walked for about seven minutes when Ez's car pulled up next to me. To my luck, the road was full of cars and I knew he wouldn't do anything stupid in public.

"Get in the car, Nina," he said as he clicked into park. I kept walking forward and heard the car door open and slam.

"Nina, get in the fucking car." He followed me, but I kept walking.

"I swear to God if you don't get in this car—"

"You'll fucking kill me? Yeah, you've said that. Here I am! Still alive! Do us a favor and go fuck yourself! You sure like to do *that*!" I yelled back.

I walked away invigorated and picked up my pace. His hand grabbed the back of my hair and spun me around.

"Fire! Fire!!!" I started to scream. "Car fire!!!!" I yelled at the passing cars. People began to slow down and turn their heads. My father once told me that if I were ever in trouble, not to yell "help," but to yell "fire." People won't bat an eye to help someone, but they will go to great lengths to witness a fire. It worked.

Ezra released me and walked back to his car, clicked it into drive, and rolled up next to me with his window down.

"If you don't get in this car, then don't ever come back. Stay out on the street, go to your father, I don't give a fuck, but don't even think about coming back. When you give birth I will be there and I *will* have rights. You will never see that baby again."

I stopped walking.

"Ez, if you don't get the hell out of my face right now, I will walk back to that gas station and call the police. I will press charges against you for domestic violence and *you* will never see this baby, period." I tucked my hair behind my ear to remind him of the marks he left.

His eyes shrunk and his face turned pale before he rolled up his window and drove away. Adrenaline sped through my veins and I picked up the pace again, walking and drinking the gallon of water I had just bought. Another hour came and went before I finally reached the center of town. I found the bank where Ezra had opened our joint account and slipped inside. The teller helped me take my name off of the account and open my own. Luckily I was listed as a secondary owner of the account and all of the debt he currently owed the bank would fall onto his shoulders. I asked the woman at the counter if I could use the bank's telephone to call my credit card. After loosely explaining the situation without giving too much detail, the customer service representative led me to his desk to use his phone. I called my credit card company and closed Ezra's card on my account. Unfortunately, I would be responsible for everything he had bought, and not five minutes prior, he had filled up his car with gas. Another thirty dollars was added to my tab, but that would be the last time.

After the bank, I continued walking to where I thought the library was. I stopped and asked for directions a few times, and people pointed me along the right path. By dusk, I was exhausted and hungry. I found a park and sat on a bench, making myself a peanut butter sandwich. The sun stretched pink and gold behind the distant hills and I knew I'd have to find somewhere to spend the night. I didn't have a phone, not that I would know who to call anyway, and the park seemed removed enough from the road. A chilly gust blew my hair back so I pulled the hood of Ezra's old sweatshirt over my head. I sat and watched children playing with their mothers and fathers on the playscape, laughing and running. Everything was moving in slow motion and I started to feel guilty. If I left, my baby wouldn't have a father anymore. What would be worse? Growing up with a mother and father who occasionally fought, or growing up with no father at all? When I reflected on single parenthood I began to panic. How would I afford this? Where would I live? *How* would I live? The thought of possibly going back with Ezra didn't seem so bad. If I could just get a job then our finances wouldn't be in shambles and maybe he would be better. I'd be out of the house every day and I'd have at least some control over my life. Maybe all of this *was* my fault? He lost his job because of *me*. I'd been living here for months and he was right, I still hadn't found work. The movie fell through. I could have looked in the newspaper and called around when he was home. This situation was just as much my fault as it was his. Ez told me that I couldn't go back, but I knew I had to try. I rubbed my baby bump and curled up on the splintered wood, laying my head between two rusted nails.

That night I barely slept on the frosted park bench. By morning I was still exhausted and just wanted to be back at Ez's apartment. At least it was warm, and the couch was much more comfortable than a bench. I reassured myself that going back would be the right decision. I would take whatever punishment Ez had in mind for me. I put together another peanut butter sandwich, drank some water and began my journey back.

As I walked, wind gusts charged full speed, whipping my face, whispering in my ears, and protesting my return. It pushed my shoulders and howled, sounding reason I wasn't hearing. It felt wrong, but the fear of being completely on my own trumped my intuition.

I walked for most of the morning before I finally made it back to the apartment. Luckily, Ezra didn't find the spare key I'd stuffed in my bag. All of the lights in the apartment were out. I stuck the key in and turned, but it didn't work. I took it out and jammed it back in, twisting and turning, but the lock wouldn't click open. I looked up and made sure I had the right apartment. The numbers matched up. I leaned over the second story railing and tried to look into the apartment. It was mostly empty and what was left was completely trashed. An old chair was turned on its side. Everything in the living room was gone. I ran over to the other side and tried to see into the bedroom. The bed was gone. I went down to the manager's office so that they could let me in.

"Excuse me," I said, "I'm in apartment 254 and my key doesn't work. What is going on?"

"Yes, Ezra requested that the locks be changed," the snarly, blond-haired bimbo replied.

"Well, I need to get in there, I live there, too."

"Sorry, but we can't let you in because your name isn't on the lease."

"But all of my stuff—where is everything?"

"I can't disclose that."

"It's *my* freaking stuff! You can't tell me where a person put all of my *stolen* belongings?"

"If the property was in his apartment, ma'am, then by law, it is technically his since it was abandoned property on your behalf."

She was so condescending. I wanted to reach across the desk and choke her. I had walked for two days eating nothing but peanut butter sandwiches and peas, and I wanted a warm place to sleep. Ezra had done his research and won *again*. I asked if I could use her phone. She pushed it toward me and stared.

"Can I have a moment of privacy please?"

"It's *my* desk," she replied.

"Whatever, lady."

I dialed my father's phone number. I should have called him at the bank, but I was too focused on getting my accounts situated and getting to the library. It went straight to voicemail. I hung up and tried his number again. Still, straight to voicemail. "Now is not the time to be forwarding my calls, Papà," I thought. His voicemail beeped.

"Papà. I am leaving Ezra. You were right about him, he's not the guy I thought he was. He raped me, Papà," I whispered. The receptionist looked up at me, so I turned my back to her and cringed. I never thought I'd ever have to use that word when talking about myself. "I'm leaving and never coming back. I need help. I need money. Please, answer your phone." I took the business cards that the police officers gave me out of my pocket and read off the phone number and the case numbers. "Call the police and they will tell you every—" The voicemail beeped again and cut me off.

I handed the phone back to the receptionist and she looked at me with soft eyes.

"I have a twenty in my purse. Just—one second." She bent down and unzipped her purse, pulled out a twenty dollar bill, and handed it to me. "Your stuff. He was here yesterday and put it all in a truck. I don't know where he took it and I haven't seen him since. I'm sorry."

"Thank you." I took the money and didn't comment on what she had just told me. I turned to walk out the door when the thought occurred to me.

I pulled the hamsa necklace out from under my shirt and swept my thumb across the sapphire. In desperation, I turned and asked, "Where is the closest pawn shop?"

"About three miles away. Go down the main drag and take a left on Belridge. You should start to see signs for it. Listen, I—"

"Thank you," I spoke over her and closed the door behind me.

I twisted the gold chain around my fingers. I had never taken the necklace off—not since the day my mother gave it to me, two days before she passed. We were having breakfast . . . well, *I* was having breakfast. Mamma had been refusing food for a week by that time. I picked at her tray of eggs and cheesy potatoes, which the hospital still delivered daily, though it usually went untouched.

She opened her weak eyes and asked me, "Do you know what your name means?"

"No, Mamma."

"Pasqualina comes from Pascal, which comes from the Latin name *Paschalis.*"

"OK?"

"Let me finish." She turned her head and looked at me.

"Sorry, Mamma."

"*Paschalis* comes from the Hebrew word פֶּסַח—pesach, which is Passover, like the holiday. You know that story." She waved her delicate hand. "Passover celebrates liberation. Freedom. You are freedom, my flower. A strong name. A good name." She took my hand and tried to squeeze.

I didn't know what to say. I'd always hated my name, but she made it sound so nice when she put it that way.

"My flower," she continued, "take this." She pointed to the necklace. "This was a gift from your father. I want you to wear it. It will keep you safe from the evil eye. Take it, flower. You can have it." She motioned for me to come closer. "Come take it."

I leaned over and scooped my hands under her wilting neck, unhooked the clasp, and slipped it from her neck. I put it around my own, and that is where it had stayed until this moment. I removed the chain and tucked the necklace into the bottom of my bag and walked two hours to the pawn shop.

"How much can I get for this?" I dangled the necklace in front of the lanky clerk. His thin gray hair was slicked back into a ponytail, revealing pieces of his scalp, and his nose was twice the size it should have been for his skinny, scruffed-up face. He took the necklace from me and looked at the charm with a magnifying glass.

"Whose initials?" He was referring to the letters carved into the back.

"My mom's. She died."

"Sorry to hear that. Sure ya want to pawn it though?"

"Yeah, I'm sure."

"This is eighteen karat gold. It's a good thing—worth more. We pay out by weight in gold. Sapphire's real. Give me a second and I'll total it up for ya." He placed the necklace on the scale. "Looks like I can give ya about four hundred fifty for it."

Four hundred and fifty might be enough for a plane ticket, but if there is one thing my father has taught me, it is that everything is negotiable.

"You can't do any better than that?" I asked.

He looked up at me, then back down at the necklace, and back up to me.

"What do ya think ya want for it?"

"I'll do six hundred." I was shooting high, knowing he would negotiate me down.

"No way. Sorry, lady, can't do it."

I looked down at my hands and studied the wedding ring I still wore. I wiggled it off and tossed it on the counter.

"How about this?"

He took the ring and twisted it in his hands. "Ten karat, can't do much with that. Diamonds are shit. No offense."

"None taken."

"I'll tell you what. Five hundred for both and that's the best I can do. If I give ya any more than that, I won't make a dime off this, you understand? Ya won't get that deal anywhere else. Five hundred is the best you'll get."

I picked the necklace up off of the scale and rubbed it between my fingers one last time. I thought about my mother, and how it fell so gracefully on her neck. I remembered looking at it as a little kid and tugging on it whenever she held me close to her chest. It was the only piece of her I had left.

"OK," I said. "Let's get it over with."

I placed the necklace in the clerk's hands and followed him to the register.

I didn't cry when he rang me out. I didn't cry when I walked back to the bank. I didn't even cry when I deposited the check. But when I paid the cab driver who dropped me off at the airport's motel, the dam that held my tears inside exploded, and all of my pain flooded out.

"Lady, I don't know what's going on, but you gotta get out of my car. I need to make some cash here, you know?" the driver barked.

"Sorry." I dabbed my eyes with my sleeve and migrated to the motel.

The lobby conveniently had a computer, so I didn't have to trek to the library, which was nice. One night cost me fifty-nine dollars, but it was worth it to have a bed to sleep in, hot coffee in the morning, and a continental breakfast. I couldn't technically check-in until three in the afternoon, so I hung around and waited for an old man to finish up with the computer. When I was finally able to log on, I opened my e-mail. I had four unread e-mails from Dave. The first two were wondering where I had gone, and asking me to call him. When I didn't, he sent an e-mail asking why I was ignoring him, and he wondered if he had done something wrong. The last e-mail was more or less a bitter goodbye. I hit reply and stared at the cursor for about five minutes, wondering where I should begin. I wanted to tell him everything, and daydreamed of him swooping in and saving the day like some superhero. But I hesitated. I was married. Pregnant.

"I'm damaged goods," I thought to myself. "No one will ever want me like this."

I settled on the vague reply:

I'm OK. Thank you for e-mailing me, and I'm sorry I didn't get back to you sooner. I've been off the grid for a while on the West Coast. Thank you for checking in. You did nothing wrong.
   —Nina

By giving him limited information, he probably would end up thinking I did some amazing backpacking trip through California or something. I'd prefer him to think that than what I had actually spent my time doing.

I had two e-mails from Karen. Both were angrily asking where I was and why I didn't show up on set. Apparently she *did* call. Several times. I should have known.

I clicked out of my e-mail and researched plane tickets. The problem was, I didn't know where to go. I thought about going to Hawaii because the tickets were cheap and I'd never been there before, but what would I do when I got there? Sell coconuts? A one-way trip to New York City was $175 on a cheap airline, so I bought that ticket. At least I was familiar with the place, and I'd figure out what to do once I landed.

EIGHTEEN

I stepped out of LaGuardia and was greeted by the stench of week-old urine and candied cashews. It was second nature for me to walk straight to the cab stand, so I approached the crowded line. The woman in front of me was nearly six feet tall with her five-inch zebra-print leather stilettos. Silky nylons hugged her tight, slender calves and traveled up under her perfectly tailored cherry-red dress. She carried a black patent leather bag with gold details, and by her side rested a designer suitcase. I looked down at the clothes I had been wearing for three days and knew I probably didn't smell the freshest. I had taken a shower at the hotel that morning, but traveling in confined cabins always made me sweat. I reached up to my neck to twirl my necklace when I remembered it wasn't there. I put my head down and wept quietly to myself.

I stepped up in the fast-moving line until I was next. That's when I realized I had no idea where I was going. Taking a cab into Manhattan would cost me a minimum of fifty bucks, and I probably should have taken the subway. I pretended to forget something and slipped out of line, going back to the airport to find public transportation. I made my way to the subway and decided that my first stop would be to get a cell phone. I needed to cancel my current phone, which Ezra still carried around in his pocket. The next stop would be to get some clothes that actually fit me. I counted some change in my hand and bought a subway card loaded with enough money to get me around for the day, then headed into the city.

Everything was exactly how I remembered it—not that I had been gone long in the first place. People walked by me on the street, bumping into my shoulder, or simply complained loudly that I was walking too slow. "Sidewalk rage" is a real thing. When I found the right cell service store, the salesman convinced me to get a prepaid phone in place of the one I canceled, after I expressed I absolutely could not pay the $540 bill that was due. My credit card was maxed out thanks to my soon-to-be ex-husband, but at least I had a means of communication. I got a simple, old-school flip phone that cost me twenty bucks, and loaded fifty minutes onto it. Money was dwindling fast, and I needed to start conserving it.

After I squared away my phone debacle, I took the 6 train up to 86th Street and popped into a cheap store, knowing they carried a few pieces of maternity wear. I bought a button-up sweater, a pair of leggings, and a maternity tunic dress, hoping each piece would last me the entire pregnancy. At least I didn't *look* pregnant yet. People would probably assume I was just fat. I wore the clothes out of the store and piled Ezra's sweats into my bag. If anything, I could use them to sleep in. Where *would* I be sleeping?

The only person in Manhattan I knew I could rely on would be Dave. Even so, I still didn't want him knowing everything that had happened. I wandered around the Upper East Side for a while until I reached Central Park. I passed by the Guggenheim, a wacky building that always fascinated me, and traveled downtown by foot until I reached Times Square. My feet brought me to Guitar Center's doorstep. I sighed, walked through the revolving door, and started down the escalator. I looked around for Dave, but I couldn't find him.

"Excuse me, ma'am?" I said, catching the attention of a pink-haired woman with a mohawk and black leather spiked bracelets.

"What's up?" she asked.

"I'm looking for Dave. Is he here today?"

"Dave—he works here?"

"Yeah."

"I've only been here two months, but I've never worked with anyone named Dave. You sure you have the right store?"

"Yeah, I'm positive. You've never seen him before?"

"No one named Dave."

"Dammit," I said, disappointed, and walked away.

"Yo, Steve!!!!" The girl shouted behind me, making me jump a little. "You know a guy named Dave that works here?"

"Oh, yeah, he quit about two months ago. Said he was joining a band or something," Steve replied. "He comes in once in a while for gear, but that's it."

"Sorry, sweets," she yelled.

"It's fine."

I turned and headed for the escalators again. My raging pregnancy hormones peeked their heads to the surface of my chest as my breaths turned shallow. My mouth scrunched up and my nostrils started to flare. Before I could distract myself, my eyes were overflowing with water like a busted reservoir. At that point, it was getting late. I had nowhere to go, nowhere to sleep, and I hadn't eaten anything but the tiny bag of pretzels on the airplane. I walked to the NYPD station in the middle of Times Square, and luckily a few officers were hanging around.

"Excuse me, sir?" I asked gently, trying to hide my red eyes. "Where is there a homeless shelter?"

"There's one a couple blocks east, down on 2nd," he replied, and turned around to finish his conversation with the seventh Mickey Mouse I had seen in about two minutes.

I walked down to 2nd Avenue, and saw a line of people outside a door that looked like a church. This had to be it. I went up to the front door and knocked.

"Um, whadduh ya think *ya* doin?" A voice behind me yelled out. "Git ya ass to da back of da line there, missy."

I turned around and saw a short, fair-skinned woman with long blond dreadlocks and yellow-crusted teeth smiling at me.

"What?" I replied, dumbfounded.

"Y'all gotta wait ya turn to git in here. Git in da back of da line!"

I looked down the side of the building and saw all sorts of different people. A mother with two small boys, a man with an amputated leg, many women in several layers of clothing. They were all mingling and talking to each other as if they'd known one another for years. All except the mother who guarded her sons close to her legs.

I didn't realize that the line was actually for the shelter itself. I mean, I had obviously never been there before. I went to the back of the line and sat down on my backpack. Finally, the curved red doors swung open. In a single file we piled into the shelter, where workers showed us to our cots. Boys to the right, girls to the left, like a sixth-grade gym class. I was happy to have a warm cot for the night. They filed us into the soup kitchen and fed us chicken noodle soup with French bread and butter, and all the grape juice we could drink. I sat with the small family of three and we ate together in silence. One of the little boys didn't like chicken noodle so he traded his brother for extra bread. They giggled as they shoved each other and kicked their feet underneath the table, their mother shushing them.

I had a clean bathroom to use and a blanket to wrap myself in. The women's wing was a large open room with about twenty cots lining the walls. In the middle of the room was a makeshift changing area with flimsy cloth dividers. I plopped myself down on my cot and rested my head on the pillow after dinner.

"If only TMZ could see me now," I thought. I began to doze off when an overpowering smell of cigarettes and body odor woke me up. The woman with dreads was kneeling down next to my cot and going through my backpack.

"Hey!" I yelled as she pulled out the brand-new sweater I had just bought. "Hey, hey!" I kept yelling until I was screaming.

"Youse ain't *homeless,*" she said as she pulled out my new stretch pants. "These still got ya tags on it!"

"Stop it!" I yelled as I snatched the clothes out of her hands.

"What in da hell are you doin' here anyways? Why don't you go back to ya *grandma's* house, little girl?"

"Stop it!" I yelled again, placing my items back into my bag. Some of the other women began to wake up and yell at us. The two boys started whining from being woken up.

"You smell like dem hotel soaps, ain't *no* way in hell you'se *homeless.*"

"Shut up, you broads!" a woman yelled, throwing an apple from dinner that smashed at my feet.

I had enough. I took my bag, packed it up, and walked to the door in Ezra's scrubby sweats. When the attendant let me out, I could still hear the woman screaming down the hall, "Ain't no way in *hell* she homeless!"

I looked up at the clock tower. It was just past midnight. I had only slept for four hours, but the brisk night air stimulated my senses enough to feel awake. I started to walk downtown again, hoping to find a bar that was still open so I could change into my new clothes, now soiled by cigarette fingers. Eventually I would need to do some laundry, but figured I could get away with a few spritzes of perfume for another afternoon. "When the city wakes up, I'll find a perfume store and collect some free samples," I thought.

I continued to walk down 2nd Avenue and turned off at some point, not noticing the street number until I came to a strip of bars. I didn't care which one I went into, I just needed to sit down, change my clothes, and grab something to drink. I picked a door and went straight to the back, where I found the bathroom. I washed my face and changed into my nicer clothes, then sat down at the bar. A band was playing in the corner, so it was loud and hard to hear, but I managed to throw the word "water" into the bartender's ear.

I sipped my drink and turned to listen to the blues band that was playing, when my heart was electrified. I grabbed the menu to look at the name of the bar, and started cursing myself and thanking myself at the same time. Behind the lead singer was a guitar player with a familiar face. Dave. I knew he had seen me because his eyes were pinned to the ground. He could feel me looking at him and didn't want to make eye contact. Fight or flight washed over my body. I wasn't prepared for a meeting with him yet. I had no idea what I would say, but in the same moment, I felt comfort in his presence.

The song came to an end, and the bartender gave a signal for last call. It was two o'clock in the morning, so I thought I would stick around to see what Dave would do. He packed his gear, completely ignoring me, and then joined a circle of his friends to talk. He still wouldn't look at me. I finished my water and stood up next to the bar, waiting a few more minutes, hoping that he would at least glance over. But he didn't. There was a girl next to him who kept flashing a smile and playing with her hair, clearly flirting with him. It was the same freaking girl from the Christmas party. "Bitch," I thought. I wanted to rip her hair out and throw her to the sidewalk for interfering with my moment with Dave. I wanted all of his friends to take a hike and leave us alone. They started laughing hysterically at a joke, and I caught Dave looking over to me for a brief flash. My heart jumped, but he immediately put his head back down. I knew my moment wasn't going to happen, and the bar was closing up, so I took my backpack and walked out the door.

Midway down the street, I heard his voice call out my name, "Nina!"

I spun around to see him jogging up to me with his guitar strapped to his back.

"Where are you going?" he asked. "How did you know I would be here?"

"Coincidence." I turned around to walk away.

"Nina, wait." He jogged up to me. "Wait!" he said louder. I kept walking. "What's the matter with you?"

"Who is that girl? Is that your girlfriend?"

"What? Nina, I don't see you for months and the first thing you do is get jealous of Sasha?"

I started crying and yelling at the same time. "I just want to know, is that your girlfriend? That's your girlfriend, I knew it, I'm a stupid moron—why would I think you would be single—what the hell is wrong with me!" I kept repeating and crying. Dave looked half-scared and half-worried when I finally calmed down enough to look at him.

"Sasha is my *cousin*."

"Your cousin?" I sobbed. Then, "Dave, I'm pregnant," I blurted out. "I'm sorry."

"*What?*" He paused for a moment and looked around. "What are you doing out here? Do *you* have a boyfriend?"

"It's a really long story. I'm out here because—because—I just am, I don't know."

His structured face started to tighten and his eyes were wandering.

"I wasn't looking for you," I said. "It really was a coincidence."

He took his guitar off his back, dropped it to the sidewalk, and stood with one hand on his hip and the other on the back of his head, in deep thought.

"You're going to have to tell me what's going on," he finally said. "But not tonight, I'm wrecked. Can we meet up tomorrow?"

"Yeah," I said with a pause. "I guess."

"Alright," he said, concerned. "Call me at this number."

He scribbled on the back of a receipt. He picked up his guitar and began walking down the street toward the train.

"Hey, Dave?" I yelled.

"Yeah?"

"Can I come with you?" My voice cracked. "I—don't have." I paused. "Can I just—can I come with you?"

NINETEEN

I woke up to Dave making coffee and flipping pancakes on his tiny hot plate, which was nearly right next to my head. His studio was about three hundred and fifty square feet, and every inch of space was utilized perfectly. It was small, but he only paid six-fifty a month for it.

"I'm moving to a house in Queens with my band next month," he had told me last night. He said they got a good deal and it was enough space to practice and live. Between the four of them, rent would be cheap enough, and the place was huge. "It even has a backyard," he bragged.

"You hungry?"

"Yeah, definitely." I pulled myself up off of the yoga mat he had laid down for me on the floor.

"There is a community bathroom three doors down," he said, "If you want to shower, or use it, or whatever."

I think he was trying to tell me that I smelled bad.

I reached into my bag and pulled out some leftover shampoo and soap from the hotel back in Oregon, and headed for the door.

"Pancakes will be done when you come back, and then, Nina? We are talking about this."

I nodded yes. I had managed to get through last night without telling him anything that had happened over the last few months, but knew that conversation was coming soon.

Using a community bathroom was a foreign experience for me. It was also co-ed, but that didn't bother me as much as the fact that I didn't have any flip-flops to wear, and the images of ringworm and athlete's foot wouldn't leave my mind. I was thankful to have a warm shower, though. I washed my greasy hair clean and scrubbed hard between my toes until I felt presentable. I used Dave's towel, which smelled like his body wash. I loved the way he smelled. I went back to the room ready to sit down and tell Dave everything. I figured, what was the worst that could possibly happen?

"So where do I begin?" I said with a mouth full of pancake. I smiled. I don't even know why I was smiling—I guess I was just happy to be out of Oregon and with Dave. We both sat cross-legged on the floor facing each other.

"Well, you are pregnant. We established that last night."

"Yes, the pregnancy," I restated. "Um, I guess I should also tell you that I'm married, too."

"*What?*" He nearly lost a bite of his food.

My eyes started to tear up again, and I knew there was no stopping the floodgates. I cried again—hard, and told him everything that had happened with Ezra, from the e-mailing back and forth to cutting the cake at the wedding. I even told him about the rape in the bathroom and me pawning my necklace. I showed him the receipt. The look on his face was hard to read until he himself started to well up. He scooted over until his legs were touching mine.

"I don't even have my guitar anymore." I wept harder. "I have nothing except this bag, and the clothes inside aren't even mine, they're his."

"His?" he shouted.

He unzipped my backpack and took out the clothes, then threw them down the trash shoot in the hallway.

"You don't need any reminders of that asshole," he said.

Dave getting protective of me actually semi-aroused me, but I quickly squashed the feeling. He was a respectful guy, and there was no way he would even so much as hold my hand knowing I was married to someone else.

"How do I go about getting a divorce?" I asked.

"You're asking the wrong person," he said. "But you can use my computer and look it up. I'm going to get ready for church and head out. You are welcome to come if you want to."

"I don't know, I think I've had enough Jesus shoved down my throat for one lifetime," I said.

He let out a long sigh and sat down next to me again.

"I want to get one thing straight with you. That man, Ezra or whatever, is *not* a Christian. And furthermore, he is *not* some prophet who hears from God. If God wants to tell you something, *He* will tell you, not some 'Joe Nobody' on the street. The Lord does not want to hurt you, he wants you to prosper and have a good happy future. It says that in the Bible somewhere, I can't remember where."

I rolled my eyes when he mentioned the Bible, like I hadn't heard that before.

"The point is, what you feel in your heart, your intuition: *That* is God. He is all around us and inside of us. Tell me, how did you feel when you were getting married to your husband?"

"Honestly? Really awful, and I wasn't sure if I was doing the right thing."

"Exactly. *That* was God. He was trying to tell you something, but you weren't listening."

"My ex told me that feeling was the Devil trying to keep me from my destiny."

"We have freedom of choice and intuition for a reason. Nina, you've got to start using it. You went from one bad relationship to the next. You need to start listening to the voice within *yourself*."

I sat there, silent for a few moments. I didn't say anything because I knew he was right, but I didn't want to admit it.

"Fine," I mumbled. "I'll go to that church with you."

"Listen, I'm not trying to convince you to come. I'm just saying, that jackass out in Oregon gave you a really bad impression as to what Christianity is actually all about. And that really pisses me off a lot."

I had never heard Dave curse before.

"So many people stand up and bash Christians because of psychopaths like him, and it really aggravates me."

He started going off on a rant.

"Jesus said to clothe the naked, feed the hungry, and help the sick," he said, counting with his fingers. "He preached that everyone should love each other, not hate each other. I'm so tired of society looking at people like Ezra and blanketing this crazy idea that Christians are bad. It's wrong."

I was starting to see his point of view.

"I mean, I spend every Tuesday at the church making over two hundred ham sandwiches so that we can hand them out to the homeless folks in Central Park. Jesus said to feed the hungry, so that's what I do."

"Dave," I said, but he didn't hear me.

"My church spends *thousands* of dollars on events that feed people for free, and all the media does is report on how crazy the Westboro Baptist Church is."

"Dave?" I said again, but he was still ranting. "Dave!" I yelled and snapped him out of it.

"What?"

"We are going to be late."

He glanced at the clock. "Oh shoot, yeah, OK, let's go."

We cleaned up our plates and made our way to Times Square. Once we rounded 48th Street, we stepped into the church and found seats. When I looked around me, I saw that the place was getting packed with people. It was a colorful audience, from black skin and white skin, red hair and brown hair. My experiences in Oregon made me feel a little uncomfortable and out of place, but I spotted a guy with a yarmulke on, and it made me feel a little better.

The lights dimmed low and the curtain opened up, like a Broadway show. The choir started singing a tune, clapping their hands, and swaying back and forth. A woman came down from the risers with a microphone in her hand and began singing along with the chorus, leading the congregation in a song that apparently everyone knew. People in the audience stood up and began to clap their hands and sing along, smiling and whistling through their teeth. I felt like I had been transported back in time to an old Southern Baptist church fueled by soul food and the Holy Spirit. Throughout the service, I started to feel the same gut feeling I got in that upper room in Israel again, and I thought to myself, "Maybe *this* is God?"

I tapped deeper into the feeling as flashes of Ezra ran through my mind. I could smell him, then a flash of the blood on the bathroom floor came to my mind's eye. I was suffocating and began breathing heavily. I felt a hand on my back. Dave's hand. Immediately the anxiety went away. It was the first time since I had seen him that he touched me. Electricity flowed from his hand straight to my chest, and my body started to tingle. Again, I was feeling aroused by him, but I had to cool myself, especially being that I was in church and all.

The message that day was about prosperity. "Putting in hard work and trusting in God will lead you into prosperity," the speaker proposed. "God will lead you, but you have to do the work," he continued. He was speaking directly to me, and he was right. I needed to get myself together. I was almost five months pregnant and I didn't even have my own pot to piss in, let alone a job, insurance of any sort, or even a pair of pajamas. I needed a job.

After we left the church, I grabbed a Sunday paper that Dave insisted on paying for. He also took me out to an entertaining lunch at a diner where the waiters and waitresses sing oldies and dance on the tables. After that, he took me to the largest department store in the world and bought me a new pair of maternity pajamas, two pairs of maternity work pants, and a blouse that would fit me clear through my ninth month. I cried when he pulled out his debit card at the cash register. Pregnancy sure makes a woman cry a lot.

"You need to look professional if you are going job hunting," he said.

When we got back to his apartment, I scoured the paper and a few online job listings. None of the businesses were open on Sunday, so I highlighted all of the places I wanted to call and set the paper aside for the next day. I used Dave's computer and looked up divorce lawyers in NYC. I couldn't believe how expensive they were, so I thought that maybe I would try representing myself in the case. I looked on the court's website and found the proper forms to file for the divorce, and get financial help to pay the three hundred dollars it initially cost. I was thankful that Dave let me use his address as my own.

By Monday morning I was on the front steps of the courthouse with my paperwork in hand. I was nervous but excited to close this ridiculous chapter of my life. I chose to file an uncontested divorce, even though I knew full well I would win in a contested matter. I didn't care though—I just wanted to be done with it. I didn't want alimony since Ezra was broke anyway. We didn't have assets, and I didn't even want any of my stuff back. I just wanted to be detached from him in every way possible. After the courthouse, I went back to Dave's and started calling the jobs I had highlighted.

Dave was in Brooklyn at his lead singer's apartment practicing for their gig that night. Apparently, they were gigging a lot, which brought in a decent amount of money, or at least more than he made working forty hours a week in retail. His band was actually really good. It was funky at times, and smooth blues at other times. They got their crowd singing and swaying to cover tunes. They even had a few originals that could have been on the radio; they were that good.

I think Dave also needed a little break from me and my problems. My issues were all we talked about. I realized that I never even asked how his life had been going for all of those months we were out of touch. I didn't even know how he got in the band. Come to think of it, I didn't really even know a whole lot about Dave to begin with. I felt like I wanted to do something nice for him, to repay him for all that he had done for me. Unfortunately, between my subway pass and a few snacks I had bought that morning, I only had about fifty-six dollars left.

It had been two days since I left Oregon, and I realized I had never called my dad to update him on the situation. I gave him a ring that afternoon and he actually answered.

"Papà?"

"Pasqualina! You had me worried to death! I've been answering every phone call hoping it was you." He started screaming at me in Italian. "I tried calling your phone and it is shut off!"

"Papà, Papà, calm down. I'm fine, everything's fine. I had to shut off my phone. Ezra never let me have it. This is my new number."

"So you didn't get my messages about your Great Aunt Marcella either?"

"No, what happened?"

"She passed away. I am in Italy now dealing with the estate. I knew something was wrong when you didn't answer your phone all that time. I'm going to murder that man! If I wasn't in Italy right now, I would kill him!"

"I know, Papà. I'm sorry I didn't call you sooner, but I'm safe. I'm in New York. A friend is helping me. I'm OK, really. I can't believe that about Auntie Marcella. How did she die?"

"Who is helping you?" He disregarded my question.

"My friend Dave, he's a great guy and really—"

"Shacking up with another boy you just met! Nina, you should learn your lesson!" He was furious.

"No, Papà, no, it isn't like that. We are friends. I've known him a while. He is safe, I promise. He is keeping me safe."

"You will let me talk to this 'Dave,' and *I* will decide that."

"He isn't home, but I promise I will have him call you."

"My flower, don't worry me like this." He sounded like he was crying. "I can't lose you, too. You need to be careful. I *knew* Ezra was trash when I met him. Please, Flower, listen to me when I tell you these things. I'm a man. I *know* other men. I can tell the good ones and the bad ones. You need to listen." His accent was getting thicker the longer he talked.

"I know, Papà, I know."

"How is your baby? What are you going to do?"

"I don't know, but I will figure it out."

"Come to Italy. I will get you a ticket."

"No, no, I can't. I want the baby to be born in America. It's OK, Papà, I mean it. I'll be fine. I promise."

After I hung up with my father, I started calling a few jobs I had highlighted, and decided to hit the pavement. How ironic that I was mainly looking for a receptionist job, and last time I was job hunting in New York, reception work was what I despised the most. At that moment, I had a different mindset, for the sake of my unborn child. The pregnancy was surreal to me. I still didn't actually *feel* pregnant. I didn't *look* pregnant, as far as I knew, and I was thankful because if anyone knew I was pregnant, I doubted I would be hired anywhere.

Walking around aimlessly looking for a "Help Wanted" sign was useless. I definitely didn't want to work at a juice bar all day, or a coffee shop with lines out the door. I couldn't imagine how uncomfortable that would be with thirty extra pounds and swollen ankles. The day turned out to be a bust, but I definitely wasn't going to give up. When I got back to Dave's he was there, packing up some of his items in boxes.

"How was your day?" I asked.

"Productive," he replied.

"What did you do?"

"Practiced with the band." He immersed himself in cardboard and packing tape.

A few minutes of silence went by, and neither of us said anything.

"Is everything OK?" I asked.

"Yeah."

More time went by without us speaking. I was starting to feel uncomfortable and I didn't know what was going in his head. Finally, he spoke.

"Nina, where are you going to go when I move?"

I hadn't thought about it yet. He would be moving to Queens in two weeks, and that wasn't nearly enough time for me to get a job and save up for my own place.

"I don't know," I said looking around. "What are you doing with this place?"

"I have someone lined up to sublet it. That's why I'm asking."

I thought about the room as I walked to the window and looked down at the street below. Six hundred and fifty bucks wasn't a lot of money for a New York City apartment, and if I could just get myself a job, I would be able to afford it. But I wasn't sure how I could pay for it once the baby came.

"How many months do you have left on the lease here?"

"About ten."

"Ten months, huh," I said, still staring at the yellow cabs and umbrellas below. It had started to sprinkle. We sat in silence for a minute.

"Would you sublet it to me instead?" I asked.

The place was extremely small, but it had enough room for a bed and a bassinet, and I didn't really need much else. It wasn't a lavish apartment on the Upper East Side or a honeymoon suite in the W hotel, but it was a space I could probably afford. A space I could consider a home. Dave stood up and placed his hand on his hip, and his other on the back of his neck again. He seemed to do that whenever he was thinking.

"I'll tell you what," he said. "I will give you one week, and if you get a job, you can have the place. I can still cancel the other tenant."

I was a little taken aback by what he said. Now I felt pressured because I had a deadline, but truthfully, I probably needed a little kick in the ass to get myself in gear.

"Deal."

That night we dined together on ramen at a noodle house. It was cheap but absolutely delicious, and best of all, it was right around the corner.

"I will be here all of the time if I get your place," I joked.

It was nice to see Dave smile. He'd seemed really bothered this afternoon, so having a normal conversation was refreshing.

"So, Dave, tell me about yourself."

"What do you want to know?" he said, grinning.

I had so many first dates that started with those exact two sentences. It wasn't exactly a date though, was it?

"Everything?"

"Well," he paused. "You know I play guitar. And, you know I'm in a band. And you know I go to church."

"Yeah, but what are you interested in? Like, what do you do in your spare time?"

He smiled and laughed to himself. "I'm actually a little bit of a craft coffee fiend. I like traveling to different shops and trying out their coffee. I'm determined to find the best cappuccino in the five boroughs."

"You speak my language!" I said. "I love coffee. I mean, I didn't always love coffee, but when I was working on *Blazing Love* I got used to it, and then I really started to love it, and now I drink it a lot. It's taking forever to get used to decaf though." I patted my belly.

"Oh yeah, I forgot you did that show."

My face changed from a smile to a blank stare fixed to the ground. I really missed working in entertainment. It's what I had dreamed of my entire life. I used to stand on my parents' fireplace hearth when I was two and act out Disney movies. While most of my peers took up sports, I took up Meisner acting classes after school, even attending a few master classes in the city, one of the only teenagers there. Getting a small taste of entertainment, even as a stand-in, was invigorating. Life would be a little different now though. It wasn't about me anymore, it was about my baby.

"Yeah," I replied.

"Well, you know, life is funny." He wanted to lighten the mood.

"Sure is . . . Hey, I filed for my divorce today. The state said it takes three months, so that's good news. I even put in for a legal separation, which was made effective immediately."

"Oh, good!" he said, trying to make the conversation lively again. "I bet you feel great!"

"Kind of. I'll feel better when it is official."

"I hear you."

It was unnaturally warm for springtime, so we decided to spend some time walking around the block and talking. I told him about my family and life growing up. He told me about his mother and life in Tennessee before he moved to New York. He said his father passed away suddenly when he was twelve, and we connected on that.

"It's tough when a parent passes away," I said. "I'll never be able to get the image of my mother lying dead in hospice out of my head. I was really pissed off when my dad decided to cremate her. I didn't like the idea of mutilating her body."

"I know the feeling. My father was hit by a drunk driver while walking on a back road one day. He was pinned between the car and the guardrail, and it crushed his body. He died on impact. I had to be the one to ID him."

"Geezes. I can't imagine that. If anything, I'm glad my mom went peacefully, hopped up on morphine."

"I've replayed the scenario in my head a bunch of times. Like—putting myself in his shoes, trying to imagine was it was like to die that way. That's what's haunted me the most."

"What was your dad like?"

"Amazing, and I'm not just saying that because he's dead. He was a solid guy, loved my mom, loved me, and worked hard at a job he was good at. If I'm half the guy he was—" His voice trailed off. "What was your mom like?"

I smiled at the thought of her and reached up to my empty neck, then dropped my hand in remembrance.

"Well, she was smart as hell. She was an amazing painter, and studied art here in the city before she met my Papà. She used to live on 72nd between 2nd and 3rd. I've actually been meaning to go there, just to see her old stomping ground, but never got around to it. It was tough, you know, for a while there. I'm glad she changed, but it took me a long time to get over her drinking. She was an alcoholic for quite some time before joining AA. Her death really screwed with me. My Papà had no clue what to do with a teenage girl, either. I'm mad at her for leaving us, but she had suffered so bad with the cancer, so I feel selfish for even thinking that. Toward the end though, she was so cool. When she started painting again for therapy, she became a whole new woman—you could see it on her face. And she was gorgeous. She had the biggest smile, like a big 'toothy' one, you know?"

We stopped walking for a minute and looked at each other. Dave took my hand and placed his other on my cheek. Our eyes locked and he leaned forward to kiss me, but I turned my face.

"No, I can't. I'm pregnant, remember? I mean, I'm going to be a *mother*. And it's someone else's kid. Geezes, I don't even have a job. I'm a wreck right now." My anxiety made my hands tingle, so I shook them and stretched out my fingers. "I'm freaking useless. I'm used up. I've got only a tiny shred of dignity left. I mean, honestly, what am I going to do?"

Dave tried to embrace me, but I pushed him away and paced on the street for a moment. My nerves spasmed and my heart raced. I looked up, grabbed my hair, and fired out a long growl at the sky.

"Screw this! None of this is fair at all. Fuck all of this, and you know what? Fuck you, God!" I looked at Dave and threw my arms in the air. "God is in control of everything, right? So he killed my mom, and then made me pregnant by an asshole that I hate—on purpose? Why the hell would God do all this shit to me! Why? What did I do?" I looked back at the sky. "What did *I* do?!" I screamed and cried until snot was flying out of my nose.

Dave placed his hand on my cheek, and I pushed my face into his shoulder. He refused to let me pull away so I collapsed into his arms.

"Why did I get pregnant? It's not fair."

"I can't imagine what you're going through. And you are right, it isn't fair. I don't know why God lets things like this happen. This world is so freaking evil—people are just downright selfish jerks most of the time."

"So then, why does he let it all happen?"

"I don't know. I guess he doesn't really *control* everyone. Would you want him to, anyway? Having some invisible force telling you what to do all of the time?"

"I guess not. I mean, you aren't really helping. No offense."

"People are assholes, and your ex is the biggest one of all."

"Well, *you* aren't."

"Your baby is still half you. Remember that." He pulled me in tighter.

"Yeah, I know. I feel guilty for saying all that."

"Don't. You're human, and you're going to be an awesome mom."

"Thanks."

"Hey." He lifted my chin.

"What?"

"Look where we are."

I looked up behind me at the street sign—72nd and 3rd.

"No way."

"Come on, let's check it out." He took my hand and we walked to 2nd Avenue.

"So this is where she lived? I wonder which one was hers." I stopped and looked around at the surrounding brownstones. "I bet—it was *that* one." I pointed to the one in front of me.

"I bet you're right," Dave smiled.

I grabbed him by the neck and brought his handsome lips down on mine for a kiss. His mouth was soft and warm. He slipped his tongue gracefully over mine and gently guided my lower back with his strong hands until my little belly was touching him, melting into paradise under the stars.

TWENTY

It was exactly one week later when I finally heard back from an office I had applied to in Midtown. I dressed up in the new clothes Dave had bought me and, still to my luck, I wasn't quite showing yet. I walked through frosted glass double doors to a parking corporation's office on the eighteenth floor of a silver skyscraper, where a flustered woman greeted me.

"Hi, are you the eleven o'clock?" She didn't bother to look up from her papers.

"Yes, that's me."

"Fill this out. The owner, Mr. Zaminski, will be with you shortly." She handed me a clipboard and jogged down the hall, jetting into an office.

I started filling out the paperwork, which basically asked everything that was already on my résumé. Why do applicants always have to fill out extra sheets like this when a résumé was already provided? "Such a waste of paper," I thought. I had brought a copy of my résumé with me, which I had printed out at the library. That same day I had renewed my library card and took out a book of Robert Frost poems that I was strangely drawn to. Poems were like songwriting, and I hoped that Frost would inspire me a little since Dave let me play around with his acoustic a few times.

"Hello, Pasqu—a . . ."

"Nina," I corrected. "You can just call me Nina." I stood up and stuck out my hand for a shake. Mr. Zaminski was a handsome man, dressed in a slim-cut pinstripe suit, spotless brown suede shoes, and a light pink bow tie.

He had one of those mustaches that curled up at the ends.

"Good morning, Nina," he said, and grasped my hand firm. "Come on in."

I walked through the towering wooden door into his corner suite. There was a long, brown, leather couch, a beautifully carved wooden table, and a few green velvet lounge chairs set up by the wall of windows. A gorgeous mantle sat over a gas-powered fireplace that housed a small orange flame. The mantle was covered with fresh flowers and family photos. I caught a picture of his wife: a beautiful, black-haired, large-breasted woman, like a Playboy bunny. I followed him through another door, which opened up to the nook of the building's corner. I sat down on a soft suede chair in front of his lavish desk amid the surrounding glass walls.

"Let's see what we've got here." He looked over my résumé. He didn't even bother to look at the paperwork I had just taken seven minutes of my life to fill out.

"You're an actress?" he asked.

"Yes, that is initially why I moved to Manhattan."

"Ah yes, one of *those*." The room was silent as he kept reading. "So tell me—I see here you worked on *Blazing Love* for a while, great show. But say we hire you, and you get a call to work on another show. Would you leave us?"

"Well," I swallowed hard. "Honestly, I'm not going to be in the entertainment business anymore, not for a while at least."

"Explain," he made a quote gesture in the air, "'a while.'"

I couldn't tell him about the pregnancy—not yet—but I had to make something up on the fly that made sense.

Before I could respond he said, "If you moved to Manhattan from—" he looked down at my résumé, "Connecticut—to pursue acting, why did you give up? Did you quit?"

Great, now he was calling me a quitter.

"No," I snapped back. "I'm not a quitter, circumstances just changed for me, that's all."

"Explain."

"Well, I guess I just grew up and grew out of it. I need to have a solid job, and small acting jobs weren't cutting it for me. I want an apartment and

I need a steady check to pay rent. I also want to settle down and have a family one day. I'd like to enroll in school and study anthropology at some point. I can't do any of that and try to be an actress all at the same time."

"I see. So why stay in Manhattan?"

"I'm not sure. I guess because I like it. I also want to go to Hunter College."

"Good school, but you could find much cheaper rent in Connecticut, and that is where your home is, after all, isn't it?"

"Not exactly." I refused to give any more details.

"Interesting. So you plan to make New York City your home . . . for how long?"

I didn't understand why he was asking me all of these questions that were completely unrelated to reception work.

"Forever, I guess."

"You guess?"

I was starting to get frustrated.

"As long as I have steady work, a roof over my head, and food in my stomach, does it really matter where I am? Life is life no matter where you are. California, life is still life at the beach. Colorado, life is still life in the mountains. And life is still life in New York City. I'm here because this is where I ended up. This is where my responsibilities are, and I see no reason to be anywhere else. 'The woods are lovely, dark and deep, but I have promises to keep.'" I quoted from Robert Frost's "Stopping by Woods on a Snowy Evening." I had just read it that morning.

"Interesting," he said again. He obviously didn't get the reference, which made me feel smarter than him. "That is a sophisticated view on life for such a young girl. So, what is your experience in reception work?"

"Well, I worked on Wall Street for a little while. In a dentist office."

"A dentist office on Wall Street, hm. And why did you leave that job?"

"It was only a temporary position and my contract ended."

"And why do you want to study anthropology?"

"I went to Israel last year and I had some really cool experiences there. Seeing a different culture really intrigued me. I'd love to study cultures and people in more depth. And truthfully, I just want to be an educated woman and do something meaningful with my life."

"I see." He paused and stood up. "Well, it was great to meet you, Nina. We will be in touch," he said, abruptly looking at his watch.

I was confused. Did I say the wrong thing? Did he like me? Did he hate me? Was he kicking me out? Was I hired? I left the office perturbed. When I got back to Dave's apartment he asked me how it went, but I didn't have a straight response to give him.

"I should let the other tenant know if you are taking the place or not," he reiterated.

"I know, I know. I'll let you know as soon as I hear back."

"Well, hopefully you will hear soon. Was that your only prospect?"

"Unfortunately."

It was true. Not one single place I applied to, other than this parking company, had called me back.

Even though I had only been staying with Dave for a short period of time, the difference between him, Ezra, Declan, and even Marco was astonishing. It seemed like he actually cared. He wasn't some asshole who just wanted to use me for my body, or wine and dine me while screwing other girls on the side. He was always home when I came back to his place. He would tell me where he was going before he left for somewhere, and made sure I felt comfortable at all time. I mean, don't get me wrong, we weren't dating. In fact, the kiss we shared was the first and only kiss we'd attempted up until that point. It's not that things got weird between us or anything. We just didn't talk about it, and we didn't do it again. I wouldn't have minded another lip-lock with the kind-hearted hunk, but I was more focused on getting my life together than anything. Once in a while we would snuggle on his narrow bed while we watched Netflix on his laptop. I lived for those snuggle sessions, because I had never felt more relaxed and safe in anyone's arms before.

A few minutes later my phone started ringing. It was a New York number I didn't recognize.

"Hi, is this Pasqualina?"

"You got my name right!" I exclaimed. "Yes! This is she."

"It's Deborah from Silver Parking Corporation."

"Yes, how are you?"

She disregarded my question.

"Mr. Zaminski is pleased to have you on the staff. He is starting you at fifty-five thousand a year with a full benefits package. If this is suitable for you, then we'd like to have you start on Monday."

I couldn't believe what I had just heard. *Fifty-five thousand* a year? I could totally afford the apartment, and anything I needed for my baby. *Finally,* something was going right. I accepted on the spot.

I looked up at Dave and told him the good news before I even hung up the phone.. He picked me up and spun me around, and insisted on taking me out to celebrate. He took a pile of clothes and told me he would be quick to return for our "date."

"A *real* date?" I smirked.

I slicked my hair back into a ponytail and brushed on some red lip gloss.

Twenty minutes later, he knocked on the door. "Are you ready to celebrate?"

He looked cute, dressed up in a navy blue button-down shirt tucked into a pair of khakis and accessorized with a brown leather belt. I took a bouquet of red roses from his hand, set them down on his bed, and invited him in. He didn't have a vase.

"So, this is what it will be like when the place is mine? You will knock on the door with a bouquet of red roses *every* time, right?"

He laughed.

For the first time, Dave was taking me out for a real, official date.

"I was thinking I'd take you out for sushi, but then I realized raw fish is probably a bad idea."

"Yeah, I don't think I can have that."

He sat down on his bed and stared up at me in a long, awkward pause.

"You look nice." I broke the silence. "I didn't think you owned any khakis."

"I take them out for special occasions."

Silence ensued.

"So, where do you want to go?" I asked.

"I don't know, what are you in the mood for?"

"Pasta, maybe?"

"Sure, I know this great Italian place called G—"

"Oh my god, please don't say Giuseppe's."

"Ew, I hate that place. Too crowded. No, it's called Geppetto's Cafe."

"Like Pinocchio?"

"Yeah," he laughed. "It isn't too far from here. Come on, we can walk."

"Sounds good."

I plopped the bouquet into a water glass before he locked up. We walked down the sidewalk with our arms linked, huddled under his black umbrella, dodging water bullets from the dark clouds. He smelled sweet, like a day at the beach, and his warmth radiated in an aura around me. We didn't speak as we walked.

"It should be right around here somewhere. I always miss it. Whoops! See, here it is, we just walked by it."

He led me down three small steps painted red, white, and green, and opened the door to a small and narrow restaurant. The few front tables were taken, so the hostess seated us in the back. We passed by a display case full of delectable desserts, where my eyes focused on a rack of black-and-white cookies. The sides of my mouth swelled with saliva. I was starving, and they looked incredible.

"This place is cute," I said.

"Yeah, it's nice."

I couldn't figure out why Dave was being so awkward.

"Is everything OK?" I asked.

"What?"

"Are you OK? You are acting totally weird."

He looked up at me and started laughing.

"Yeah, sorry. I just feel dumb in these clothes."

"You look handsome!"

"I guess, but I feel like a nerd."

"Well, you *are* a nerd."

"Oh really? Then what does that make you?" He smiled.

"A girl who dates nerds."

"You're ridiculous," he laughed. "What are you going to have?"

"I'm going back and forth with the lasagna and spaghetti and meatballs."

"Just order them both."

"Really?"

"Yeah, absolutely. I mean, no one will look twice at you since you're pregnant," he chuckled.

"Then, that's happening." My cheeks ached from smiling.

The waitress came over and took our order.

"Lasagna and spaghetti and meatballs for the lady, and a small pizza for me. Cheese with banana peppers, jalapenos, and pineapple."

I looked at him strange. Banana peppers, jalapenos, and pineapple? Was he kidding?

"And a side of black-and-white cookies, please," I added.

"Oh, and two cappuccinos," Dave added.

"Make mine decaf."

"Yes, she needs decaf."

"I'm pregnant," I said, tapping my still small bump.

"Aww, congrats, you two! Parents-to-be, how sweet," the waitress said before walking away.

My eyes grew big. "I am *so* sorry."

"It's fine, don't worry about it," he patted my hand.

The waitress came back with two glasses of water and a plate of cookies.

Dave picked up a cookie and held it up in the air.

"To a new apartment, and new beginnings."

I held up a cookie. "And lasagna."

"And pizza," he said, tapping his cookie with mine.

The more we talked, the more Dave loosened up, but it still seemed like something was bothering him. Our food came and filled up the table with all sorts of delicious flavors. Except, of course, his disgusting pizza.

"Are you really going to eat that?" I asked.

"I know, it's a weird combination, but you shouldn't knock it until you try it." He waved a slice in my direction.

"No! Thank you, but no. I puked enough in my first trimester, thanks very much. That pizza is *all* you, buddy."

He winked at me and took a huge bite.

"So, um," he rubbed the back of his neck with his hand. It was a cute trait I'd grown accustomed to. "I don't really know how to do this."

"Do what?" I asked.

He reached into his pocket and pulled out a small black jewelry box, and placed it on the table. My eyes widened.

"Oh, Dave, I'm separated and all, but I can't—"

"No!" He startled me. "I mean, no, it's not a ring. I'm sorry. Here, just open it."

I felt like an idiot for assuming this was a proposal, but slid the box in front of me and popped it open. Immediately my eyes flooded with salty water that dripped on my lasagna below. In the box was a golden hamsa hand with a sapphire in the middle. I flipped it over and revealed my mother's initials. I covered my mouth with my hands, stood up, walked to Dave, and pushed my way onto his lap. I threw my arms around his neck and wept into his chest.

"How did you get it?" My voice was muffled by his shirt.

"I took the receipt you showed me and called the shop about buying it back. No upcharge. I only paid what you sold it for since it was within sixty days. It's too precious to let go of, Nina. I know why you pawned it, but you deserve to have it back."

He took the necklace out of the box, brushed my hair to the side, and secured it around my neck. I thumbed the sapphire and kissed it.

"Thank you," I whispered.

When we got back to the apartment it was dark. I walked in and reached for the lamp, but Dave stopped me with his arm around my waist. He stood in front of me and stroked my forehead with his fingertips. My body surrendered to his touch and he pulled me in to his lips. We shuffled our feet toward the bed and dropped ourselves onto his mattress. I wanted him—all of him. I unbuttoned his shirt and uncovered his tattooed chest. He loosened his belt, threw his pants to the ground, then hesitated.

"I want you so bad," he whispered.

"Me, too."

He slipped his hands under my dress and pulled the silky fabric up over my head. I felt his fingers on my back unhooking my bra, now too small for my growing body. I felt relief when he pushed the straps off my shoulders and tossed it to the ground. His mouth found my neck and my breath shook.

"Please, I can't take it, I need you now," I trembled.

"I'm nervous," he replied, his mouth so close to my ear. "Your baby, is this OK?"

It was more than OK. I needed him. I wanted this moment. I deserved to feel the warmth of a man who cared about me, and I wasn't going to take no for an answer. My fingers traced his body until I found him, and pulled him inside of me.

❧

The next morning, we lounged in bed for a while. I snuggled into his chest and we talked for hours. I felt like I was truly connecting with someone for the first time. It felt even deeper than what I had with Declan. We had so much in common, and I felt like he genuinely cared about me and my well-being.

Dave let his tenant know that the apartment was no longer available. It was unreal when he signed the keys over to me two weeks later. I couldn't believe his apartment was now mine. I'd never actually had my own apartment before. I'd never actually lived by myself either. On moving day, Dave packed up the rest of his stuff into his band's van, and with a goodbye hug, he was off to Queens. The room felt strange without him. I really didn't want him to leave, and in fact, I was secretly hoping he would decide to stay. I knew he wouldn't, though. He was getting some pretty great opportunities with his band, and even had a gig that night at the B. B. King Club, which I planned on going to. Mr. Zaminski gave me a sign-on bonus of a few hundred dollars to "buy a nice wardrobe," since I would be the "face of the company," so I had some cash in my pocket. I walked back to the empty apartment and realized that I would need to buy a few things to get by. Rather than spending the money on clothes, I grabbed the water taxi and headed to a massive warehouse store in Brooklyn known for selling affordable furniture. Dave had left me the hot plate and microwave, since his new house had a stocked kitchen, so I bought myself a twin storage bed, a few pans, some sheets, a few towels, plates, silverware, and a lamp. The total cost was just over two hundred dollars, which still left me with quite a bit of cash.

When the delivery team pulled up and started to unload the items into my new place, I couldn't stop smiling. I smiled as I washed the plates and put them in the only closet in the room, alongside my towels and clothes. I smiled as I put my new bed together, and even smiled when I washed my new sheets at the Laundromat before the gig. By the end of the day, everything was in its place. It was tiny and the walls were still bare, but it was mine, and everything in it was mine.

I sat down on my bed and looked around the room. A few minutes went by before I started to think about Dave. I missed him, but I knew us "shacking up" together, as my father so nicely put it, was not going to be a permanent situation. Dave had his own life. His band was doing great. They were being looked at by a major record label, or so I had last heard. He was amazing, but I had to let the idea of him go. I still had some loose ends to tie up with Ezra, and with divorce court in three weeks, taking care of myself was the priority. My belly was starting to swell, too. I was nearing the end of my second trimester, and at this point I was definitely showing. I had bought a few more maternity shirts, which landed me some cockeyed looks at work, but no one asked if I was expecting. I had scheduled a prenatal visit at the hospital for the following week, which I was extremely excited about, considering they would tell me the gender of my baby at the appointment. I never got to go to my final appointment in Oregon, and I couldn't wait to see the ultrasound images, because the baby was still surreal. I knew seeing a picture would help.

I had to tell myself several times not to text Dave, and I repeatedly tried to stop thinking about him. The excitement of my new apartment dissipated when I realized how lonely it felt. When Dave was around it felt like home, but now, it was just four walls and closet. I had to somehow find comfort in my loneliness, but it was hard. I gave up and reached for my phone, but before I could send him anything, a text came through.

Dave: Can I come over?
I knew it. He missed me.
Me: Absolutely.

An hour later, Dave buzzed my intercom and I let him up. Before he could even get through the door, I grabbed his strong arms and kissed him.

"Did you miss me already?" I joked.

"It feels so weird in here now." He put his guitar and gear down. "I hope you don't mind," he said motioning to his stuff. "I'm going to go straight to the gig."

"Sure, of course."

"I like what you did with it." He walked around and inspected all of my new purchases.

"I got it all from the warehouse that has that water taxi thing."

"Not bad."

"I won't lie to you Dave. I'm pretty much scared shitless to be on my own here."

"Well, you won't get a better deal than this in Manhattan. Plus, you'll be making more than enough money to survive. It's a tiny place, but tiny living is, like, 'cool' now, anyway, right?"

"I guess. It's just, what happens when the baby comes? What if I can't work? Who is going to take care of him? Or her? Did you know that day care costs like five hundred bucks a week around here? It's insane." In fact, five hundred was on the "cheap" side of the spectrum when talking day care in New York City. I couldn't believe the prices I saw when I scoped them out.

"You have a good job, it pays well, everything is going great for you. You'll be fine."

"Will I, though?"

He took my head between his hands and kissed my forehead.

"Repeat after me. I'm a strong, independent woman."

"I am a strong, independent woman."

"— and everything will be OK."

"Everything will be OK."

He embraced me and I took a deep breath, inhaling the cologne on his shirt and pulling him in tighter to me.

"I have a surprise for you," he said.

"Really? What is it?"

He unzipped the case to his guitar and put it over his shoulder, sat on the bed, and took a pick out of his pocket.

"I wrote this the other night and took it to the guys. I think we might record it."

He what? He wrote me a *song*? Judas priest, I'd never had anyone write me a song before. This was definitely the most panty-dropping moment I'd ever experienced, and I wanted to savor every second.

Buzzzz. The intercom interrupted our moment.

"Were you expecting someone?" Dave turned toward the door.

"Um, no. No one even knows I live here. Were *you* expecting someone?"

"Not that I can remember."

"Hello?" I said into the speaker.

The other side was dead quiet.

"Hello?" I repeated.

"Ninaroni?"

My face burned, and my legs felt weak. I turned to look at Dave as the blood fled from my face, turning my skin pale white.

"Nina?" Dave said, concerned.

"It's him."

"Who?"

"Ezra."

"*What?*" he shouted.

"Oh my god, you can't be here. You can't be here! You have to go. He's going to kill me if he sees you. You've got to go, Dave."

"No way in hell—I'm not leaving you here with this psychopath. Are you nuts?"

"Oh my god," I repeated.

"Nina, you don't have to let him up if you don't want to."

The intercom buzzed again.

"You don't have to let him in," he said softly.

The buzzer went off once more. I pressed the intercom button.

"Ezra?"

"Can I come up?" he asked, sweetly.

"Why are you here, and how did you get my address?"

"From the court papers."

"Shit," I silently mouthed at Dave.

"It's up to you," Dave whispered. "But I'm not leaving."

I buzzed the latch open for him. Two minutes later he was at my door and walked in without inhibition.

"Oh my god," he smirked. "This is *so* small. Are you serious? Why would you get such a small place? You know we have a baby coming soon." He approached me, put his arm around my shoulders, kissed my cheek, and put his hand on my belly.

"We?" Dave chimed in from behind the opened door.

Startled, Ezra replied, "Yeah. *We.* Me and my *wife*, here. Who the hell are you?"

Ezra released my shoulders and pushed himself away from me, then looked back and forth between Dave and I.

"I knew you were cheating on me, you stupid bitch! I come all the way out here to New York City to try and repair our *marriage*, and this is the shit you pull? Are you *fucking* kidding me? I come here to get you back, and you are spreading your disgusting legs for a piece of shit moron over here?"

I had started to back away into the corner when Dave came between Ezra and me.

"I want you to get out of here right now, before I call the cops," Dave said.

"And I want you to get out of here before *I* call the cops. This is my *wife*! Who are they going to believe? You? Her boy toy? Or me, her *husband*?"

"Stop it. Ez, what do you want? Why are you here?"

"I already told you, I'm here to save our marriage. I had a gift for you and everything, and I'd like to give it to you," he paused. "Alone."

"I'm not going unless she wants me to." Dave pointed at me.

They both looked in my direction, awaiting my response.

"It's fine. I'll be OK," I said to Dave.

Dave walked to me, took my hand, and whispered, "You do whatever you feel is right. I'll be in the hallway, right outside that door, and I will be back in five minutes to check on you. Remember. You are a strong, independent woman."

"Time to get out now," Ez said sternly as Dave walked by.

Dave left his guitar and gear in the room, and walked out. Ezra slammed the door behind him.

"I got you a gift."

"You've said."

He pulled a white box out of his suitcase and gave it to me. I was curious as to what kind of gift would actually "save our marriage," as he claimed. When I opened it up, I pulled out a self-help book. I read the back: It was a thirty-day program for someone who wanted to repair their marriage. I peeked at the pages, and landed on day twenty. "Buy your spouse something nice as a gesture of kindness and to let them know you are thinking about them." I flipped to day five, which read, "Listen to your spouse speak today and ask questions rather than talking about yourself. Put all of your energy into your significant other to show you are interested in him/her."

"There is something else in there, too," he said.

I reached my hand in and pulled out a red-and-black buffalo-checked men's button-down flannel shirt. I was completely confused by the gifts.

"What do these things even mean?" I asked.

A sour look came over Ezra's face.

"The book is for you, so you can read it and help save this marriage. I bought a plane ticket and came all the way out here, you know. You could put in a little bit of effort too."

"So you want me to read through this book and do all of the things it says?"

"That's the idea."

"What's with the shirt?"

"That is your favorite pattern right? You said you like it when men wear this pattern. You said it a long time ago, but that's what you said." He was quick with his speech.

"I mean, yeah, I think I mentioned it once. But what's the shirt for? For me?"

"Yeah. I'm going to wear it, and you will be attracted to me. So, you know. You'll be turned on, I hope."

I sat for a second, trying to piece all of it together.

"So, if I'm understanding correctly, you bought a shirt and put it in a box to give to me to open, but the shirt is for *you* to wear so that I'll have sex with you?"

"So that you will *want* to have sex with me."

"But this isn't a gift for *me*, it's a gift for *you.*"

"No, it's not. It's for *you.*"

"How do you figure? You gave me a book with a list of tasks I have to do that only benefit *you*, and then you gave me a shirt that *you* get to wear. This entire gift was for you."

I could sense the steam beginning to form behind his eardrums.

"Listen, a shirt isn't going to make me want to have sex with you. It's not a piece of clothing that turns me on, it's the person inside I'm attracted to, and I wouldn't have sex with you if you were the last person to ever have sex with! And you gave this book to me? *Me?* Did you forget what you did to me on the bathroom floor? And now I have to, what, go buy you dinner or something? Are you out of your fucking mind?"

The sides of my small belly were twitching and sore, so I grabbed them.

"What's wrong?" He jumped up.

"*You*. You are what's wrong. I don't want you back, Ez."

He started to take his shirt off and put his new checkered shirt on.

"Ez, that shirt isn't going to change how I feel about you."

He started to undress until he was completely naked but the unbuttoned shirt.

I covered my eyes.

"This isn't working, Ez. Just stop it and go away. I'm not going to have sex with you!"

"Yes, you are. I came out here and you are still my wife, damn it!"

"No, I'm not. You said you got the divorce papers. That's it, Ez. I'm done. We are legally separated. I don't owe you shit!"

"So you would rather just walk around and fuck anyone else with a dick, then? Like that shaggy idiot that was in here? I bet you suck his dick and he pays for this piece of shit apartment for you like a goddamn pimp," he said, closing in on me.

He was getting harder, and pressed himself into me, grabbing both of my arms. He slid his dick across my leg until it was throbbing. He grabbed himself as he pinned me to the wall, and started jerking himself off.

"Stop it!!!" I screamed at the top of my lungs.

I caught my breath and the door swung open. Dave grabbed Ezra by the shoulders and flung him into the hallway, slamming the door shut and locking it. I gathered his clothes and shoved them back into his suitcase while he pounded on the door.

Dave took the suitcase and stormed into the hallway. He grabbed half-naked Ezra by his collar and pushed him up against the elevator door. I followed behind, clicking the down button. By now, anyone who was home was sticking their heads outside of their doors.

What a great, neighborly, first impression, I thought.

"Is everything OK, Dave?" an elderly gentleman asked, standing in the hallway with his bathrobe and slippers on.

"It's OK, Walter. I'm just taking out the trash," he said as he struggled to keep Ezra in place.

The doors opened and Dave shoved him in.

"Don't ever fucking come back here," he demanded.

The doors closed in Ezra's face. I began to walk back to the apartment when Dave came up behind me and gently took my hand.

I led him back into the room and the door latched behind us. We stared at each other for a moment before he put his hand on my cheek and embraced me against his chest. I loved it when he did that. At that moment, I let all of my reservations go. I didn't have to be strong because Dave was my strength. He held me up and cradled my head as I soaked his favorite band T-shirt. Neither of us said anything. We didn't have to. I lifted my head when I noticed that Dave's eyes were red and puffy.

"What's wrong?" I asked. He kissed my forehead several times. "Dave, it's OK. I'm OK."

"It's not that," he sniffed back.

"What's the matter?"

"Nina, I have to tell you something."

I stood confused.

He continued, "I was hoping that we could have a great night tonight because I was supposed to tell you that I won't be seeing you for a while. But now, with this prick here, I'm afraid to leave you."

"What do you mean, leave me?"

"This band, this gig."

"I know, I'm going with you to the gig."

"No," he said softly. "It's not just *this* gig." He paused. "I'm going on tour. For six months. I was going to play you this song, and that stupid asshole ruined it. Jesus, I'm crying like a freakin' baby. I need to stop this." He rubbed his temples and sniffed up his boogers.

A single blink lasted an eternity.

"This gig is the first stop on our tour. I came over to tell you the news, but now I'm not sure I want to go with this psycho here."

I couldn't say anything. He wasn't the father of my child. He wasn't my husband. He wasn't even my boyfriend—at least I didn't think so. I didn't even know where we stood, to be honest.

"Let's go," I said, picking up his guitar and putting it back in his case.

"Give me that," he smiled through tears. "You can't carry stuff like this." He picked up his amp and took the guitar from my hands. "If that lunatic is still outside, I am giving you fair warning right now that I'm going to kick his ass."

It still made me laugh when Dave cursed.

"I give you my full blessing for that."

Luckily when we left the building, Ezra was gone. We hailed a cab and set off to his gig.

❧

That night, Dave killed it. His band was incredible. It turned out that he had landed a spot on a tour with a fellow blues band that had a large following out West. The band would be driving to California in the morning to tour up and down the coast. I envied Dave. He wasn't tied down to anything or anyone. He could just up and leave on a whim, and pursue his dream. Any girl would be lucky to have him. I wished that girl was me, but we were just at two different places in life. I wondered though, if I wasn't pregnant, what I would have done. Would I have packed up and followed him, like a pathetic groupie? Or stayed behind and survived on my own, like I would do now?

In the middle of the set the band left the stage for a quick break—all but Dave. He sang backup vocals, but he approached the front man's microphone in the middle of the stage, and adjusted the height.

"I meant to play this song earlier today, but never got the chance, so I'm going to play it now if you all don't mind." The crowd cheered for him.

I stood in the front row and his eyes locked with mine. He began picking at the strings, playing a beautiful, slow ballad and his raspy voice began singing. I soaked up every word of the song, and swayed with all of the other women who suddenly had eyes for someone other than the lead singer. The chorus kept repeating in my head, even long after the band joined him for the rest of their set. *It's a beautiful thing, rocking with you, rolling with you / No road can stop forever with a girl like you.* I couldn't stop smiling. Maybe he *did* want this to work?

After the gig, we met up backstage to say goodbye.

"So, I guess this is it," he said.

"Oh geez, come on. You are going to end tonight with a cliché?" I playfully hit his arm.

Dave did a polite "I'm-laughing-so-I-don't-cry" laugh.

"I wish you had told me sooner," I said solemnly.

"I'm sorry. I honestly just found out a few days ago myself. The headliner wasn't sure if they could afford to take us or not, but with this label looking to sign us, it seemed like a no-brainer."

"Yeah, so, what's up with this label thing?"

"It's actually pretty much a done deal. Our lawyers are looking everything over, and we should be signing within the week. It works out that we will already be in California anyway."

"Yeah, I guess so," I said quietly. "I mean, that's super awesome." I perked up. "I'm sorry, I should be way happier than I am."

"No. I mean, I get it," Dave said.

"I loved that song, Dave. It was beautiful."

"Just like you."

I smiled and pushed my hair back with my hands.

"So," I started. "Call me?"

"I'll call you." He kissed me.

It was the most perfect kiss. His tender, smooth, ChapStick-covered lips made my body tingle.

Dave hailed me a cab and handed the driver a twenty. I watched his cute butt walk away as the cab door slammed shut.

TWENTY-ONE

The next two months at my new job went surprisingly well. I liked the work, and everyone at the company was super nice, especially when they all realized I was carrying around another person. I was able to avoid the questions until I was midway through my sixth month, then all bets were off. I expected my boss to be pissed off at me for not telling him in advance, but instead he bought me a huge gift basket with diapers, bottles, clothes, and all sorts of other baby necessities. The staff pitched in one day around my thirty-week mark, and surprised me with a cake and gifts. The room was drenched in pink, since I found out soon after Dave left that I was having a girl. My father and I spoke daily now, and he was beyond elated about the news of a girl. He sent me a children's necklace with a 14-karat gold Italian horn on it as a gift from Italy, since he was still there. Apparently, my great aunt's house was in a disheveled condition, and he extended his stay to fix it up for a higher resale price. He told me that he would be back before the baby was born, and planned to fly in around my thirty-eighth week. He wanted to book it early, just in case.

Ezra ended up sticking around after the night of Dave's gig. He tried to come back to my apartment several times, but by then I had filed a temporary order of protection against him. The police were called, and on two separate occasions he was physically removed from the property. Finally, I felt like I was winning when it came to Ezra, and I felt like I had control over the situation.

On the day of the divorce hearing, I was nervous. I had to take the day off from work, and I told my professor that I would have to skip my English class that day. I had finally started taking night classes at Hunter and it was going well, but I knew I'd most likely be an emotional wreck. She gave me the work ahead of time, and I told her I'd hand it in the following class. The assignment was to write an essay about a role model or someone inspirational, and how the person impacted your life. I thought I might write about my mom, especially since I was thinking about her more often with my baby coming and all.

The courtroom was packed with mothers and young children not old enough to attend school yet, couples who looked in love, couples who looked like they hated each other, and courtroom mediators calling people's names. The judge hadn't entered yet. I scanned the room, but didn't see Ezra, so I sat in the corner, took out some lined paper, and began writing my essay. I was interrupted by two hands on my shoulders. I looked up behind me. Ezra.

"Hey."

"Hey."

"What are you writing?"

"An essay for school. Listen, you shouldn't be anywhere near me. I know you don't respect *me,* but you won't even respect an order given by the courts? Clearly not. I want you to get away from me right now."

"Well, the problem with that is, you gave me a *temporary* order of protection, which you know is completely bullshit anyway. If you were even the slightest bit observant, you would have realized it was only effective for twenty days, and that ran out two days ago. Maybe next time you won't be so stupid about it."

I packed my papers away in my bookbag and without saying anything, I walked to the other side of the room. Luckily the judge came in, and everyone had to stand up anyway. When the judge sat back down, I took a seat, and Ezra squeezed himself in next to me. I was stuck. I took my papers out and started to write again, but the bailiff came over and told me that I had to put everything away. Ezra rolled his eyes and shook his head at the bailiff, said, "Sorry about her," to him, and snickered at me. Then he whispered "stupid" under his breath. I stood up to leave when our names were called for mediation.

We sat in a stuffy room with a woman who attempted to mediate a divorce agreement between us. We'd have to come back to court to establish child support and visitation once the baby came, but I knew if I didn't put his name on the birth certificate, none of that would be necessary. I wasn't about to let him in on that knowledge, though. It was my little secret, the one piece of ammo I had that might blow him out of my life for good.

"What about alimony?" the mediator asked.

Ezra scoffed. "We weren't married long enough for her to get alimony. Nice try."

"You don't even have any money, you nitwit. You only have money now because you stole all of mine!" I yelled.

"Enough!" the mediator said. "If you can't keep yourself under control, then I'm going to continue this case and you'll have to come back another time."

Like fucking hell I was going to go through mediation again.

"I'm fine. I won't yell again," I said.

Ezra rolled his eyes at the mediator. "See what I had to deal with? And you wonder why we are getting divorced."

The blood inside of my body was seething with anger, but I kept my composure.

"I will not be pursuing any alimony. He doesn't have a job anyway," I retorted.

"Great. Let's move on to assets," she said.

Ezra scoffed again. "We have none. She destroyed them all."

I destroyed them all? I was gearing up to go full-throttle Joan of Arc on his ass when I realized what he was doing. He was *trying* to get a rise out of me. He *wanted* the hearing to be continued, and I was not about to let him win at this game.

"There are no assets to split. Let's move on to the next section, please." I smiled at Ezra, and I could see the fire forming behind his eyes.

Every section of the mediation was met with some sort of opposing remark by Ezra, and I simply smiled and agreed to whatever was suggested by the mediator. No continuance necessary. All points were met and agreed upon, whether Ezra liked it or not. At that point I already had everything stripped from me, and I didn't have anything left to lose, except my composure, which

I kept in check. Ezra looked like he was ready to throw himself out of the fourth story window by then.

After our mediation, the court had a quick recess for lunch. I took my bag and ducked into the flood of people, and lost Ezra behind me. I rushed down the steps and out the main doors, across the street and down an alley, where I found a quaint English tea shop. I popped inside and ordered a decaf tea, and a cucumber and watercress sandwich. I kept my eyes on the window at the street, but didn't see Ezra. I had finally lost him. I pulled out my papers and finished the assignment while I munched on my sandwich.

An hour later I shuffled back into the courtroom with everyone else, in hopes that my case would be heard. I really did not want to come back the following day. I just wanted everything to be over. Luckily, our names were called first. The judge beckoned me to the stand, since I was the plaintiff, and I swore to be truthful on the book that had ensnared me so many times.

"Do you, Pasqualina Panicucci, agree to the terms of this agreement as you have discussed and agreed in mediation between yourself and Ezra Alto?" the judge asked.

"I agree." I looked over at Ezra and his face was maroon. He was wiping his eyes with his sleeves, putting on a show for anyone who cared to watch.

"OK, then as of today, you are officially divorced as decreed by the State of New York. Good luck."

"Thanks."

I grabbed my bags and walked by Ezra, avoiding eye contact. He was still crying.

"I'm always going to love you, Nina!" he shouted as he walked out behind me. "Nina!" he yelled again.

I held onto my bag and dashed down the stairs, out the courthouse doors, and ran down the sidewalk. I ran around several corners and crossed intersections. I ran down the subway stairs and through the gates. I stopped on the platform to catch my breath. A train was coming and as soon as it stopped, I walked through the doors without even the urge to look back. They closed behind me, and the train brought me home a single woman.

TWENTY-TWO

Two nights later I walked into the classroom at Hunter and set up my space. I had a tiny little sliver of a desk attached to the rock-hard chair in an off-white room that smelled like fresh paint. I sat and briefly meditated, ready to learn. Everyone had a laptop except for me, which was fine for now since I hand-wrote everything and then stayed after work to type all of my essays up and print them out. Mr. Zaminski gave me his blessing to use the company's printer. In fact, he said if I got an A in my classes, the company would pay for a percentage of them, which was extremely generous. Everything about the company was so great, and it really made me feel like I was part of a family. I didn't see myself leaving the job for many years, and I felt that was Mr. Zaminski's goal, too. His generosity was not a typical trait for a boss in New York City. I decided that I'd strive for a 4.0, and if I did get money back from the company, I would purchase a laptop. It was a small goal, but achievable, and I was determined to put in the hard work. I felt for the first time like I truly was the strong, independent woman Dave knew I could be.

All of the students filed in and the professor began with a short writing exercise, which was to summarize what we wrote in our essays in one paragraph and then share out. It was tough for me to stuff my mother into five or so sentences, especially because my essay was three pages in length, but I did my best. When it was my turn to share, I stood up, nervously wrapped my necklace around my fingers, and read from my paper:

My mother was one of a kind, a humble, beautiful, strong woman who overcame addiction and lived out what few days she had left loving people. If she could see me today, I know she would be so proud of all that I have accomplished. Oftentimes, when I am sitting in my tiny apartment, alone and wondering what the hell I'm even doing in this world, what my purpose is, and why God has thrown such crazy situations my way, I get a bit down, thinking that everything seems to be so out of reach. All of my dreams and aspirations are too far away. I feel like I'm reaching for stars that just never seem to be close enough to grasp. If my mother were here, she would hug me and encourage me and tell me, "My flower, the stars are not out of your reach. You have a good job, a beautiful baby girl on the way, a roof over your head, and you are pursuing a good education. The stars are already in your hands. You just have to pull them down so they light your way."

It was hard for me to concentrate on the rest of class thinking about everything that had happened. The divorce, Dave being gone, my due date getting closer, work, school. At the same time, they were all good things, except Dave being so far away. That was the only thing I wished I could change. I reflected on what I had read in front of the class. I really *did* feel like I had reached some stars, but was I ready to have them light my path? They were different stars than I originally anticipated for my life. I thought I'd be an actress, or maybe a model. Now I was working in corporate America and studying anthropology.

Then I remembered, without darkness, there is no light. And maybe, in life, it's the dark paths that teach you the most. You live, you learn, and you move on to brighter paths once you pull down the right stars. My choices led me to an abusive situation, and I wasn't happy about how everything transpired. I mean, who would be? But I was happy in the end that I learned something from them, and I'd sure as fucking hell never make those same mistakes again. And maybe some people have *more* than one path. Who's to say I can't be an actress years from now, after my child has grown up? Right now, corporate America guaranteed me money, shelter, food, and a future, and that sounded like a damn good path to me.

After class, I took the train into Brooklyn to check out a temple. I had been e-mailing with the rabbi and he said I could come to the office to ask him questions, and he would show me around. I liked Dave's church and all, but I decided that I would look for a temple to attend regularly. I remembered what Grace had told me. Since my mother was Jewish, technically I was too, and I wanted to explore more of my Jewish heritage. The rabbi was elated to greet me, showed me the temple, and told me what to expect when I came back on Saturday evening. I was excited to start this new chapter in my life, and my father was just happy that I was engaging in a religion at all, especially after what happened with Ezra. After all, "Jesus was Jewish, too," he said. The rabbi gifted me with a mezuzah and I hung it in my doorway that night.

On my way back to the subway, I spotted a trendy baby store and popped in for a look. I was starting to enter into my "nesting" stage, you know, when an expectant mother feels that animalistic urge to create the perfect nest for her baby. Now, I couldn't exactly set up a nursery for her, and probably wouldn't be doing that for a while since my apartment was so tiny, but I *could* buy her a bunch of really cute clothes. I figured I would save as much money as I could to get a real apartment by the time she was three. It was another good goal to strive toward. I had been penny-pinching since I started my job, but that night I just wanted to splurge a little, and what better excuse than for my little bun in the oven? I spent an hour in the store, moseying around, rubbing the sides of my belly, and walked out with three pairs of newborn shoes, two little dresses, and the cutest little pink spring jacket.

"Do you want any of this monogrammed?" the clerk asked.

Life had been so crazy that I hadn't thought much about a name for my daughter. Once in a while I'd refer to her as my "bun" or my "little lioness," but I couldn't really come up with any names I liked. If she were a boy, I had about six different names picked out, but nothing had struck me yet for a girl's name.

"No, thanks, I'll take it as is."

The whole thing came to two hundred dollars, which didn't put a huge dent in the thousands I had currently banked. It was nice to have a little cushion in my account, "for a rainy day," my father joked, which was appropriate since it had started to drizzle by the time I left the shop.

Dave was good about checking in with me every day, but he was also busy with his music stuff. After his band signed with the label, they immediately started recording an album, which kept them in California indefinitely, it seemed. He called me when I was on my way to my thirty-fifth-week appointment with my midwife, Ginny.

"Hey, Mamma!" he said playfully.

"Hey, Dave. How's it going?"

"Dude, you are going to freak out when I tell you this. Are you ready?"

"OK?"

"Remember that song I wrote for you?"

"Umm, yeah, how could I forget *that*?"

"Well, we recorded it with the full band, and that's our first single off of the album. They told us it's going to be premiered on a radio station out here tonight!"

"What! No way! Dave, that's incredible! Gosh, I can't believe it." I felt so proud.

"I know! Hey man, how's it going?"

"What? You already asked me that."

"Yeah, man, sounds good. I'll catch up with you later."

"Huh?"

"Sorry, I just ran into one of my buddies from this club I started going to out here, and it is so rad."

I didn't realize Dave had been in California long enough to have "buddies."

"That's OK. Sounds like you are busy. So, do you think you will be coming back here at all?"

"I know, I know, you ask me that every time. Honestly, I don't know. The tour went so well, and with this new album coming out, they are promoting us big time. We have a few shows lined up and we are headlining now. It's tough to say."

"Yeah, OK. I hear you."

I'm sure he could sense my disappointment.

"So how's the little soccer player?" he asked.

"Ha!" He was always making me laugh. "She's definitely kicking! I feel huge."

"Stop it. You are beautiful, and you know it. That picture you sent me— so gorgeous. And a solid heart to match it. How much time do you have left?"

"About six weeks."

"Are you stoked or what?"

"Stoked? You say 'rad' and 'stoked' now? You've been in California way too long."

"Yeah, whatever," he laughed.

"I'm really excited. I just want to see what she looks like."

"She's going to be beautiful because she's going to look exactly like you."

"Did you see the ultrasound picture I sent?"

I had texted him a snapshot of the ultrasound a week ago, but never heard back.

"Oh, shoot. Yeah, I saw it. I'm sorry. I was in the middle of a session when I got it and I totally forgot to write back."

"It's cool."

I realized that he still hadn't answered my question about New York.

"So," I treaded lightly. "What's going on with your place in Queens? Are you guys going to sublet it, or what?"

"Nah, we are keeping it. The plan is to make it back there eventually."

"So you *are* going to come back?"

"Eventually."

"I really miss you."

"I miss you, too. I wish you could come out here and see all of this."

"Oh yeah, let me just walk into a bar with a huge belly on me. The looks I would get? No thanks. At least the bars in New York know I only drink root beer now."

"Actually, our drummer's girlfriend just came out here and she's pregnant too. You'd probably get along with her."

Girlfriend. That word again. He has used the word to describe everyone else's significant other, but he never used the word with me. I was still confused as to what we were. I was sick of the distance, but I was happy that all we had for contact was a phone. Every relationship I'd ever had turned sexual so quickly. Once I had sex, the talking and "getting to know you" part sort of disappeared. Even though we'd had sex, once, it was nice talking so often. I was actually getting to know him in a deeper sense, and with every conversation, I fell for him even harder. It was just confusing because I wasn't sure what *he* thought about us. My situation was complex given that I was now considered a "package deal." Maybe Dave didn't want kids? Or, maybe he just didn't want to take care of someone *else's* kid. Either way, the word was tossed around but never used as a label, not for me at least. But I didn't push the issue.

"Well, the preggo girlfriend and I already have one thing in common," I replied.

"I'd say so. I'm being real, though. Would you ever come out here?"

"To visit or to live?"

"Both, I guess?"

"I would probably come out to visit, but I don't know about moving. I have a good thing going with the parking company, and my apartment."

"Yeah, how *is* the old crib?"

"It's fine. I had my first official 'I've fallen and can't get back up' moment with Walter."

"Good ole Walt—what is he? Ninety now?"

"Ninety-two on Halloween. The poor guy. He had fallen in his apartment and was banging on the wall for like five minutes before I realized he was probably trying to get my attention. I could barely lift him up, so I had to get Adrian and Todd to help, too. They moved in last month."

"You shouldn't be lifting things right now anyway, especially people."

"Yeah, I know."

"Well I'm glad everything is going great," he said.

"I'm glad everything is going so well for you, too. I miss you but I'm really happy for you."

"Thanks, love."

I sighed at the sound of "love" coming from his lips.

"Hey, I'm at the doctor's office now. Can I talk to you later?" I asked.

"Of course. I'll be out with the guys later on, but you can always text me."

"Alright, cool. I'll talk to you soon."

"OK."

"OK."

There was a small pause. I wanted to say "I love you," and at times I felt like he wanted to say it too, but it never happened.

"Goodbye."

"Bye."

After I hung up with Dave, I rode the elevator up to the fourteenth floor, to my midwife's office. Ginny was a young, soft-spoken midwife with red, curly hair who I started seeing after I finally got on the company's insurance plan.

"Hey, Nina! Good to see you again," the receptionist declared. "Six weeks to go. How are you feeling?"

"I'm OK. A little nervous."

"Oh, honey, you will be just fine. I've had five kids, and remember how hard it was at the end."

She was a sweet lady, but she was always reminding me that she had five kids, as if she deserved a medal or something.

"It's very uncomfortable," I replied.

A few minutes later the nurse called me in and took my weight. I had gained over forty pounds at that point and my ankles were like redwood trunks.

"Oh *god*." I stepped off the scale onto the cold tile floor, reflecting on the scale's flashing number.

"Don't worry about it, you will lose twenty pounds before you even leave the hospital."

"Really?"

"Yup. You have the baby, which is around seven pounds, or more, by the time you deliver, then the placenta, the water, blood—You know, all the gross stuff. You will probably pee out five pounds of water the day after. I'm not even kidding."

"That makes me feel better, sort of," I said.

"Is there anything specific you want to talk to the midwife about today?"

"Not really."

"Alright, she will be in shortly."

"Thanks."

I thumbed through a magazine on the white quartz countertop.

"They even Photoshop pregnant people, for Christ's sake," I thought.

The door swung open and in walked Ginny.

"Hey, Nina!" Her smile was abnormally white. "It's the final stretch! Six weeks left."

"Yeah, six to go."

"Let's take a listen to this little girl, what do you say?"

She helped me up to the table and put her instrument on my belly. Immediately I heard the "whoosh whoosh whoosh" sounds of my daughter's heart beating.

"It still sounds nice and strong," she commented.

"Good," I relaxed.

"Have you come up with a name yet?" she asked, making small talk.

"Not really. I have a few in mind, but nothing solid yet."

"Well, you've got plenty of time."

"I guess, yeah."

"We got your test results back from the lab."

I had gotten some blood work done after hearing how many partners Ezra had. Although I was usually pretty good about having protected sex, I'm not so sure that was the case with him, and I wanted to be sure I was still part of that 20%. I had unprotected sex with Dave too, and it just made me feel better knowing about it.

"You are clean down the line," she said. "I can't stress enough how lucky you are. You must have someone watching over you."

"Thanks, Mom," I whispered.

She handed me a thin blue folder with some papers inside.

"This your birth plan. Make sure to mention if you want an epidural or a natural birth, and here is the section where you can ban visitors. I know we talked about that a little bit last time."

At the last appointment, I had a full-on mental breakdown in the middle of her office because Ezra had e-mailed me asking to see an ultrasound picture. I e-mailed him back with a few pictures, and commented that the baby had the cutest little pouty lips, like Marilyn Monroe. I don't know why I felt obligated to send them to him. I should have just ignored his request because his response was uncanny. His e-mail attacked me right away, the subject line stating, "Skewed beauty." He accused me of having a skewed vision of what beauty is and said that I was unfit to be a mother if I was going to make comments like that. I cried for half an hour in her office that day. Rather than rushing me along, she sat next to me, put her arm around my shoulder, and let me cry it out. She skipped her lunch break to console me, and that is when I knew I had picked the right woman to walk me through this life-changing journey.

"Are you still having a hard time with your ex?" she asked.

"I was, but I changed my phone number and my e-mail address so I don't have to deal with him anymore. He was texting me nasty messages at least once a week. I couldn't take it anymore."

"Good for you. You need to stand up for yourself because this *is* an abusive situation. Like I said last time, you can put him on the 'banned list.' That decision is up to you. Even if he comes out here and tries to get in, they will turn him away. If the police need to get involved, we will do that as well."

"Wouldn't be the first time. Plus, I don't think he will waste his time coming out here for the birth. He just wants to say hurtful things to me to make me upset. I don't think he has any intentions of actually being a father."

"You have all the tools to be an independent woman. Remind yourself of that daily," she said firmly. "And if he is only going to make you upset, then you did the right thing cutting him loose. If he cared about the baby then he would care about your well-being. That's not the case, and you need to do what is best for you."

"Thanks." I cradled my head and rubbed my eyes.

"What about Dave?" she asked, remembering his name.

"Oh, he's good. Really good. Still in California," I perked back up.

"You really like him, don't you?"

"I think I'm in love with him, actually, but it's not like I can say anything about it. I don't even know if we are together, or what."

"It's still hazy, huh?"

"Unfortunately. But, honestly, I'm just glad he is in my life, no matter what part he plays. I will love him as a friend, and I will love him as a partner. It's really up to him to take it further. I think I just want to focus on myself, the baby, my job, and things like that for now."

"Very responsible. You see? All the strong and independent tools are right here," she pointed to my head, "and right here," she pointed to my heart. "You've got this. Now let's check to see if you are dilating yet."

She helped me lean back and I laid my head against the crinkly white paper. I put my sockless feet in the unfriendly stirrups and took a deep breath in as she reached up to feel my cervix. Though it wasn't the most welcoming feeling, Ginny's gentle touch and soft voice walked me through it.

"You are about a centimeter dilated!" she exclaimed. "But don't get your hopes up for an early delivery. This is fairly normal. And anyway, I'm leaving for Texas in a few hours, so you better keep that baby cooking until I come back," she joked.

"Um, *what?* When will you be back?"

"Don't worry, I'll only be gone for a couple of days. I promise I will be there for your delivery."

"Ginny, please, I don't want anyone else."

"Don't worry, kiddo, it's fine. I'll be back before your next appointment."

Her persistence put me at ease. I was finally comfortable with someone fiddling around down there, and I didn't want to have a random stranger touching my love canal to deliver my child. She finished the exam, and on my way out I made an appointment for the following week. I didn't feel like going back to work and I had already taken a half day, so I decided to walk to the bar at which Dave used to play. By now the bartender and patrons were used to seeing a girl the size of Venus grace a bar stool for a cup of root beer and some blues tunes. They always had a band playing, even midafternoon. That day I decided to take a seat at a table, since my lower back was exceptionally sore. Pregnancy really beats the hell out of a woman's body. I plopped my feet up onto the chair next to me and sipped the smooth, sugary brew while the band played a chilled-out version of "Ain't No Sunshine." I closed my eyes, bobbed my head to the groove, and zoned out for a moment or two, when, of course, I had the sudden urge to pee. I stood up and—

Splash!

I spilled my root beer all over the floor—or so I thought until I looked at my pants and realized my water broke. A strong pain surged from my lower back and crept over to my belly button.

"Oh hell," I said, clenching my stomach.

"A little help here!" the woman next to me yelled. By now everyone in the bar was looking at me, and the music stopped playing.

"Call 911!" someone yelled at the bartender.

I stood in the middle of the room, shocked at what was happening. "Wait! No!" I yelled. "It's too soon! It's not supposed to happen now!" I kept yelling.

People crowded around me. A woman grabbed my elbow and held me up as I doubled over in pain: a second contraction. I threw my phone at a gentleman with a long beard and a leather vest on.

"Call Dave, please," I asked through my "hee hee whos."

He called Dave, and I overheard the pathetic conversation.

"Some lady here wanted me to call you. She's having a baby. Yeah. (*Pause.*) No. (*Pause.*) I don't know. (*Pause.*) Look, I don't know, she didn't even tell me what to say, she's just having a baby or something."

Click.

About ten minutes later an ambulance picked me up and hauled me away to the hospital. I was having flashbacks of my stomach bug episode.

"Hello, Miss." I was greeted by the ER receptionist. "Let's get you registered. Can you tell me what's happening?"

"Obviously, I'm having a baby here," I barked.

"Yes. And what would you say your pain level is right now?"

"How about an 'I'm having a baby' level of pain?"

"Between one and ten, please, one being a dull pain and ten being—"

"Ten! OK, ten!"

"Listen, ma'am, I know you are in pain, but most people preregister at a hospital when they know they are having a baby."

"Oh yeah? Well, most people don't have their babies a month and a half early!" I yelled back.

She gave me a hard stare, looked at her computer, and asked, "Place of employment?"

"If you don't get me to labor and delivery right now, I swear to god I will—"

"Nina, you can come with me," a man said to me as he pulled on the back of my wheelchair. "I will take it from here," he said, glaring at the receptionist.

I gave her a side glance as he spun me around and pushed me down the hall.

"I'm one of the nurses up in the maternity ward, Nurse Enfield," he explained. "I'm sorry they put you in with reception. Usually people who come by ambulance don't have to deal with that."

His soft and caring voice was a nice change of pace, and his face was easy on the eyes. He was a bit cliché, but tall, dark, and handsome never goes out of style. His long, black, wavy hair was slicked back in a man bun, and his scruffy five o'clock shadow framed a skinny smile. He had a strange accent, sort of a mix between Boston and British. Australian, maybe. He patted me on the shoulder as another wave of pain contracted over my daughter's bones, and reminded me to breathe as he raced me to my room.

"Listen," I started. "I'm thinking we go straight to an epidural, like stat."

"You got it."

He whisked me into a room and helped me out of the wheelchair, then handed me a gown.

"I think I can take it from here," I said.

"Sure thing. I'll put in for your epidural right now. Shouldn't be long, just hang tight."

I carefully pulled my soaked pants off, trying not to let them touch my legs on the way down. Another contraction rounded my body and I yelled in pain.

"What's the matter, Mama?" Nurse Enfield peeked his head through the door. He was at my beck and call, which was sweet but also really fucking annoying, since my ass was out in the open and I was still leaking uterus gunk.

"You sure you don't need help?" He walked in and put a cup of ice chips on the bedside table.

"I guess I do."

"The anesthesiologist was in the on-call room, and is on her way," he explained as he helped me out of my shirt and draped the gown over my arms. I'd never felt so humiliated while a man undressed me. When I was settled in the bed, he hooked me up to an IV.

Ten minutes later the anesthesiologist came, dressed in pink scrubs two sizes too big for her tiny frame, bothered that I had woken her from a brief slumber. She made me sign a waiver and told me to pound back a really disgusting drink. As gross as it was, I didn't care what they made me do, I just wanted the pain to stop as soon as possible.

"I want you to curve your back and stay completely still. If you move, I could paralyze you. *Do not move.*"

Nurse Enfield came to my aid and held my hands. I felt her stick my back and, of course, that's when my body started to contract again. I squeezed my eyes shut and breathed hard.

"Breathe, honey. Breathe and keep still," he cooed. "It's almost over, keep breathing."

"All done," the anesthesiologist announced. "You should feel much better in a minute or so." She helped me lay back onto my pillow. Nurse Enfield fixed my sheets, and they both walked toward the door.

"The doctor will be here in a little bit to check on you." They left the door slightly ajar, which was annoying now that I couldn't get out of bed to close it. Suddenly I couldn't feel my toes, and within seconds, my feet were numb. I yelled like a banshee, but by the time Nurse Enfield ran back into the room, I couldn't feel or move anything below my belly button.

"Don't worry, it's fine. It's totally normal and it will wear off," he said as he adjusted my drip.

"How long?" I asked. "I knew it would take the pain away, but I literally can't feel *anything*. I'm paralyzed. I think I'd rather feel the pain. Can you take this thing out?"

"Mama, you don't have to be a hero." He embraced my hand. "And once you make the choice you are kind of stuck with it. That stuff takes a good while to get out of your system. You're better off just keeping it. Are you doing OK? I checked your chart. Where's your family? You've got one heck of a list of banned visitors." His accent killed me.

"Yeah." I looked down, fiddled with the crisp white sheet, and thought of Dave. "I'm alone."

He touched my forehead and brushed my bangs out of my eyes. "Everything will be OK."

I craved a man's touch, and his hand felt nice. His dark fingers were soft and warm. His smooth voice was powerful and kind. He couldn't be much older than thirty, but I could tell he was an old soul.

"You don't have to be alone. I'm here."

I shook my head. "I wish my mom was here." I thumbed my necklace, which I refused to take off, and I dared anyone to challenge me.

"Where is she?"

"Heaven."

"Oh." He looked sorry for asking.

"Yeah, and my dad is in Italy, but I'll call him once I know more of what is going on."

"There you go. Dad will make it better."

Dad will make it better? He was hot, but his bedside manner was a little awkward.

"Yeah."

Just then a high-pitched scream bounced through the hallway. I heard the footsteps of several nurses running down the hall, dashing into a room.

"Oh my God," I heard a man say calmly, just before a loud thud.

The woman kept screaming inaudible gibberish.

"I'll be back to check on you," the nurse said as he released my hand and left.

The woman's screams made me cringe. My hands started shaking, and soon my arms were vibrating involuntarily. I broke out in a sweat, and my throat dried up, so I reached for some ice chips.

The doctor came in and began reading off of my chart.

"Pask—er—"

"Just call me Nina," I said.

He was an older guy, definitely not as hot as Nurse Enfield, and definitely not as nice either. I had never seen this doctor before.

"I thought I was going to be seen by—"

"I'm the one on call right now, no one else. You're stuck with me, so let's get to know one another." His voice was scratchy and it annoyed me. "Is it just you today?"

"It's just me." I wanted to throw the ice chips at his face.

I didn't expect to be alone and I was tired of the reminders that I was. I had daydreams of this day, holding Dave's strong hands and exchanging sweet kisses, but those dreams faded with every hour I spent on the bed by myself. I had texted him about a hundred times with no response.

The doctor examined my body. I could feel his cold hands through the latex gloves. I hated him. He inspected my chart and recorded my vitals.

"I know Ginny's not on call, but I really prefer to have a midwife."

"Well, she isn't here, and there aren't any in the building right now. I'm more than capable, and I have to be in the room anyway, regardless of who is helping you. Please just try to relax. That's the best thing to do right now. How are your legs?"

I stared at him and squinted my eyes for a moment, debating whether I should go off on him for being such an insensitive asshole. "They are still numb. I can't move them."

"The feeling will come back; it's normal," he paused. "Well, little miss, it seems like you've got a ways to go. I'll come back in an hour or so." He removed his gloves and tossed them into the bin by the door.

Little miss? He seriously addressed me as "little miss?" What a dinkwad. I should have cussed him out.

"Before you go, can you please just call Ginny? Please?"

"Listen, I'm not going to bother a midwife who isn't on call. We have a schedule and it's just how things work here. You get what you get. I've been delivering babies for over twenty years. You are going to be fine. That baby will come out no matter who delivers it."

I raised my eyebrows.

"No matter who delivers *her*. It's a girl."

"Yes, of course." He closed the door.

I reached over to my phone and called my father. He answered on the second ring.

"Ciao."

"Papà! She's coming!"

"Pasqualina? It's too soon. No, no, I have to be there."

"I know. But my water broke and she's coming now. I'm already at the hospital ready to go."

"Flower, I can't miss this. I can't."

"I know, I don't want you to miss it either." I thought about it for a second. "How about a video chat? I mean, no offense, but I'm not going to let you see her come out." I started laughing. "But you can at least see what's happening in the room."

"Yes, please, Pasqualina. I would love that. Thank you. My first grand-baby." He started crying.

"Oh Papà. Don't cry. If you cry, then I'll cry." It didn't take long before I was in tears, too. "I can't believe she's coming now. I really miss Mamma too."

"She's there, flower. She's right there with you."

"I know, Papà. I can feel her." It was true. Ever since I entered the room I sort of felt a strange but warming presence. It had to be her. She would never miss the birth of her granddaughter. I clasped the hamsa in my hand. "I will call you again when it's time."

"I will wait right here by my phone. I promise. And flower?"

"Yes, Papà?"

"Thank you for letting me be a part of this."

"Of course, Papà. I love you so much."

"I love you, too."

When I hung up with my father, I tried texting Dave again, but noticed that none of my text messages were going through. Not a single one since I got to the hospital showed up as "sent."

"What the hell?" I tried sending four more messages, and all were stuck in the invisible cloud above my head, and it sucked because I really wanted to talk to him. Aside from Papà, he was the *only* one I wanted to talk to. I turned on the TV and channel surfed until I settled on a program about Mars. I looked at the machine that monitored my contractions and it was going completely berserk, but I didn't feel a thing. Some of my contractions were nearly, literally, off the charts, but I was sitting happily unaware as I chomped on another piece of ice. A few hours passed, and the doctor came in a few times to check on me. I hadn't progressed much so they put a shot of Pitocin in my IV to speed up the process. Nurse Enfield told me to get some rest and save my energy for pushing, so I took a long nap. I woke to the doctor flicking on the lights. It was just past midnight when he announced that I was ready to go.

He called in his team and they prepped me to be transferred to a room that would no doubt change my life. I looked for Nurse Enfield, but he wasn't there. I checked my phone one last time, but still no messages.

"She said she would be here for me," I said, panicking, but no one responded.

They pushed my bed into the hallway, and I started crying and shaking my head "no." The doctor kept repeating: "We're here to help you," and "You're going to be just fine." I clenched the rails until my swollen knuckles were blue. I was nervous. We rolled down the short corridor and turned the corner.

"I've never done this before," I muttered. "I can't do it, not without Ginny. I don't know what I'm doing. Where is she?" I cried. "Where's Ginny? She is supposed to be—"

The team of nurses pushed me through the double doors, and I saw a flash of white light. I closed my eyes at the sight and opened them only to address an unexpected question from a familiar voice.

"Would you like me to set up a mirror, so you can watch?"

"Ginny!" I screeched as I spotted her bouncy red hair.

"I told you I would be here, didn't I?"

"But what about your trip?" I asked.

"You are lucky that I hadn't left yet. I was finishing up with my last patient when I got the voicemail you were in labor. When I got here, you were out cold, so I just let you sleep."

"You put off your trip for me? Oh my god, the doctor actually *called* you?" I looked over at the doctor, who had now completely redeemed himself, and cried, "Thank you." He nodded.

"I'm still going, but I changed my flight, yes."

I relaxed my fists and gave her a hug.

"So would you like the mirror? You'll be able to see her come out."

"That's a little weird! But yes, I want to see her. I can't wait." I was finally beginning to relax. I finally spotted Nurse Enfield in the corner, and tossed him my phone. "Video chat my Papà, please. But if you send him any footage of my crotch, I'm going to kick you in the balls."

"OK, OK," he laughed.

They positioned my bed into the delivery room and pulled up the stirrups where my legs would rest. I couldn't feel anything from the waist down at this point, so hot Nurse Enfield had to hoist them up onto the padded platforms. How freaking embarrassing. I begged him in my mind not to look at my hairy, haven't-shaved-in-two-months hoohah. Ginny, all dressed up in her disposable gown and gloves, examined my pelvis and yelled for a birth kit.

"She's further along than I thought," she whispered to Nurse Enfield after glaring at the doctor, who was now back on my shit list.

They hurried and prepared everything needed for delivery as Ginny lifted her head and gave me a reassuring smile.

"Are you ready?"

"No, I'm really not." I wanted Dave. I wanted him there with me, holding my hand and helping me breathe. Where the fuck was he? Why wasn't he calling?

"It's OK, Nina. Whether you are ready or not, this is happening, so you need to give me one big push if you can. Hold on to these handles and bear down."

"I've got your dad here!" Nurse Enfield exclaimed, but I was a little too busy at that point.

I grabbed the handles on the sides of the bed and tried to push as hard as I could, though I couldn't feel anything so I didn't know if I was doing it right.

"She has so much hair!" Ginny exclaimed. "Would you like to feel her head?"

I reached my hand down and looked into the mirror as I patted the top of her tiny head.

"That's her?" I started to hyperventilate and cry.

"That's your girl. Let's get the rest of her cute little head out. Give me another big push with the next contraction. Ready? Go!"

I squeezed the handle and pushed my tailbone down into the vinyl bed.

"Good job, flower!" I heard Papà say, and it comforted me to feel like he was in the room with us.

"We have her head," Ginny said calmly. "Now I want you to give a little push for her shoulder."

I pushed down again and my daughter slipped out into Ginny's hands.

"Oh!" she yelled. "OK! Here she is!"

She placed my baby girl down on my chest and I watched her skin turn from blue to pink. Eight hours and three pushes had turned me into a mother. Tears fell onto her cone-shaped head.

Ginny handed me a pair of scissors and showed me where to cut along the leathery umbilical cord. Removing her for what seemed like forever, they weighed her in at four pounds, seven ounces.

"Look at you. You are so beautiful. My baby, you are so sweet," I sang, stroking her chalky hair. Nurse Enfield hung up with my father and told him I'd call him later. My little girl's cries turned to gentle coos, and when she was calm, I fed her. She latched on to me like a dart on a bull's eye and suckled down the sweet serum my body was eager to produce for her. After my daughter was finished with her first meal, I swaddled her in a blanket and watched her eyelids slowly close into a peaceful slumber.

Nurse Enfield wheeled my bed into the recovery room and closed the door. I cradled my baby and whispered lullabies into her tiny ear. I wasn't alone anymore, and I never would be ever again. For the first time in my life,

I felt real love. There, in the sterile, ugly, hospital room, staring at my little creation, my heart finally found a home.

I heard a gentle knock at the door.

"How are we doing in here?" Ginny whispered.

"She's amazing. I can't believe she's mine." She was sleeping soundly on my chest, her head beside my necklace.

"Look how beautiful she is." She reached out and touched her small hand. "You did a great job."

"Thank you."

"So what are you going to name her?"

I pushed the blanket back from her cheek and stroked my thumb over her furry eyebrow.

"Aliyah."

"The most beautiful name," I heard a deep voice say.

I turned, and in the doorway stood Dave, holding a little pink doll and a bouquet of red roses, and I completely lost it. He walked in, kissed me on the forehead, and a tear formed in the corner of his eye when he looked at Aliyah.

"I love you," he whispered in my ear.

"I love you, too."

And in that moment, my path was illuminated.

About the Author

BETH MARIE READ is a writer and photographer born and raised in central Connecticut with experience in film and television. She is a wife and mother to two daughters, and lives in Newington, Connecticut. For more information, check out @bethmarieauthor on Instagram and www.facebook.com/bethmarieauthor.

woodhall press

Also available by Woodhall Press

AWARD-WINNING

The Astronaut's Son

Tom Seigel

FOREWORD REVIEWS
2018 INDIE AWARD WINNER!

On the eve of the 50th Anniversary of the Moon Landing comes a novel in which a Jewish astronaut must reassess his moral compass when forced to confront NASA's early collaboration with Nazis and the role it may have played in his father's death.

Jonathan Stein, the CEO of Apollo Aeronautics, is an ambitious polymath who has spent a lifetime determined to accomplish two tasks: First, to complete his father's unfulfilled mission to reach the moon, and second, to forge a relationship with the reclusive Neil Armstrong. Despite a heart condition, he's on the verge of his first goal, but has gotten nowhere with the second. Armstrong has never responded to any of Jonathan's dozens of letters.

Avi Stein was an Israeli pilot specially chosen to command Apollo 18 in 1974, but suffered a fatal heart attack before launch. Now, months from being able to realize his father's dream, Jonathan discovers a "lunar hoax" conspiracy website offering a disturbing reason for Armstrong's silence: He knows Jonathan's father didn't die of natural causes.

While researching his father's last days in the National Archives, Jonathan expects to confirm the official cause of death, but what he uncovers instead is a motive for murder. To get to the truth, Jonathan must confront Dale Lunden, his father's best friend and the last man on the moon.

ISBN: 978-0997543780

HILARIOUS

Flash Nonfiction Funny: 71 very Humorous, Very True, Very Short Stories

Tom Hazuka and Dinty W. Moore

From Dinty W. Moore, founding editor of the popular journal Brevity and prolific and pioneering author of several books of creative nonfiction, including *Between Panic and Desire, Dear Mister Essay Writer Guy*, and *Crafting the Personal Essay*, and Tom Hazuka, editor of the anthology *Flash Fiction Funny*, comes a new book that will make you laugh out loud in 750 words or less! *Flash Nonfiction Funny* explores the exploding form of very short creative writing and offers an accessible anthology that's perfect for individual entertainment or in a classroom setting. Teachers are increasingly embracing the very short form because it lets them use brief pieces to illustrate various styles and structures. The anthology includes work from both new and established writers from all over the world. It's like they always say: It's funny because it's true!

ISBN: 978-0997543742

woodhall press

ILLUSTRATED
Alice's Adventures in #Wonderland
Illustrator: Bats Langley
Editor: Penny Farthing

Alice's Adventures in #Wonderland re-imagines Lewis Carroll's classic stories through the digital lens, down the rabbit hole, and beyond the smartphone glass. With the help of Penny Farthing and illustrations by Bats Langley comes a new adventure for Alice.
ISBN: 978-1949116106

The Rose Island Lighthouse Series:
The Curious Childhood of Wanton Chase
Lynne Heinzmann
Julia T. Heinzmann
Michaela M. Fournier
Marilyn T. Harris

Wanton Chase lived with his grandparents at the Rose Island Lighthouse from 1910 to 1916, from the time he was 1 to 7 years old. Later in life, he recorded his memories of his adventures on the island, which he shared with the Lighthouse Foundation. His recollections are the basis for the story chapters of this book. The history chapters contain additional information and photographs to provide context for the stories.
ISBN: 978-1949116113

woodhall press

REFLECTIVE
A Lion in the Snow
James M. Chesbro

When his wife was pregnant, James M. Chesbro started having daydreams of seeing a lion in his street, padding toward his house through the snowflakes of a New England storm. He felt more like a son, still grieving over the early loss of his own father, rather than a prepared expectant-dad. In these essays, Chesbro finds himself disoriented and bewildered by fatherhood again and again as he explores the maddening moments that provide occasions for new understandings about our children and us.

A Lion in the Snow is a contemporary father's field guide, a husband's compendium, and a wife's glimpse into the turning mind of a spouse in the grounded prose of domestic conflict.

ISBN: 978-1949116007

Man in the (Rearview) Mirror
LaRue Cook

At a time when American identity is increasingly fractured, LaRue Cook explores a deeply personal journey through love, loss, and self-discovery, using the lens of a physical journey across the United States, and abroad, by a former corporate sports-editor-turned-Uber driver.

Part voyeuristic, part inspirational, sometimes hilarious, always thoughtful and probing, Man in the (Rearview) Mirror is a book about learning how to love yourself (and others) at a time in America when it is often too easy to hate. With compassion for his passengers and himself, Cook carefully navigates us to a place of forgiveness, patience, and, hopefully, peace.

ISBN: 978-1949116021

woodhall press

PERFECT FOR THE CLASSROOM

Mentoring Teenage Heroes:
The Hero's Journey of Adolescence
Matthew P. Winkler

Matthew P. Winkler's viral TED-Ed lesson "What Makes a Hero?" introduced the Hero's Journey to millions of viewers. His debut book guides parents, teachers, coaches, and other adults toward a fresh understanding of adolescence as a heroic quest - a rite of passage as old as the ancient myths that metaphorically describe it. Those myths echo through contemporary books and movies and the real-world experience of growing up. For most adults, daily life is a routine grind. For teenagers, it's an epic struggle for identity.

ISBN: 978-0997543711

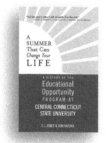

A Summer That Can Change Your Life:
A History of the Educational Opportunity
Program at Central Connecticut
State University
C.J. Jones and Tom Hazuka

As of the 2017-2018 academic year, more than 2,000 students have participated in the Educational Opportunity Program at Central Connecticut State University. Thousands more have been part of similar programs at other Connecticut colleges, including Southern and Eastern Connecticut State Universities, and Wesleyan University. This book is a celebration of all those students. Fifty years after the program was created at CCSU, the students who have passed through its doors—largely first-generation college students from minority populations—are a testament to how far the program has come since its early days, when its mission was often called into question. The histories chronicled herein shed light on a program that has achieved a lasting, generational impact, and which, over the course of successive summers, has indeed changed thousands of lives.

ISBN: 978-1949116045

POETRY

Oysterville: Poems

edited by Laurel S. Peterson

In August of 2018, eleven Norwalk poets stepped into the recording booth to capture their voices so that audiences could experience their poetry out loud. The project was conceived by Poet Laureate Laurel S. Peterson and Marc Alan of Norwalk's Factory Underground Studios. This companion chapbook brings the poems to the printed page. Oysterville: Poems the Album is available for download on iTunes, Amazon, Spotify, Soundcloud, YouTube and most major retail/streaming platforms in about 100 countries.

ISBN: 978-1949116083

Woodhall Press
Norwalk, CT
WoodhallPress.com
Distributed by INGRAM